"I see you

"I always research people I'm ~~going to~~
with." Farmington folded his hands tog~~ether~~

Shoving the paper at him, Julie snapped, "Forget it."

He smiled back coldly. "Don't rush into a decision
you'll regret. I'm very good at getting my way." He
swiveled on his feet and headed to the door.

As soon as he left, Julie ran into the bathroom and
splashed water on her face with hands that still
trembled. She had no idea how she was going to
fight one of the richest men in America. Numbness
spread throughout her body as realization hit her.
She really did need that miracle to happen or she
was going to lose everything.

The bell above the shop door chimed and rage
pummeled inside her. What now? Had Farmington
returned to drive the stake in even harder?

"You know what," Julie yelled as she ran toward the
front of the store, "you can just get the hell ou—"

She stumbled as she came to an abrupt halt, her
mouth hanging open in shock.

"And here I thought you wanted me to visit,"
Jake Reynolds said, the smile on his face matching
the one on her poster. "Julie Alleen, I do believe you
offered me a challenge. Well...challenge accepted."

Dear Reader,

When you were younger, did you ever love a boy band? Now picture that the boy band is from your hometown. Imagine growing up with them, going to school with them. In *His Small-Town Challenge*, Julie is at her wit's end. She's a struggling small business owner, trying to fight off a corporation from taking over her store. In desperation, she posts a video online asking her former classmate/longtime crush/now-famous singer to return home and visit her store for some much-needed publicity. She never expects him to accept her challenge.

The idea for *His Small-Town Challenge* came from my own love of boy bands. When I was a tween, I was *obsessed* with a particular band. I'd always wanted to see them in concert, but no one would ever take me (which I still gripe about to my siblings, LOL). Fast-forward *many* years later, and the band came to my hometown. I decided I would finally see them in concert, and after I bought the tickets, I started to wonder... What happened to them after their heyday? Did they get married? Did their spouses know who they were when they met? A light bulb went off over my head, and the premise for my book was born.

I hope you enjoy reading about the Holiday Boys as much as I've enjoyed writing their stories. For more, you can visit my website, kellistorm.com, where you can also subscribe to my newsletter.

Kelli

HIS SMALL-TOWN CHALLENGE

KELLI STORM

SPECIAL EDITION

Harlequin®
SPECIAL EDITION™

Recycling programs for this product may not exist in your area.

ISBN-13: 978-1-335-40239-4

His Small-Town Challenge

Copyright © 2025 by Kelli Du Lude

For questions and comments about the quality of this book, please contact us at CustomerService@Harlequin.com.

TM and ® are trademarks of Harlequin Enterprises ULC.

 Harlequin Enterprises ULC
22 Adelaide St. West, 41st Floor
Toronto, Ontario M5H 4E3, Canada
www.Harlequin.com

Printed in Lithuania

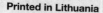

MIX
Paper | Supporting responsible forestry
FSC® C021394

Kelli Storm's debut novel, *His Small-Town Challenge*, was inspired by her love of boy bands. She graduated with a BA in public relations from Grand Valley State University. In a former job, she did publicity for a dog rescue and had press releases used by *People*, I Heart Dogs, MSN and Yahoo. Kelli resides in the Great Lake State with her three rescue dogs and a fourteen-year-old fish named Henry O'Malley.

Books by Kelli Storm

Harlequin Special Edition

Challenge Accepted

His Small-Town Challenge

Visit the Author Profile page at Harlequin.com.

For My Dad

Chapter One

Julie Alleen stared hopelessly at the large pile of bills sprawled on the worn, gray laminate counter in front of her. Things were not going well.

Her store—her whole life, really—was swiftly going down the financial drain. Between business being slow and her mom's increasing living expenses, Julie was headed for serious trouble soon, unless a miracle happened.

The bell above her shop's door rang, and despite her worries, her face relaxed as a familiar teen entered, carrying a decorative crate-size cedar chest.

"Morning, Ms. A."

"Good morning, Dylan."

Julie shoved the bills under the counter and walked toward him. Although Dylan and his family only recently moved to Holiday Bay, he was already one of her favorite people. The tall, fifteen-year-old had floppy brown hair that always fell into his hazel eyes and a sweet, introverted nature that Julie could appreciate, being a quiet person herself.

"Shouldn't you be in school?" she asked.

"Half day for parent-teacher conferences."

Julie admired the pattern of Petoskey stones embedded on the chest's lid. "Dylan, this is beautiful."

"Thanks," he said proudly. "It's—uh—my dad's latest creation. He wanted me to bring it in."

Julie made her way over to the large storefront window and moved a bedside table covered in white chalkboard paint. "You can put it right here."

Dylan set the chest down, angling it in a way that caught the sunlight streaming through the window, making the fossilized rocks shimmer. Julie stared in awe as she always did whenever Dylan brought in a new piece.

She didn't know much about Dylan's dad, except that he was a true craftsman. She hoped that she would get to meet him one day, but the man was a bit of a mystery. He was some big shot who traveled a lot and was much too busy to speak with her directly. Instead, he had his son drop off his work once or twice a month.

Normally, Julie worked closely with the vendors who sold their products in her store. Her connection with them was personal. Strong business relationships were the cornerstone of what made her shop a great experience. Julie's store sold unique items ranging from antique furniture to farmhouse decor. Pieces of Home had that bit of human touch you couldn't get from big online stores, and her customers and vendors were like family to her.

But she had yet to meet Dylan's dad. Julie got the impression that father and son didn't get along very well. The teen tended to change the subject whenever she pressed him for details.

Dylan adjusted the chest one more time before glancing out the window. "Did you see Baxter's is for sale?"

Julie paled at the announcement. "No, I didn't. That happened fast."

Baxter's was the coffee shop neighboring her store. That was one more property for Harris Farmington to get his greedy hands on. Only a few more businesses stood between him and his takeover of the town, her shop being one of them.

"Are you okay?" Dylan asked.

Julie blinked several times, trying and failing to hide the worry, fear, and mental exhaustion that had crept into her expression.

"Oh yeah," she said, forcing herself to sound casual. "Baxter's seriously has the best raspberry mocha lattes around. It's heartbreaking to know I'll have to resort to my boring coffee from home.

Not that she could afford to buy lattes on a whim. It was usually a very special treat for her.

Dylan nodded before turning to look at her store. Julie followed his gaze, taking in the changes she'd made that morning. She moved all the seasonal items to the front, things such as crocheted lemons and hand-carved wooden bumblebees, giving the space a nice summer vibe.

She loved her shop. The building itself was over one hundred years old. In its lifespan, it had been a post office, malt shop, drugstore, and now, her store. Julie's eyes drifted over the scuffed pumpkin pinewood floors, original to the building, admiring how they gleamed under the drum-shaped metal chandeliers that hung in four different places around the ceiling.

"It's looking good in here, Ms. A." Dylan pointed to a large poster on the wall opposite from where they stood. "That doesn't exactly fit in."

Pushing aside her unease, she looked at the picture of Jake Reynolds and smiled. Julie and the mega famous singer had both grown up in Holiday Bay. When they were children, they sometimes hung out together through mutual friends who were neighbors. She'd always liked him as a person, but it wasn't until Julie turned fourteen that her feelings deepened, and she developed a massive crush on Jake.

"That poster has been up since the store opened," Julie said.

Her best friend, Meg, had hung it up as a joke. Julie's neverending love for the Holiday Boys—and specifically Jake Reynolds—was well-known in her inner circle. Julie had planned to take the poster down at some point, but never got around to it. Now, it was a part of the store, a collection of homemade Holiday Boys merchandise underneath it, sold by various vendors from town. Tourists loved the connection the band had to Holiday Bay, and the poster had become a talking point.

"Still doesn't fit the look you're going for." Dylan folded his arms over his chest as he stared at the picture. Every time he adopted that pose, he reminded her of someone, but for the life of her, she couldn't think of who. "I heard he's a jerk," he said. "Completely full of himself."

"Yes, I know, you've told me…at least a hundred times in the three months we've known each other." Julie patted Dylan on the arm before grabbing a string of sun-shaped lights from a nearby plastic tote bag. She strode over to the poster. "When you've loved a band for as long as I have, not many people are going to change your mind about them. That's twenty years of loyalty. Jake here was my first crush. We went to high school together, though he was a senior when I was a freshman."

"Yeah, you've told me…at least a hundred times in the three months we've known each other." Dylan smirked, throwing her words back at her. Julie snorted. She really did like this kid.

"Just wait until these lights are up," she assured him. "Then Jake will be as festive as the rest of the store."

"Sure, Ms. A., whatever you say," Dylan replied before changing the subject. "I'll be bringing in a table soon…well, it's more of a nightstand."

"That'd be great. I look forward to seeing it."

He said goodbye and left her to finish her work. After stringing the lights around the poster and turning them on, Julie snickered at the way the suns formed a sparkling crown around Jake's head.

Julie had so many wonderful memories associated with the Holiday Boys. As an excitable teen, she used to sing and jump on her bed, blasting their CDs on repeat until she had every lyric memorized. As schoolgirls, she and Meg spent hours taking quizzes in magazines to see which Holiday Boy would be their perfect match—she always got Jake.

It was a time of innocence. A time before her father's passing and her mom's descent into Alzheimer's. It was a time before Julie recognized her sexuality for what it was.

A dead end.

If she was honest with herself, she never took the poster down because Jake and she never took the poster down because Jake and her love of his music encouraged positive thoughts. Thoughts that didn't involve worrying about how she was going to pay the store's heating bill in the winter, or finding the money to replace her mom's missing glasses for the hundredth time. Memories that didn't involve a corporate billionaire hell-bent on destroying her livelihood, or the weary acceptance that she'd grow old alone due to her asexuality. All Julie had to do was glance at the poster, and things in her world didn't seem as heavy.

After giving the picture a fond pat, she walked back to Dylan's trunk to see if his dad had placed a price on it. He had for one hundred dollars. He always lowballed his own work. Julie grabbed a pricing gun and marked the trunk up another hundred dollars.

She wondered again what the mystery man did for a living. He obviously wasn't concerned about getting the best price for his work. She had theories about him, her favorites being that he was either an international spy or some trust-fund baby who jet sets around the world.

Julie went back to setting up the rest of the shop for the holiday season, ignoring the unrelenting worry that was turning her stomach into acid. She grabbed some dried sunflowers from the storage room in the back and secured them to either side of the front entrance, completing the summer look.

She opened Pieces of Home ten years ago and poured so much of her time, energy, and money into it. Julie was proud of what she'd accomplished in that time, but business had slowed over the past couple of years, especially since Farmington Stores, Inc. had opened a brick-and-mortar store in the neighboring Traverse City.

The irony of it all. Farmington was one of the largest online retailers in the world, driving small businesses like Julie's straight into bankruptcy. And now that they had killed off most of their competition, they were buying up buildings across the country at little cost, ripping them down and turning the spaces into cold, monster-shopping complexes.

To make matters worse, Harris Farmington, Farmington's CEO, had his eyes set on Northern Michigan. Aside from the store in Traverse City, he wanted to set up a distribution center in her hometown of Holiday Bay. Specifically right where Julie's store was.

Julie was doing everything she could to stay afloat, but the past few months had been especially brutal. Holiday Bay always saw their fair share of tourists in the past, thanks to their location near Lake Michigan. But between the rise of larger online retailers and Farmington doing everything he could to pull people to his store in Traverse City, customers were a rarity these days. The heart of Holiday Bay was their community of small business owners. Once the stores were demolished, everything positive Julie loved about her hometown would be gone.

A few customers trickled in throughout the rest of the day. She managed to sell several items, including the chest, which went to someone on their way home from the Upper Peninsula. While she was happy to make a quick sale, she was a little sad to see the beautiful piece go so soon.

Around closing time, she strolled over to the Jake Reynolds poster to unplug the lights. As she reached for the cord, the bell above the door rang.

"What in the ever-loving world? You gave him a crown?" Meg said from behind her. Julie turned to see her best friend staring at Jake's poster, amused disbelief on her face. Julie laughed, despite the stressful day.

"Someone was in here earlier and said Jake's picture didn't fit with the holiday decor, so I decided to make him look a little more festive for the season." Julie unplugged the lights before turning back around to face Meg. "I thought we were meeting at the restaurant."

Despite the changes that came with growing up, Meg and Julie were as close now as they'd been when they first met back in kindergarten.

Meg shifted from one foot to the other. "Okay, so there's something I need to talk to you about, and I didn't want to do it in public."

Julie raised an eyebrow. "Do I need to be worried?"

"Maybe?" Meg said in a cautious tone. "What do you think of the color orange?"

"As in?"

"As in the color of the bridesmaid dress."

Julie let out an incredulous laugh before lifting a strand of her wavy crimson hair. "With this?"

"I know." Meg raised her hands in a placating gesture. "But Clarice has her mind locked on it."

Meg had waited years for her boyfriend, Lucas, to propose. He was everything she'd ever wanted in a husband. His mom, not so much.

Julie let out a quiet sigh. She was going to look awful in orange, but it wasn't worth causing Meg more stress. Meg was already anxious enough lately, trying to organize her dream wedding while dealing with an interfering future mother-in-law.

"Fine, if that's what you want."

Meg narrowed her eyes. "You gave into that relatively easy. I thought I was going to have to do more convincing."

"It's your wedding." Julie walked over to her best friend and gave her a hug. "*Your* day. Not Clarice's. If orange bridesmaid dresses are really your choice, then I fully support it."

Meg pulled back and stared into Julie's steel-gray eyes, a frown forming on her face. "What's going on?"

Julie pivoted away from her friend and walked behind the counter to grab her purse. "Nothing."

"Slow day again?" Meg asked.

"It's always a slow day."

Meg walked over to Jake's poster. Her hand skimmed over a few Holiday Boys knickknacks on the shelf below——handmade beanies with the name *Holiday Boys* embroidered on the brims and wood lithograph boxes with the faces of the different band members plastered across them.

Julie's eyes drifted to Jake's poster again, thinking about Dylan's earlier comment. "Do you think he's turned into a jerk?"

"Who?"

Julie nodded at the poster.

"Well, if town gossip is to be believed," Meg said, "Jake allegedly broke up Holiday Boys so he could have the spotlight to himself as a solo artist. And you know there was a lot of speculation after he and his wife divorced. Rumor has it he's a bit of a womanizer, which is why his marriage broke up. Of course, that's all hearsay."

Julie huffed. "Everyone in this town loves a hero, but loves when their heroes fall even more."

"That's society in a nutshell."

Julie stared at the poster, trying to reconcile the guy she fell for as a teen with the man people said he was today. The person Julie knew was always kind to everyone in school, no matter how cool or unpopular they were. She didn't care how famous Jake was these days, she couldn't believe he'd grown into a self-involved, egotistical jerk.

Meg picked up one of the lithograph boxes that featured Jake and examined it thoughtfully.

"You know what this town needs?" she said.

"Hmm?" Julie murmured as she rummaged through her purse for her keys.

"Some much-needed publicity. Something that will put Holiday Bay back on the map like it was when the boys were at their peak. Do you remember how fans used to show up here in carloads?"

It was hard to forget. Three out of the five members of Holiday Boys were from Holiday Bay. The town attracted a lot of people when the band was at its peak. Traffic had been a nightmare.

"That was twenty years ago," Julie pointed out.

Meg whirled around to face Julie, Jake's lithograph box clutched to her chest. She had a look in her indigo eyes that Julie knew well. It was an expression that usually got Julie grounded when she was a kid.

"I have a brilliant idea," Meg said.

Julie looked cautious. "Will I end up in jail?"

"When have I ever gotten you in jail?"

"What about that time you convinced me to do the Naked Mile Run—"

Meg rolled her eyes. "This again?"

"—and we showed up, *buck naked,* only to find out that they had canceled the race four years prior."

Meg gave her an exasperated look before putting Jake's picture box back. "I told you a million times that I had the day correct, I simply forgot to check the year. Besides, Officer Pete was very understanding. He only gave us a warning. It's not like we actually went to jail."

Meg hurried over to Julie, pulled her purse off her arm, and began searching inside, ignoring Julie's "Hey!"

"Do you remember our mantra when we were younger?" Meg asked before letting out a triumphant noise as she pulled out Julie's phone.

"Which mantra of the many are you referring to?" Julie asked.

"WWJRD."

Julie folded her arms over her chest. "What would Jake Reynolds do?"

"Exactly." Meg unlocked her screen.

Julie *really* needed to come up with a different password other than her birthday. She glanced at the poster, taking in Jake's warm blue eyes and crooked smile.

"You want me to close up my store, leave Holiday Bay, and never look back?"

Meg angled the phone so it went into landscape mode. "No. I'm talking about the fact that Jake Reynolds, at the tender age of seventeen, had a dream, my friend. He formed his band and made history. Nothing got in his way and now he's one of the most famous singers in the world."

"Pretty sure I'm the one who told *you* all that." Julie reached for her phone, but Meg stepped out of reach and began to fiddle with some of the features. Julie let out an exasperated breath. "I'm not sure I'm tracking where you're going with all this."

"You'll do anything to save your store, right?"

"Of course."

"Jake Reynolds draws a crowd wherever he goes. His biggest rival is Harry Styles, and even there, he has the edge. Jake is ten times more popular now than he was twenty years ago. If you can get him to return to Holiday Bay, think of what kind of boost that'll give the town. What it would give your store."

"What makes you think anything I say would get Jake Reynolds back here? He didn't know I existed in high school and that was *before* he became an internationally famous singer."

"It couldn't hurt," Meg said as she waved the phone. "What's the harm in making a little video, asking him to come for a visit?"

"Why don't we ask Tyler to come into town while we're at it?" Julie retorted. Tyler was Jake's best friend, former Holiday Boy, and Meg's old neighbor. Their parents still lived next door to each other. He also happened to be Meg's greatest childhood nemesis.

"Like he'd ever help anyone besides himself. Besides, his mom said he's busy with a project in LA. I ran into her yesterday at the grocery store, and she told me he's collaborating with some up-and-coming hotshot." When Julie continued to stand there, Meg let out an exaggerated sigh. "I'm not moving until you ask Jake to come visit your store."

Julie didn't know why she hesitating. Jake had over 150 million followers on Instagram. Even if she did post whatever Meg wanted her to say, it wasn't as if he would ever see it. But maybe some people would. Potential customers.

The mounting bills she'd shoved under the store's counter entered her mind. And with it came a sense of anger. Anger at the fact that she was on the precipice of losing everything she'd worked so hard for. Making a stupid video that no one would see was better than doing nothing at all, and as pointless as the effort was, at least it felt like she was doing *something* to save herself.

With a nod, Julie said, "Roll it."

Meg grinned and hit the record button.

Flicking her red hair over her shoulder, Julie stared into the camera.

"Hello, Jake Reynolds. My name is Julie Alleen. I know you probably don't remember me, even though we attended the same school. I'm sure you don't remember a lot of people from Holiday Bay. It's been years since you've been back here. And yet…" Julie walked over to Jake's poster on her wall, waving a hand in front of the homemade Holiday Boys merchandise. "The town hasn't forgotten about you. Holiday Bay is suffering, Jake. Corporate America is knocking on our door, wanting to buy up all the local businesses and destroy everything that makes Holiday Bay what it is. We've fallen so far off the map that most people don't even know we're here—despite one of the biggest boy bands to have ever existed naming themselves after us." Julie paused, emotion making her voice tight. "And so… I put this challenge out to you. Come back to Holiday Bay for the holidays. Help people remember we're here. Visit my store, Pieces of Home, while you're at it. We need you, Jake. *I* need you. What do you say? Will you accept my challenge and come home?"

Meg stopped recording and opened a different app on Julie's phone.

"What? You're posting it now?" Julie covered her mouth as Meg put the video on Pieces of Home's Instagram page. She also tagged Jake in the post.

"Let's see if this does anything." Meg closed the app and handed Julie back her phone, looking smug.

Julie panicked for several seconds. What if Jake or any of his followers actually saw her video? What would they think of her?

She shook her head.

She had nothing to worry about.

There was no way Jake Reynolds would ever see that video.

Chapter Two

Jake Reynolds woke with a pounding headache. His mouth tasted like something had died in it. The scent of stale beer and sex covered his skin. Bile rose in his throat as his hangover hit in full force. He tried to focus his blurry eyes on the bright flamingo-printed wallpaper opposite him, but the sharp colors made his headache even worse.

He rubbed at his forehead, questioning his poor life choices.

Yesterday had been the anniversary of his divorce, and he'd marked the occasion the same way he always did—getting drunk and finding someone to spend it with. It wasn't something he was proud of. It reminded him of how his father had solved his problems—having meaningless sex to escape how miserable he was.

Taking a shaky breath, Jake glanced across the motel bed and peered at the naked brunette still sleeping soundly. Carefully pushing back the sheets, he stood and quietly got dressed. As he made his way across stained green carpet, he stepped over the woman's black dress, lace underwear, and a couple of torn condom wrappers. He would have felt like an ass about leaving without speaking to her first, except he'd made it clear to the woman—Christ, he couldn't even remember her name—that this was a one-off and she'd happily agreed.

Most women did.

Jake made no illusions that his success with women had

anything to do with him personally. The women he'd slept with over the past five years since his divorce were more interested in sleeping with Jake Reynolds, famous singer, rather than Jake the person.

He left the motel room and walked to the bar he'd been at the night before, relieved to see that his black Camaro was still there and hadn't been towed like he half feared. He hopped inside, started the muscle car, and began the twenty-minute drive home. As he entered Holiday Bay's city limits, he passed the old diner his mom used to work at. God, he hated that place and everything it symbolized. It was there that his parents' marriage officially died.

Jake's phone rang and he welcomed the distraction. That was until he scanned the display screen on his dashboard and saw his ex's name.

Groaning softly, he pressed a button on the steering wheel and said, "Hey, Angelika."

"Where have you been?" she asked, her tone impatient. "I've been trying to get a hold of you all morning."

"I was busy."

"And what was her name?"

There it was. The main reason why their marriage ended after eleven years. Every time Jake came home after a long, exhausting tour, Angelika would be at the ready, throwing accusations of infidelity at him—accusing him of sleeping with some groupie or his manager, Lori—despite the fact that he'd remained faithful to her the entire time they were together.

He actually enjoyed being married and still missed being in a serious relationship. He missed having someone to connect with on a deep, personal level. To share his worries or concerns about how a tour was going, or if the stove needed replacing because the back burner never worked. He missed sharing his life with someone. But his relationship with Angelika had always been rocky, even in the best of times.

His head pounded even harder. "What do you need?"

Angelika was silent for a moment before she asked reluctantly, "Is our son with you?"

Jake grew instantly alarmed. "No. He's not with you?"

"We...had a disagreement earlier. He's not answering his phone."

Jake turned into the hidden drive that led to his newly purchased mansion. As he sped down the paved path that cut between large, towering pines, he said, "I just got home. Let me see if he's in the shop."

Angelika made a tsk-tsking noise. "I really wish you wouldn't indulge that little hobby of his."

Jake's fingers tightened on the steering wheel. "He loves woodworking. He's really good at it."

"It's a waste of his time," Angelika retorted. "He needs to focus on his studies so he can get into law school."

As Jake reached the end of the drive, he let out a pent-up breath. Dylan's turquoise moped was outside the workshop attached to Jake's garage.

"He's here," he said.

"Good." Angelika sounded relieved. "Tell him to come home."

"You know," Jake said, "have you ever asked Dylan what he wants to do with his life? He's never expressed interest in becoming a lawyer to me."

"When have you ever been around long enough to know what his interests are?"

Jake's jaw clenched. It was true. He hadn't been around much when Dylan was growing up, nor was he there to support Angelika. Sure, she was the one who suggested Jake branch out into a solo career after the Holiday Boys broke up, but neither of them anticipated he would be gone as much as he was. He'd left his young wife and infant son behind to record album after album and to do worldwide tours.

After Jake's own upbringing with an abusive father and a mom who'd worked three jobs to support Jake and his sister, Jake became obsessed with making sure Dylan never experienced what he had. But in his efforts to give his son everything, he neglected to give Dylan the one thing that was most important. His presence.

"I moved back to Holiday Bay to be closer to Dylan," Jake gritted out, "despite my feelings for this town, which you were well aware of when you chose to move here—"

"I know this is hard for you to believe, Jake," Angelika said, "but the world actually doesn't revolve around you. We moved here because the school system is good and my family is one town over."

"—and," Jake continued, as though she hadn't spoken, "I'm going to support my son. Why are you so set on him going to law school anyway?"

"Carl can get him into any school he wants," Angelika said.

It still stung that Angelika married her divorce attorney soon after her marriage to Jake officially ended. Not only did she get married, but they also had a little girl together, and that was after Angelika insisted for years that she didn't want any more children.

"I'm sure Carl means well," Jake said tightly, "but maybe he should let us—you know, Dylan's parents—decide what's best for our son."

"Oh please. Carl's been more of a father to Dylan than you've ever been."

Ignoring the pain that comment caused, Jake said, "You know what? I've got to go. I'm supposed to be in the recording studio in an hour."

"Of course you are," Angelika snapped before asking, "Will Lori be there?"

Jake's shoulders tightened. "Well, yeah. She's our manager."

Her only response was, "Tell Dylan to come home now!"

She disconnected the call. Jake laid his head against the steering wheel, pushing his brow against the hard surface in an attempt to relieve some inner pressure.

God, he hated fighting with Angelika. Scratch that. He hated *anyone* fighting. A therapist once told him he had PTSD from his childhood. For a long time, he'd have to leave the room whenever people started fighting, the sound of angry voices putting him on edge.

With a heavy sigh, Jake got out of the car and walked toward the two-story red-brick mansion he'd purchased the month before. The home once belonged to Riley Chamberlin, a huge silent movie star from Michigan. The place came with impressive views of the bay, a tennis court, an Olympic-size swimming pool, and most importantly…privacy.

Jake entered the grand hallway. Marble floors and wainscoted walls greeted him. In the middle of the hall was a large staircase made of the same marble, with ornate black railing. A gigantic crystal chandelier hung high from the ceiling above, casting sparkling light everywhere. The cleaning service must have come in that morning because the entire foyer smelled like fresh-cut lemons.

He took the stairs to the second level and headed to his room. Stepping inside the master suite, he breathed in the mixed scent of fresh paint and newly polished wood. Everything was new in here, from the dark wood furniture to the thick gray carpet. Glancing at the clock on his bedside table, he swore. He was going to be late if he didn't get moving soon.

Jake rushed into the white-tiled bathroom to wash off the night before. He spared a few minutes to stand under the warm water descending from the rain showerhead. As he hung his head and briefly closed his eyes, he tried to let some of his frustration with Angelika drain away.

He wasn't lying when he told her he needed to leave for the studio soon. After a lot of recent talking and reminiscing, the members of Holiday Boys had decided to reunite for a new record. It would be the first time the band performed together in fifteen years.

Jake had always been notoriously late for events and recording sessions when he was younger. He spent a lot of time in those early days either wrapped up in a song he was writing, or on the phone with Angelika, trying to assure her that he was behaving himself. He didn't want to start on the wrong foot with the guys. They were already doing him a huge favor by coming to Michigan to record the album so he could stay close to Dylan.

After dressing, Jake hurried to the kitchen to grab some painkillers for his headache before proceeding into the workshop. Large windows on the north side of the room allowed natural light to filtrate through the entire workspace. Every woodworking tool imaginable lined one wall. Various saws and benches rested against the wall opposite Jake. To his right was a door that led outside and another bench, which Dylan used for his finished projects.

Dylan was hard at work, going over his latest creation with an electric hand sander. Sawdust covered the cement floor beneath his beat-up Vans. The Craftsman-style nightstand he was working on looked incredible, considering he'd only recently started making furniture.

If there was one thing Jake was grateful for regarding his childhood, it was the many hours Jake's maternal grandpa had spent teaching him woodwork. It was something he grew to deeply love and a passion he'd passed on to Dylan. More importantly, it gave Jake and his son something to bond over.

Sometimes they worked on pieces together, but Dylan had begun making things on his own as he gained more confidence in his abilities. Next to his workspace was a pile of Petoskey stones. Adding Michigan's state stone to every project was Dylan's signature.

People can take a piece of Michigan wherever they go, he had told his father in one of his more talkative moments.

"Hey," Jake called out before noticing Dylan had his earbuds in. As he stepped close enough to hear the music blaring, he winced at the damage Dylan was probably doing to his eardrums. Not that he was one to criticize. Between his shows' pyrotechnics and the screaming fans, God knew what damage he'd done to his own ears over the years.

He tapped Dylan on the shoulder to get his attention. Dylan dropped the sander and swung around with a startled expression, which turned to caution once he noticed his dad.

"Uh, hi," Dylan said. He grabbed the sander and turned it off. He pulled out the earbuds and placed them in his jeans pocket, the music still softly playing through the material of his pants. "I hope it's okay that I'm here. I wanted to work on this and Carl doesn't have the equipment you do."

Jake's jaw tightened at the mention of Dylan's stepdad. He was happy Dylan had another loving father figure in his life, but he couldn't help but be a little jealous. Woodwork was *their* thing...their only thing.

"It's fine," Jake said. "You know you're always welcome here whenever you want. My house is your house as long as you're not—"

"Using the saw," Dylan responded. It was one of the few rules Jake gave his son to use the workshop. He wasn't allowed to use any of the more dangerous machines unless an adult was there.

Dylan didn't say anything else as he stared awkwardly down at his feet.

Jake stared at the top of his son's head, trying to think of something to say. He finally settled on, "What are you listening to?"

Shrugging, Dylan tapped on his Apple Watch. The music

stopped blaring from the earbuds. "The Accidentals. You wouldn't know them."

"I've heard of them. They're from Michigan, right?"

Dylan nodded but continued to stay silent.

"They've got a good sound. Mellow," Jake said, eager to talk to his son about music. *This* was a subject he knew well. "I'm surprised you're not listening to something more hard-core. Maybe a little Rage Against the Machine or something."

Dylan stared at him blankly. "Who?"

"Ouch," Jake muttered. Now that he was living closer to his son, they were going to have to do some serious work on Dylan's musical education.

Jake began tapping his thumb nervously against the work-bench as Dylan eyed his project again, probably eager to get back to it. Jake really didn't want to say what he needed to. Even if their current conversation was awkward as hell, he'd rather have that than any fighting.

Knowing he couldn't put it off any longer, Jake said, "You know, your mom's looking for you. She called me."

Dylan turned to pick up the sander again, his back to his father. "That must have been painful."

Jake ignored that. He moved so he could see Dylan's profile. "She's concerned about you."

Dylan rolled his eyes. "More like she's worried that her grand plan for my life might be in danger. She wants me to become a lawyer. I keep telling her that's not what I want to do."

Jake ran a finger across the smooth surface of the leg Dylan had just finished sanding. "What *do* you want to do?"

Dylan fiddled with the cord of the sander. "I guess I want to do this. I… I want to open my own store so I can sell my stuff."

Jake nodded. "You know, I could help you with that. Once you're of age. I can give you the money—"

"No thanks," Dylan said, his tone short. "I want to do it on my own."

Jake tried to think of something else to say. It was crazy. He could win over a crowd of ten thousand people just by saying *hello* into a mic, but he couldn't make small talk with his own son. He peered around and noticed there was an item missing from the bench where Dylan stored his completed projects.

"What happened to the chest you were working on? Did you finish it?"

"Yeah. I gave it to a friend." His shoulders hunched as though he expected Jake to be mad or something.

When he didn't say anything further, Jake tried again. "I hope they liked it."

Dylan rested his hand on the workbench. "I'm almost done with this and then I'm going to start staining it. D-do you want to help?"

Jake wanted nothing more than to stay home and spend time with his son, but he'd already committed his afternoon away.

"I'd really love to, but I need to head to the studio."

Dylan stiffened before Jake even finished his sentence, as though he anticipated his dad's rejection.

"Yeah, sure. Whatever."

"I already made the commitment," Jake said. "The guys from the band are coming into town today, just for this record. What if you and I meet here on—"

"It's fine," Dylan interrupted. "I'll try to put it in your calendar next time."

"Dylan, come on—"

"You know? I better get going." Dylan brushed the dust from his hands before grabbing his moped helmet off a nearby table. "I should go see what Mom wants."

"Dylan—"

Dylan left without looking back, slamming the door behind him as he went.

Jake massaged his shoulder, trying to relieve some tension. The silence in the room after Dylan's abrupt departure taunted

Jake. Sawdust was everywhere. He was half tempted to grab the shop vac and clean it up, but he didn't have time. He hurried back to the kitchen. He never thought anyone could beat his own father in the running for Worst Father of All Time, but he knew Dylan would vote for him in a heartbeat.

After downing a Toaster Strudel, he hopped back in his car to do the hour drive to Charlevoix. After reaching the city limit, he drove to one of the mansions along the lakeshore. His friend Trevor—another Michigan native—was a renowned music producer. He'd converted his basement into a dream studio, which had some of the best acoustics Jake ever had had the pleasure of recording in.

After the housekeeper let him in, Jake walked down the grand hall with its rich, warm dark wood floors and bright red-painted walls. He took stairs covered in pink carpet down to the basement level and entered the control room. Some of Jake's tension left his shoulders at the sight of Trevor sitting behind the large multitrack mixing console, talking to one of the audio engineers.

He got up when he saw Jake. "Hey man."

They hugged, slapping each other on the back before Jake pulled away, then looked through the glass window that separated the control room from the live room.

His best friend, Tyler, was already inside, holding a guitar. Tyler and Jake's friendship dated back to elementary school. They, along with Jake's cousin James, were the founding members of Holiday Boys. As Jake moved to the glass door separating the rooms, he noticed his other bandmate, Zan, was also there, leaning against the wall with a grimace on his face.

"Yes, Bob, I understand," a voice said behind him.

Jake looked over his shoulder and saw the band's manager, Lori, enter the room on her phone. She stopped when she saw him. She didn't end her call, but she didn't break eye contact with Jake. He turned to leave, but she held up a finger, gesturing that she wanted him to wait.

"Of course the record will be on time," she said before laughing in a way that sounded insincere to Jake's ears. The person on the other end of the conversation said something and Lori's eyes narrowed on Jake. "Of course. That won't be a problem."

She ended the call and said, "Jake, you're here on time. Will wonders never cease?"

"Good to see you again, Lori," Jake said. He didn't mean it. If he never saw Lori again, he'd be fine with that.

Lori started with the Holiday Boys as their assistant manager, working under her father, "Big Poppa" Phil Cummings. Big Poppa was the one who discovered the Holiday Boys. His passion and commitment helped the band reach the level of stardom that they had. More importantly, he'd become the father figure to Jake that Jake never had. He was devastated when his mentor retired due to terminal illness.

Before he died, Big Poppa made Jake promise that Lori could take over managing the band. He'd come to regret that decision.

Lori had always been flirtatious with Jake, even while he was married, but she'd never crossed a line, despite Angelika's paranoia that the two were having an affair. Jake had made sure they always maintained a professional relationship.

It wasn't until after his marriage ended that Jake made the mistake of sleeping with Lori. They'd run into each other at an awards event, which also happened to be on the anniversary of his divorce. He'd handled the day like he always did, by getting drunk, and they'd wound up in bed together. At the time, he didn't think about the consequences. He never thought Holiday Boys would get back together or that Lori would be a part of the reunion package.

"You know…" She sauntered over to him, her low-cut black

top barely covering her breasts. She lifted her hand and ran her fingers through his hair. He stepped away from her and her eyes flashed with something ugly. Her voice went cool. "You could try to make yourself presentable for these sessions. I want to take pictures of you guys recording for the website. It looks like you just stepped out of the shower."

"That's because I did." He glanced at the live room, longing to join his friends.

She jutted out a hip. "If you ever need some help washing your back, give me a call."

His expression turned to stone. Lori was fantastic at her job, but her behavior around Jake had become increasingly inappropriate since the band reunited. When she wasn't finding excuses to touch him, she made inappropriate remarks like this.

"I can wash my own back, thanks."

Her turquoise blue eyes burned before she flipped her jet-black hair over her shoulder and returned to her phone to make another call. He didn't get why she kept flirting with him. Half the time, she looked like she couldn't stand him.

The air in his lungs loosened a little as he finally escaped the control booth and entered the live room. White insulated panels hung on the walls. Bright overhead lights caused the maple wood floors below to shine. The sound of screeching guitar riffs greeted Jake's ears.

"After all these years," he said good-naturedly to Tyler, "you still haven't learned how to play an instrument."

Tyler put down the guitar and walked over to him, then lifted him into a bear hug. Though the two weren't as close as they were when they were kids, with Tyler living in LA as a prominent songwriter, they still kept in touch whenever their busy schedules allowed.

Zan sauntered over and slapped Jake on the shoulder. "Thanks for the invite, oh exalted one."

Jake laughed, knowing there was no malice behind it.

While Jake may have been the most successful of the group, Zan had his own success as a bestselling author.

"How are Mary and the kids?" Jake asked.

"Probably glad to finally have me out of the house for a while," Zan joked before pulling his phone out and showing Jake the latest pictures of his kids.

Jake observed the photo, noticing how much the kids had grown since he last saw them. "They're getting big."

"Don't I know it. Alexander keeps hitting growth spurts. Mary has to get him new clothes every other week. And Alice added another boyfriend to her collection. She's up to five now."

"Don't worry, Papa," Tyler said. "She's in kindergarten. I don't think you have to plan any weddings anytime soon." He looked at Jake and frowned. "You don't look happy for someone who probably spent a more enjoyable night than either one of us did." He waved his hand between himself and Zan.

Even though the band didn't see each other that often, they all knew what Jake's tradition was on the anniversary of his divorce.

"So, did you find the next Mrs. Reynolds?" Zan asked.

"Not really looking for one," Jake reminded them. One bad marriage had been enough. Was Jake lonely? Absolutely. Did he still wish he had that special someone to grow old with? Definitely. Was he willing to go through the pain of dating, of trying to find someone who wanted to be with *him* and not a superstar? Hell no.

"Who's the next Mrs. Reynolds?" A voice said from behind them, and Jake grinned as his cousin, James, walked into the room followed by their other bandmate, Paul.

"No one," Jake muttered before asking James, "Mason come with you?"

"Nah, he decided to stay home," James answered, a familiar fond look on his face whenever he mentioned his husband. He pointed a thumb over his shoulder at Paul. "He and the block-head over here came up with a home-improvement show featuring me. Mason is at the townhouse working out the details."

"The show's going to be great." Paul waved his hand in the air for dramatic effect. "Former boy band member turn rugged construction worker. The ladies and gents will go crazy over it, especially when they find out you've been restoring old historic homes in Detroit. And with Mason on board, given his past experience as a reality TV star, not to mention I hired one of the best directors in the biz to lead the project, I'm telling you, HGTV is already salivating."

"What about *First Comes Marriage*?" Zan said, elbowing Paul lightly in the stomach. "How will the world continue without you filming a bunch of horny strangers marrying each other at first sight?"

Paul raised an eyebrow at Zan. "The show's on hiatus and don't mock it. We're number one in our timeslot."

"Has anyone actually stayed together from your show?" Zan asked.

"Hey, our recent contestant winners are still going strong. They just celebrated their one-month anniversary."

"Wow, a whole month," Zan said dryly. "That *is* a record, considering the show has been on the air for what, six years? You know, Mary had a great idea. She said you should be on the show, but pick a girl from one of our meet and greets à la *The Bachelor* style."

"First of all, do you recall that I was voted Hottest Holiday Boy by *Teen Beat* magazine? Why would I need to pick up some chick from a reality TV show?" Paul always loved to throw that in their faces whenever the guys got together. "Second, why would I want to settle down, especially with a fan who's probably obsessed.

"Hey!" Zan glared. "They aren't all like that. I met Mary at a fan meet and greet and she's perfect."

Trevor's voice came across the room's sound system, interrupting their squabbling. "You guys about ready?"

"I have to take a piss," Paul said before leaving the room through a side door.

"Classy as always, Paul." Tyler went over to a workstation set up in one corner. "Jake, come here for a second. I wanted to get your thoughts on a change I'm thinking we need to make to 'Starry-Eyed.'"

While all of the guys in the band contributed songs, many people considered Jake and Tyler to be the McCartney-Lennon of boy bands—labels they were happy and honored to accept.

They began to discuss some of the lyrics for the song about an obsessive fan. It was based on an experience Tyler went through a few years ago. The fan had broken into his house and worn his dirty underwear like a hat. Jake never understood what drove a person to go that far. It made him thankful all over again that his new house offered him privacy and safety, thanks to the plethora of security features he'd added before he moved in.

Jake's eyes briefly met Lori's through the glass but he turned away.

"Okay, 'Starry-Eyed' is definitely going on the album." Jake moved over to the piano and sat down. He began to play a melody that drew the guys over.

"I like it," James said. "Is that for Tyler's song?"

"No, this is something I wrote for Dylan." Jake didn't look at his bandmates. "It's called *Little Man Grown*."

His friends looked at him with varying expressions of sympathy. James clasped the back of his neck and gave a comforting squeeze.

"He'll love it," his cousin said.

Paul returned to the room, laughing at something on his phone. "Jake, you've gone viral."

"What?" Jake jerked his head up, dread filling him. Lady

Gaga had said it best when she had called social media "the toilet of the internet." He couldn't think for the life of him what he could have possibly done to go viral. Unless it was the woman from last night. Had she recorded them?

"Look." Paul handed him the phone.

It was a video of a woman. Her hair glimmered like molten lava. She had gunmetal-gray eyes that shone like melted pewter. Her full mouth held a bitter smile for some reason, but it only emphasized her high cheekbones. She was beautiful.

A wrinkle formed on Jake's forehead. He didn't think he'd ever had the pleasure of meeting her. He hit Play.

Hello, Jake Reynolds. My name is Julie Alleen. I know you probably don't remember me, even though we attended the same school—

Jake pressed Pause. "Holy—."

He *did* know Julie. It had been at least twenty years since he last saw her back in high school. He hadn't recognized her at first because she'd obviously grown up—her face had matured—but he did remember that unique, beautiful hair.

She'd been in the background all his life—everyone who grew up in Holiday Bay knew each other in some capacity—but he always viewed her as a kid when they were younger.

The first time he felt like he really *saw* her was in high school. Julie had been walking down the hall with her books clutched to her chest. As she'd tilted her head back and laughed at something her friend said, her glorious red hair cascaded over her shoulders. Jake could still remember how his breath caught as he watched her go by.

He wanted to talk to her then, but his life was already on a different path. At the time, his focus was on getting the hell out of Holiday Bay and never returning. The town held a lot of bad memories for him, thanks to his dad's scandalous behavior, which had been a source of malicious gossip for years. He wouldn't have even named the band *Holiday Boys*, but Tyler and James had insisted, their memories of their hometown more positive than Jake's.

Jake had never told anyone, but he'd written a song about Julie called "Enchanted," about that day he had seen her in the hall. Most people thought the song was about Angelika, but he hadn't met her yet. They met a few days later at a gig and became a thing soon after. "Enchanted" was what helped the band gain the attention of record labels, not to mention it became their first major hit.

"Do you know her?" Zan asked, nodding at the video.

"Didn't we go to school with her?" James moved his face toward the screen so he could get a better look. "Wait, I think that's Meg Archer's friend? You remember? They'd sometimes hang out with us when we were kids. I dated Julie's sister for two weeks years before I came out."

"Meg?" Tyler pushed his way closer to the phone. "Is she in the video?"

"Why do I know that name?" Paul raised an eyebrow at Tyler. "Wait…you grew up next door to her, didn't you? Didn't you say you two were super competitive when you were kids?"

"Yeah, Meg was a regular pain in my ass," Tyler said, but the fond smile on his face took away any malice in the statement.

Jake ignored them and hit Play again. He watched the video, his mouth curving upward as it continued. Julie still had the power to enchant.

And so… I put this challenge out to you. Come back to Holiday Bay for the holidays. Help people remember we're here. Visit my store, Pieces of Home, while you're at it. We need you, Jake. I need you. What do you say? Will you accept my challenge and come home?

"Well, isn't it convenient that you're so close to her now?" Paul smirked.

Zan whistled as he looked at the hits. The video already

had over seven hundred thousand views and two thousand comments. Some people were nice and encouraging; others not so much, accusing Julie of being desperate and attention seeking. A few even called her a stalker.

"Boys." Lori's impatient voice came over the speaker. "Can we please get to recording so we can get the hell out of Michigan someday?"

"You know we're all from Michigan, right?" Paul said, as he, Tyler, and Zan moved to their microphones.

James nodded at the phone. "What are you going to do about that?"

Jake leaned back, thoughtful, as he stared at Julie frozen on screen. He took in her delicate features, not missing the worry lines around her mouth and eyes.

He really didn't want the publicity. On the other hand, if it hadn't been for Julie Alleen, "Enchanted" never would have happened. In a way, he owed his career to her.

Decision made, he got up from the piano bench and tossed the phone back to Paul.

"I think I'll accept her challenge."

Chapter Three

Julie's phone buzzed, followed by two more vibrations. She impatiently turned it off, then opened her purse and shoved it inside before heading into the assisted-living residence her mom lived in. Her phone had been buzzing nonstop ever since Meg posted that stupid video a few days ago. Last time Julie checked, it had over one million views. Much to her dismay, people also tagged Jake's and the Holiday Boys' Instagram pages. They hadn't responded yet, and she prayed to every deity out there that they either hadn't seen the video or hadn't taken it seriously.

The whole thing was completely out of Julie's comfort zone. She only hoped that the situation passed soon. Overall, people had been kind to her, wishing her the best of luck with her shop. The store's website had even tripled in traffic over the past few days and online ordering was up, which she was grateful for. But it hadn't brought many people into the actual location. For her to stop Farmington, all the shops in her surrounding area had to stay strong and survive. To do that, they collectively needed more business.

And then there was the seedier side of social media that felt the need to comment on her video. Some people called her an attention-seeker. She even received a few death threats telling her to leave Jake alone or else…because *she* was clearly the one with issues.

Julie entered the main hallway, walking across the laminate faux-wood floor. Red Oaks was the only assisted-living place in the area that had a memory-care unit. Her mom wasn't at that level yet—and God knew how they'd be able to afford it when the time came—but they would need that option for her eventually.

Julie breathed in the fresh floral air freshener as she moved past the clean dining room, situated to the right of the entrance. To her left was an entertainment area, where two residents were playing checkers while another watched TV. An island off the kitchen area offered fresh cookies and bowls of popcorn for their residents.

"Those better be good," Julie muttered as she eyed the cookies, thinking about the extraordinary amount of money Red Oaks charged for that level of attention.

The rent for her mom's apartment alone was well over five thousand dollars a month, even before her Alzheimer's got as bad as it was now. Julie had long accepted the place was a racket, sucking up more and more of their money. But it was either this place or another facility that took Julie over forty-five minutes to get to.

"Ms. Alleen, a moment?"

Julie silently groaned before turning to face the administrator. The woman—*call me Aubry*—looked like she was right out of college, with a youthful face that hadn't experienced any of life's hard lessons yet. She tapped something rapidly on her phone before turning her attention to Julie with an insincere smile.

"I was hoping I would run into you. We need to schedule your mom's six-month assessment."

Julie's heart sank. An assessment was code for *Let's add another six hundred dollars a month to the bill*. "Sure. Sometime next week?"

"That'll be wonderful. I'll call you with a time," Aubry said, going back to her phone as she walked away.

Feeling bone-tired at the idea of facing yet another financial burden, Julie walked into her mom's apartment. If there was one thing she did like about where her mom lived, it was the cute setup of the place. Upon entering the space, a person walked right into a living room. The walls were in a warm cream color, the carpet a soft brown. To her right was a bathroom with a private full shower, which was a feature most of the other assisted-living places Julie had toured didn't offer. Other facilities only offered a toilet and sink with community showers down the hall.

To the left of the entrance was a kitchenette area, which had a sink and a small refrigerator, though Julie had to continuously check it in case her mom snuck food into it. Lord knew the staff never did. Her mom once left a tuna sandwich inside that went undiscovered for weeks. The smell saturated the interior and no amount of scrubbing could remove it. Red Oaks ended up replacing the refrigerator…charging Julie for the damage, of course, because the money her mom received from her pension and social security benefits didn't even cover her rent, let alone extra expenses.

Kitty-corner to the main entrance was a bedroom, which again, was a nice addition that several other assisted living residences lacked. Most places she'd visited only offered studio apartments with the bedroom and the living room in the same space.

Julie smiled when she saw her mom in her favorite brown recliner. Julie's childhood dog had chewed holes in the arms when she was a puppy. Her mom never bothered to replace the chair, stating at the time that it was still comfortable, even if it was an eyesore.

Her mom rocked herself with her foot as she worked on a crossword puzzle, humming as the recliner creaked. Julie felt hope blossom inside her when she noticed the puzzle. When her mom did something of her own free will, it meant she was having a good day.

It also looked like she wore fresh clothes, consisting of a soft purple sweater and black pants. Her mom's clothes were one of the many battles Julie had with Red Oaks. When she first moved her mom in, her memory wasn't as bad, but her mom refused to wear clean clothes on a regular basis. Staff wouldn't tell her to change because she was still "aware" and might get offended. It made Julie irate, as she was always the bad guy who made her mom change outfits during her weekly visits. She sat down on a beige love seat next to the recliner. "Hey, Mom."

Her mom glanced at her, eyes wary, and the hope in Julie's chest drained. Her mom didn't recognize her.

Julie forced a smile anyway. "How are you feeling today?"

Her mom set the crossword puzzle in her lap. "Are you the nurse who keeps stealing my pens?"

"No, Mom. It's Julie. Your daughter."

Her mom's eyes narrowed. "My daughter's name is Veronica. I don't know you."

Julie swallowed over the painful lump in her throat. Julie's older sister, Veronica, had always been closer to their mom, but she'd found it too hard to be around her as the disease progressed. She had moved to California under the guise that she needed to go for her job, and she took their mom's only grandchildren with her. Julie would never have any. It was something her mom never understood about her.

When she was younger, she used to tell her mom that she didn't feel like she'd ever get married. Her mom always replied with *You just haven't met the right man yet. Someday, you'll change your mind.*

It took Julie a long time to figure out she fell under the asexual spectrum, specifically that she was graysexual: someone who experiences little to no sexual attraction. She did find people physically attractive. She could pass a man and literally have her breath taken away by how much she felt drawn to him. But the thought of actually engaging in sex was a turnoff for the most part. She wasn't exactly sex-repulsed like some aces. She considered herself more sex-positive. While she enjoyed aspects of intimacy—a man kissing her neck always got her pulse racing—she didn't understand the appeal of actual intercourse.

It was a viewpoint hard to explain…that a healthy thirty-four-year-old woman had absolutely no desire to have sex. And if most people couldn't fathom the concept, there was no point in trying to explain it to a parent in the depths of a disease that made them forget their own child's name.

"You're right, I'm not Veronica," Julie finally said before pointing at the crossword her mom was working on. "Is that a new puzzle?"

The defensiveness in her mom's face dropped and she picked up the book. "Yes, my daughter gave it to me." She frowned. "Her name is… Julie. Yes, that's it. Julie."

Julie smiled. "She must love you very much."

Her mom nodded, her face proud. "She does. I'm lucky to have two loving daughters."

Julie stayed for another hour. Her mom told her all about the puzzle book. Over…and over…and over again. They had the same conversation at least ten times before Julie couldn't take it anymore. Getting up from the love seat, she dropped a kiss on her mom's head.

"I have to go now, but I'll see you again next week."

"Okay," her mom said, already lost in her puzzle.

Julie's stomach twisted with guilt as she all but ran from the building. She knew it wasn't her mom's fault that she was how she was. It made Julie sick to admit, but there were days she just couldn't handle the same repeated conversations. It made her feel like the worst daughter in the world, and she had to remind herself to be more patient.

When Julie was inside her car, she called her sister.

"Hello?" Veronica said, her voice sleepy.

"Hey, I thought you'd be up by now. Aren't the kids going to school today?"

"Greg took Jesse to school." Veronica mentioned her husband and son. "Vanessa has the flu. I was up all night with her."

Julie grimaced. Her sister was probably not going to be in the mood for this conversation, but it had to be done.

"Listen, I'm calling about Mom."

"Did something happen to her?" Veronica sounded a little more alert.

"No, she's okay. But Red Oaks said it's time for another assessment. You know they usually hike up her rent during those."

"What do you want me to do about it, Julie?"

"I need to know if you'll help me cover this."

"My money is already tight. They recently did a hike in tuition at the kids' private school, and the insurance on Greg's Porsche went up after his DUI. I'm not in a position to help you out any more than I already do. Why don't you move to that place in Clarington?"

Julie ground her teeth. They'd had this conversation before. "I told you, that place is a dumpster fire. It's dirty and they were cited for patient neglect last year. Not to mention it's a forty-five minute drive."

"Then move her to your house and hire a nurse."

"Mom needs twenty-four-hour care, and you know the size of my house. I don't have room for one additional person to live there, let alone two."

"Well, you'll need to figure it out. There are options out there, you just don't want to do them. Now, I can hear Vanessa throwing up in the bathroom. I have to see to my sick child. Goodbye."

Veronica disconnected the call. Julie rubbed at her forehead before glancing at the clock in her car. Meg wanted Julie's help picking out a wedding dress, and Julie was going to be late for the appointment if she didn't get going. She cracked her car window open and drove to the town's only bridal shop, hoping the late-spring air would revitalize her after the depressing visit with her mom and conversation with Veronica. Thankfully, the shop wasn't too far from her own, so Julie parked next to her store and walked the short distance to Bridal Barn.

The first two people she ran into were Meg's future mother-in-law, Clarice, and her spoiled daughter, Opal.

"Well, thank goodness you finally arrived," Clarice said in a condescending tone. "I thought we'd have to start without you, which would have been *such* a shame."

"I'm sure," Julie replied, doing her best not to roll her eyes.

Clarice Beaumont was the mayor's wife. Richard Beaumont had been mayor for as long as Julie could remember. He'd run for governor once when she was a kid, but there had been some scandal regarding him and his assistant.

Julie murmured a hello to Opal, who smiled in a way that looked like she was sucking a lemon. The thing about both women was that they could be beautiful, with their stylish blond hair and brown eyes, but jealously and pettiness made their faces twisted and ugly.

"Hello, Julie," Meg's mom called out from across the shop. Finally, a friendly face.

"Hi, Greta." Julie walked over and gave her a hug. Greta had always been like a second mom to her. "Where's Meg?"

"In the changing room," she said before lowering her voice. "Thank you for coming today. I think Meg is going to need all the support she can get."

Julie winked at her before taking a seat on a yellow-and-white-striped chair next to a large pedestal and mirror.

"Julie, is that you?" Meg called out.

"Yep, I'm here," Julie replied as the other three women sat down in various matching chairs.

Jessica, the shop's owner, came out from the changing room. She wore a French twist in her gray hair; her blue silk blouse and matching skirt were impeccable. She gave Julie and the other women an impersonal nod, despite being on the local businesswomen's association with Julie for years. She pulled back the curtain to reveal Meg. Julie's eyes grew misty as her best friend stepped out with a look of pure happiness on her face.

Meg wore a mermaid-style strapless dress that hugged her curvy figure. The bodice had a V-neck that went down to her navel. Lace and sparkling beads covered the dress everywhere with the exception of the sides, which had peekaboo lace windows cut into them. It was daring, fun, and so Meg.

"What do you think?" she asked as she stepped up onto the pedestal, tossing her honey-brown hair over her shoulders.

"Sweetheart, you look beautiful." Meg's mom had tears streaming down her cheeks as she stared at her only daughter.

"It's perfect," Julie added.

Clarice scoffed. "Perfect? Are you getting married by showgirls in Vegas, or in a church in front of God and my son? No. That dress is much too trashy."

Greta's face flushed with anger. "I don't think it looks trashy at all."

"You look gorgeous," Julie insisted.

Clarice inspected her nails. "Well, if I had Meg's shape, I certainly wouldn't want to show off that much skin, but I've always been blessedly thin."

"Listen—" Greta started to say, but Meg interrupted.

"Mom, it's fine." Meg's excitement had already dimmed

as she took another look at the dress. "I guess I can try on another one."

Clarice waved her hand dismissively while Opal smirked. Julie was half-tempted to reach across the aisle and throttle both women. Clarice had done nothing but criticize Meg for the past eighteen years. Now, whenever the woman was around, Meg turned into a shell of herself.

The appointment went on this way for another two hours. Clarice picked apart everything Meg tried on until Meg finally caved and put on a dress that Clarice loved. It was matronly and looked better fitted for an eighty-year-old woman instead of someone in her midthirties. Meg agreed to the dress for no other reason than to be done with the appointment. Nodding in satisfaction, Clarice turned and left, Opal trailing behind her.

Julie and Greta walked over to Meg.

"Sweetie," Greta said. "Are you sure that's the dress you want? It's not really…you."

"It's fine." Meg looked defeated, her shoulders sagging. Her earlier happiness was completely gone. "I could be married in a burlap dress as far as I'm concerned. I just want to marry Lucas.

"Eyes on the prize?" Julie joked.

Meg gave a smile that didn't quite reach her eyes. "Exactly."

She left to change out of the awful dress, leaving Greta and Julie alone.

"One of these days… I swear…" Greta muttered.

Julie let out a shocked laugh. Greta was one of the most laid-back, passive people she'd ever met. It was ironic that she'd raised someone like Meg, who was known for her wild child ways growing up.

Julie nudged Greta in the side with her elbow. "I'd be happy to help."

Meg returned a short time later in her jeans and sweater.

Greta leaned over and kissed her on the cheek. "Come over

for dinner this weekend, okay? You're welcome, too, Julie, if you don't have to work."

"Thanks, Greta," Julie replied. "I'll see if I can make it."

"Thanks for coming, Mom."

Greta waved at both of them and left. Julie's heart ached as she took in her best friend's misery.

"I'm going to look like a country bumpkin," Meg muttered, slouching down into Julie's vacated chair as she waited for Jessica to ring up the dress.

"You don't have to get that one, you know. To hell with Clarice. I keep telling you, it's *your* wedding day, not hers."

Meg stared up at the ceiling, her face bleak. "I don't want there to be problems. I just want a happy, peaceful wedding day. Once I'm married and Lucas's wife, I'll tell Clarice she can kindly shove it and stay out of our marriage."

Julie was silent, and then voiced something she'd never said before. "Do you think that'll really happen?"

Meg let out a loud, tired breath. "I hope so. Because I won't be able to take her crap for the rest of my life." She gave Julie a grimace before she lit up again. "You know, I saw a dress earlier that screamed your name."

"A bridesmaid dress?"

"Not exactly." She grabbed Julie's hand and led her over to a stunning A-line satin dress with off-the-shoulder sleeves draped in delicate lace.

"Uh." Julie stared at it. "This is a wedding dress."

"Try it on," Meg said.

"What's the point?" Julie responded. "It's not like I'll ever get married."

Meg was one of the few people who knew Julie was asexual. It wasn't that Julie wasn't out about her sexuality. She didn't try to hide it. But people always looked at her with complete confusion or disbelief when she tried to explain, so she had stopped bothering.

"You never know," Meg said. "Just because you don't want to get into anyone's pants doesn't mean you don't feel romantic attraction. Remember Charlie?"

Charlie had been a sweet guy Julie had met in college. They had dated for three months and Julie fell hard for him—his sense of humor and kindness was addicting to be around. Then they'd started having sex. At the time, Julie hadn't understood or recognized she was asexual. She only knew she felt empty afterward. When she told him she preferred if they didn't have sex again, Charlie dumped her.

"Yeah," Julie said. "And how many guys have I dated since Charlie?"

She could count on one hand how many dates she'd been on in the past twelve years. Hell, she could count on one hand how many serious relationships she'd been in her entire life. Two.

"Pleeeeease try it on," Meg said, batting her eyes obnoxiously. "I'd love to see someone in a beautiful dress today."

"That's emotional blackmail," Julie grumbled, even as she grabbed the delicate gown. "I'm sure Jessica doesn't want people trying on dresses unless they're actually engaged."

"Hey, Jessica," Meg called out. "Can Julie try on this dress for a minute?"

"That's fine," Jessica said, her face friendlier now that Clarice was gone. She strolled over to Julie, taking it from her. "This way."

Ten minutes later, Julie found herself standing in the changing room, the gown clipped in place to emphasize her small waist and full breasts. It really was a dream dress that seemed made for her.

"You do look gorgeous in this," Jessica said. "Your hair is such a lovely color and the dress complements you. There's no lucky man or woman in your life?"

Julie laughed derisively. "Nope, just me."

"Come on, I want to see," Meg called out from the sitting area.

Jessica opened the curtain and Julie stepped out.

"Oh my," Meg murmured. "Julie, you look perfect. Exactly how a bride should be."

Julie stepped up on the short pedestal and turned to look at her reflection under the bright lights of the shop. The dress was so lovely. It pained her to know that this would likely be her only experience wearing it.

Glancing at the clock on the wall, she saw it was half past one, and jolted. "Oh—I didn't realize it was so late." Smiling at Jessica, she said, "Can you help me get this off? I need to open my store."

"Of course."

After changing back into her clothes, Julie hurried to where Meg was waiting for her.

Julie hugged her best friend. "Rethink that dress, okay? Get something you really want."

"Maybe," Meg murmured.

She gave Meg's shoulder a comforting squeeze before raising her voice. "Jessica, will you be at the meeting on Thursday night?"

Jessica came back into the lobby with Meg's bill in her hand. "Yes. It's my turn to bring the dessert."

"Great, I'll see you there. Meg, I'll call you later."

Julie waved goodbye before rushing outside and heading toward her store. She was crossing the road when she noticed Harris Farmington waiting for her. She stopped midstep in the middle of the street. A car horn honked at her and she jumped into motion again. Julie reached the shop, her eyes on its door so she wouldn't have to look at the odious man.

"Hello, Mr. Farmington. What can I do for you?" she said as she pulled out her keys.

Harris Farmington was well into his sixties, with balding hair and a paunch at his waistline that he tried to hide with boxy suit jackets.

"The sign on your door says your store opens at one p.m. And yet, it's past one thirty. If this is how you normally do business, I can see why you're struggling."

Julie clamped her lips shut as she unlocked her door and entered the shop. Harris followed behind, not allowing for much personal space. She hurried around the counter, but put her hand up when he tried to follow her.

"What do you want?" she asked.

"Julie, Julie," he said in a smooth, oily voice. The man truly was an entitled creep. "You know that Baxter sold his little coffee shop to me."

She hadn't known that anything was firm, but she had a feeling he'd end up buying her neighbor's store.

Farmington's face was filled with satisfaction. "In fact, you and a few others are the only holdouts."

"Why Holiday Bay?" Julie asked. It was something she'd wondered about ever since she heard Farmington Stores, Inc. was buying property in town like it was a free-for-all. There were neighboring towns that had plenty of property for sale.

"Convenience." Farmington shrugged. "The bay will allow easy access for shipping, and the distribution center I'll build on this site is only a short drive to Traverse City."

"So, you're going to tear down my store and build some ugly warehouse while causing environmental damage to the bay."

"Not ugly," Farmington countered. "I can't have my brand associated with something ugly."

She noticed he didn't say anything about the environmental impact his business would have on the area.

Julie folded her arms over her chest. "Why are you here instead of one of your minions? I thought you'd be too busy to bother with a peon like me."

"I'm vacationing in Charlevoix and heard you were being stubborn. I thought I'd pop over and make you an offer you couldn't refuse."

He reached into his expensive suit and pulled out a piece of paper. He placed it on the counter and slid it over to her. Against her better judgement, Julie flipped it over. Her eyes bulged at the amount.

"Think about what that money could do for you," Farmington said. "No more worries about your mom running out of money. No more worries about if it's time to take on a second mortgage so you can keep this little business going and still afford food. You can start over somewhere else, somewhere fresh."

Julie stared at the figure, anger building inside. How did he know so much about her? Had he hired investigators to spy on her?

Her hands began to shake. She felt violated. "I see you've done your research on me."

"I always research people I'm trying to make a deal with." Farmington folded his hands together.

Shoving the paper at him, Julie snapped, "Forget it."

He smiled back coldly. "Don't rush into a decision you'll regret. I'm very good at getting my way." He swiveled on his feet and headed to the door. He paused before leaving, glancing over his shoulder to look at her. "This is going to happen. The quicker you accept it, the better it'll be for you."

As soon as he left, Julie ran into the bathroom and splashed water on her face with hands that still trembled. She had no idea how she was going to fight one of the richest men in America. Numbness spread throughout her body as realization hit her. She really did need that miracle to happen or she was going to lose everything.

The bell above the shop door chimed and rage pummeled inside her. What now? Had Farmington returned to drive the stake in even harder?

"You know what?" Julie yelled as she ran toward the front of the store. "You can just get the hell ou—"

She stumbled as she came to an abrupt halt, her mouth hanging open in shock.

"And here I thought you wanted me to visit," Jake Reynolds said, the smile on his face matching the one on her poster. "Julie Alleen, I do believe you offered me a challenge. Well… challenge accepted."

Chapter Four

Jake stared at the woman in front of him, taking in the angry flush on her otherwise unnaturally pale cheeks. His memory of Julie Alleen and the video she'd posted hadn't done her justice. Even ticked off, she was beautiful, her startling gray eyes hypnotizing.

She still hadn't moved, staring at him like she was being visited by the Ghost of Christmas Past.

"Is this a bad time?" he asked.

"I…" She finally unfroze and moved over to the counter, gripping the edge of it until her knuckles turned white. "I'm sorry, I wasn't expecting…"

"Me?" Jake pulled his phone out of the pocket of his jeans and opened an app, turning it so she could see her video playing. "Pretty sure you and half the world should've expected me by now. My social media has been blowing up for days, telling me that if I didn't visit your store, I'd be the 'biggest prick on the planet who only thinks of my own self-importance.' I do believe that's a direct quote from one of your many fans."

"Oh my god." Julie buried her face in her hands. "I'm so sorry. I never expected…"

Jake hid a smile. She was mortified but so dammed cute about it, he was half tempted to go over and give her a reassuring hug.

"That's the thing about the internet," he said. "Your fans

KELLI STORM 53

were adamant about defending your honor, especially to my—er—overzealous fans. It was starting to become very *West Side Story* on my feed."

"I don't have fans," she mumbled, her voice muffled by the hands still covering her face.

"On the contrary." He finally gave into the urge and moved closer to her, leaning against the counter. "Your little video had the hashtag #TeamJulie trending for six hours."

She lifted her face and he was startled to see tears in her eyes. "I didn't mean for any of this to happen. I honestly didn't think anything would come of the video."

His heart did a funny little jerk, and protective instincts he didn't even know he had surfaced. Jake cleared his throat, pushing the unexpected emotion aside.

"I'm not really mad, you know," he finally said.

"How can you not be?" Julie didn't meet his eyes. "All this attention has been horrifying."

Jake cocked his head. "If you didn't want the attention, why did you post the video?"

"I..." Julie paused before she left the safety of the counter so that she could pace in front of him. Her hands waved frantically as she talked. "Everything was piling up and I just... I needed to feel like I was doing something to fight off the inevitable."

"What's inevitable?"

Julie stopped moving, her expression akin to horror as she seemed to remember that Jake was *someone*. Not a stranger she was spilling her heart out to. Not a former classmate she hadn't seen in years. But someone of importance in the eyes of the world.

Jake hated that look. He witnessed it too many times over the years. People had a tendency to treat him like he wasn't human once they remembered he was famous. He became something else in their minds, too far out of their league to converse with normally.

"Julie," he said, impatience making his tone sharp.

Her cheeks reddened. "I'm sorry," she said again. "I shouldn't be taking up your time, burdening you with my problems. It was very kind of you to come visit me, but I know you must be busy."

Jake's eyebrow lifted at her attempt to dismiss him. Most women would be flirting with him ad nauseam by this point in the conversation.

"I *am* busy." He straightened from the counter. "But you invited me to visit your shop, so here I am. You could offer me a tour before I go."

"Oh…" She looked around the store. "There really isn't much to show."

"I'd like to see it."

She bit her lip before giving him a hesitant nod. "Okay, if you'll follow me."

She started walking down one aisle. "I started Pieces of Home about ten years ago. I've always loved this building. It has a lot of history, you know?"

"It used to be the pharmacy, right?"

She looked back at him with surprise on her face. "You remember?"

It was hard to forget. He used to come here to pick up his mom's antidepressants.

"I'm surprised the pharmacy went out of business," Jake said. "It was the only one in town as I recall."

"A Walgreens opened in Clarington," Julie replied. "It offered better prices and customers started going there. The pharmacy couldn't compete and ended up closing."

"I noticed there are a lot of businesses in town that aren't here anymore. Patty's Diner closed, huh?"

"Yeah, Patty retired a few years ago and no one wanted to

take over the restaurant. She put the property up for sale and moved to Arizona. It still hasn't sold. I think because it's too far on the outskirts of town."

Jake was glad Julie couldn't see the look on his face, the brief flash of fury as he thought about the diner.

"That's too bad," he forced himself to say. "I'm sorry people lost their jobs."

Julie stopped to straighten a couple of glass turtles on one of the shelves. "Not a lot of people come to Holiday Bay anymore. We were once a premier destination, especially when Holiday Boys were huge. People used to stop in town on their way to Mackinac Island."

Jake glimpsed the unhappiness in Julie's profile before she started walking again. They passed a stand selling incense and he breathed in the mixed scents of lavender, jasmine, and rosemary.

"My mom and sister told me people used to line up in front of my old house to take pictures," Jake said.

Julie smiled faintly back at him. "I remember that."

They finished going down the last aisle and headed to the front of the store.

Julie waved her hand toward the window, and Jake could see she was pointing to an empty business across the street. "When the state built the new expressway five years ago, that's when things started to dry up around here. It's easier for people to take that instead of driving through smaller towns like ours. Between that and bigger businesses, like Farmington Stores, Inc. moving into Traverse City, there's very little reason for people to come here anymore."

"And that's why you made the video," Jake said. "To give people a reason to come here."

"It was stupid, I know. But I figured if we could draw some attention here, maybe it would give my shop and the surrounding businesses a boost to our economy."

"It's actually pretty smart."

She gave him a startled look, and he offered her a slight smile. "There's nothing wrong with trying to do what you can to save your store."

"You don't think it was a little mercenary?"

Jake laughed. "I mean, if you have an idea, there's no reason not to explore it. Having a business in today's economy is a bit of a gamble. You never know what will happen unless you throw the dice."

Her face softened for the first time since he entered the store, and Jake felt his heart do that little lurch again. He cleared his throat before walking toward an old, industrial table clamp in the window display. He bet Dylan would love it. Twinkling lights caught his attention and he turned his head only to come face-to-face with a poster of his teenage self. He had a vague memory of seeing a poster in Julie's video, but his focus had been on her, not what was in the background.

"What...oh..." Julie's voice filled with embarrassment. "I, um, guess I forgot to unplug those last night."

He gave her a sideways glance and wanted to laugh at her expression. She was staring at the poster with large, horrified eyes.

"Personally not my favorite one," Jake said. "There's another one out there where I'm lying on a faux leopard-print rug and wearing red holiday pajamas. It was ridiculous but our manager at the time thought it would be a huge hit with our teen audience. From what I remember, it was a sellout."

"I think I had that one," Julie confessed before slapping a hand over her mouth.

Jake did his best not to crack a smile as he took in her dismay. Who knew spending any time in Holiday Bay would be so pleasurable? He was having more fun than he could remember. He wondered what Julie was thinking, and if she was finding their conversation as enjoyable as he did.

* * *

Julie wanted to die on the spot.

Apparently, being in front of Jake Reynolds turned her brain into mush and made her lose her natural filter.

She couldn't believe he was standing in her store, and that he was talking to her and not slapping a restraining order against her.

She gave him a pleading look. "I swear I'm not a stalker. My friend put that poster up as a joke when the store first opened because she knows I love Holiday Boys. Tourists enjoy your connection to the town, so I never took it down."

"Julie, if I had any concern you were a stalker, I wouldn't be here."

"I still can't believe you actually came to Holiday Bay."

"I was actually in the area already," Jake said.

He didn't elaborate any further, and Julie didn't feel like she had a right to ask, despite her curiosity. As far as people in town knew, none of the members of Holiday Boys had been back in years. Jake's family had moved away shortly after he hit it big. Tyler's parents still lived in town, but they usually flew out to wherever he was. James used to visit his family, but these days, they tended to travel to him.

Julie bit her lip as she took in the shop, wondering how it looked through Jake's eyes. She was glad he hadn't gone out of the way to come here. While she was proud of her store, she couldn't imagine it was a place the superstar would normally be caught dead in…unless he had a taste for farmhouse decor.

"So…" Julie said, unsure what to say next.

"So." Jake regarded her before giving Julie his signature smile that never failed to speed up her heart. "I should take a picture with you."

"With me?" Julie squeaked.

"Sure. You asked me to visit because you want to draw people's attention to your store, right? If we're both in the picture, it'll be proof that I actually came here. Not to mention that if people see I'm okay with this, that'll get some of the less pleasant people who've been responding to your video to back off."

"Oh…right."

Jake pulled out his phone and turned on his camera. Glancing up from it, he gave Julie a concerned look. "Don't let those people bother you. The internet can be a toxic place, and if you give them a taste of your blood, they'll only crave it more. Don't respond to anyone or let them know they got to you, no matter how this plays out."

Switching the camera to selfie mode, he moved closer to Julie. When she stood there stiffly, he raised an eyebrow at her. "Mind if I put my hand on your shoulder?"

"Uh, no. Go ahead." Julie's heart galloped as he leaned against her. She tried to ignore the delicious scent of his aftershave, which reminded her of an ocean breeze. He wrapped his arm around her back, his hand warm as it rested on her shoulder.

He held up the camera. "Smile."

His breath tickled her ear, sending goose bumps down her arms.

Julie automatically grinned and heard the camera shutter sound effect. He pulled the phone away and showed her the picture. If it was just Jake Reynolds, her high school crush, standing beside her, and not one of the most famous people in the world, she would have admitted they looked good together, her red hair and naturally pale complexion complemented by his dark features.

But there was no point in letting her mind drift into that territory.

Jake was rich, famous, and could have any woman he wanted. If rumors were true about him, he already had. Having a crush on Jake the superstar was much safer to her heart than developing feelings for the flesh-and-blood man next to her. Because nothing could come of it. He would never be interested in her, especially if he ever found out she was ace. She'd never have to worry about all the beautiful women in his life who would freely give him all the sex he wanted. Liking a celebrity from afar would never make her question if she was enough. But falling for the man behind the fame was a dangerous line she refused to cross. After tonight, she knew she would never see him again, and that was that.

Jake pulled up his Instagram account. He quickly typed out a message, encouraging his fans to stop by Pieces of Home, one of the coolest shops in Michigan, and included the hashtags #SupportLocalBuisnesses and #PiecesOfHome. He posted it and the response was immediate, being shared and liked by hundreds of people within the first few seconds.

Julie could hear her phone start to buzz where she'd left it behind the counter. She hurried over and pulled her cell out of her purse, and opened up her store's account. Her eyes grew misty as she saw the new follows her page was getting. Her eyebrows pulled together when she also saw the hashtag #Julake, posted in the comment section. Clicking on it, her face flamed.

"What?" Jake walked over to her. He laughed when he saw her screen. "We already have a ship name?"

"What's a ship name?" Julie asked.

Jake snorted. "Fans combine two people's names together when they think they're dating."

Julie placed one hand against her hot cheek. "Why on earth…"

"It's just a trend," he said lightly. "Don't give it too much thought." Jake placed his phone in his pocket and looked around the shop one more time, and then his gaze settled back on Julie. "I guess my work here is done. I should leave before the masses descend on you."

"You actually think they will?" Julie glanced out the window.

"Knowing my life and fan base, it's pretty much a guarantee." Jake's lips twisted cynically as though an unpleasant memory had popped in his head. "I need to get going."

Julie nodded, sad to see him leave. "Thank you for doing this. I don't think I can ever repay you."

Jake nodded and turned toward the door, his movements slow. He paused before he swung back around. "Would you like to have dinner with me?"

"What?" Surprise etched across her face. "Why?"

"Why not?" Jake countered. When Julie didn't say anything and the silence became awkward, Jake added, "Look, you're right. Holiday Bay isn't what I remember. It's practically a ghost town and despite my personal feelings for the place—" Julie's curiosity grew, but before she could ask him for more details, he continued "—I don't want to see you or anyone else lose their business. Maybe there's something I can still do. Something that'll benefit not only your store, but give the local economy a boost."

"What do you have in mind?"

"Have dinner with me and we can figure it out."

Somewhere in the distance, Julie could hear tires screeching. Jake frowned as he looked out the window. He grabbed for the door handle but paused as he waited for her reply.

"Okay," Julie said quickly.

Jake grinned. "I'll get a hold of you."

"Do you need my—" Julie started to ask but Jake was already out the door "—number?"

She was still standing there when a group of women in their early twenties hurried into the store a few minutes later.

"Was Jake Reynolds seriously here?" a girl with ombré hair asked. "How long ago? Is he still around?"

She cranked her neck around the store as though she expected him to jump out from behind one of the displays.

Julie forced a professional smile to her lips.

"Sorry," she said. "You just missed him-feel free to look around the store, though. We have some amazing Holiday Boys merchandise available."

Chapter Five

Jake grabbed his phone off the bedside table and rolled over on his mattress. He stared at the ceiling as he tried to think of something clever to say to Julie. As he pulled up his social media, he could see #SupportLocalBusinesses trending. It hadn't stopped since he had posted his picture with her the day before.

A text from Paul popped up on his screen. Are you sure I can't have you and Julie on my show? Better yet, we could start a new show, Love Reunited. Former classmates reunite, sparks fly...

Jake rolled his eyes. Paul had been sending him texts since Jake had posted the picture. It was seriously too early for this.

For the last time, I'm not doing a reality TV show with you.

He could see Paul was in the middle of responding when his phone rang. Jake grimaced when Lori's name popped up on his caller ID. He really didn't want to deal with her right now.

"What's up?" he said in way of greeting.

"I saw that picture you posted." Lori's tone was short.

"And?"

He could practically hear her seething over the phone. "You know you have to run all publicity for the band through me."

"For the band? I agree. But what I do on my personal social media is none of your business."

"Are you seeing her again?"

"Again, none of your business."

He disconnected the call, done with the conversation.

He pulled up the phone number for Julie's store and tried calling her, but heard a busy signal. Jake threw back his sheets and went into the bathroom to take a shower. After he finished getting ready, he tried calling the store again, but heard the same busy signal. He wondered if she was receiving a lot of phone calls after their picture. He should have gotten her cell number before he left the shop.

Jake checked to see if Julie was on Instagram. She wasn't, so he pulled up Pieces of Home's account and saw that her store followed him. He opened up his direct messages and began composing a message, asking Julie if she wanted to meet for dinner that Saturday. Once he finished, he stared at the draft DM for several minutes. Did it come off as needy? Too desperate? Writing a hit song was easier than trying to message Julie Alleen.

"Pull yourself together." He hit Send and headed down to the kitchen to make coffee. He was acting like a teenager with a crush.

To be honest, he hadn't felt this excited in a long time, but something about Julie drew him in. Sure, she was attractive, but there was more to her than that. She was an intelligent woman, not afraid to put herself out there to survive. He respected that, and he wanted to do whatever he could to help her. And if that meant he got to spend a little more time with her, then that was even better.

His phone buzzed a few minutes later and he pulled it out of his pocket, hoping it wasn't Lori again. It wasn't. He had a notification from Julie.

I can meet you after I close the store. Does 8 p.m. for you?

Jake couldn't type his response fast enough.

I'll meet you at Florentina's. See you then.

Jake drummed his fingers on the kitchen counter, feeling restless. He didn't have to be at the studio for another two hours, but he found he couldn't relax in the quietness of the house. After finishing his breakfast, he hopped in his car and drove aimlessly.

Another call came through and he smiled when he saw it was Rich Morgan, the man who acted as his manager when Jake wasn't in Holiday Boys.

"Rich, hey," he said.

"How's my favorite superstar?" Rich said.

Jake snorted. "Can't complain."

"You know, there's a little rumor going around the industry right now. You know how managers love to gossip."

"What's that?" Jake said absently as he turned down a side street.

"Rumor has it that Lori is doing everything she can to manage your career in between your gigs with the Holiday Boys."

That made Jake snap to attention. "There's no chance in that."

Rich had Jake's back more times than he could count. Aside from their business relationship, the two had become good friends over the years.

"Look, Jake, I know how loyal you are to Cummings. Big Poppa gave you the break you needed to get into this industry—"

"Rich," Jake interrupted. "The only reason Lori is managing the Holiday Boys is because she was with us from the beginning. Trust me, she's not getting anywhere near my solo career."

"Okay, okay," Rich said. "How are things going with Dylan?"

Jake hesitated. "We're getting there."

"I'm glad to hear it. You know I'm here to talk if you need it."

"I know, thanks Rich."

They disconnected the call and Jake continued to drive. Before he knew it, he found himself pulling into the parking lot of Patty's Diner.

It was just as he remembered. The outside of the building was made of green metal. Neglect had caused portions of it to rust, while the previously trimmed bushes under the building's large windows were overgrown. Jake knew from memory that the inside looked like something out of the 1950s. The flooring was made of large black-and-white tiles. The booths had deep red seats that matched the stools, which lined up along the counter.

Jake slowly got out of his car and walked around to the back of the building.

As he stared at the back entrance of the diner, an image popped in his head against his will. He'd fought hard over the years to repress that day...the day his father went too far and his parents' marriage died.

He'd found his mom in this very spot, leaning against the dumpster, not seemingly aware of the rancid smell of rotting trash, or the fact that her waitress uniform was streaked with grease. Her eyes had been completely empty, nicotine stains visible on her fingers as a pile of cigarettes lay at her feet.

Through all the abuse his father threw at them, his mother never broke...until that day.

Jake wished he could erase how she'd looked in that moment from his mind. A mere body standing there, her soul obliterated after too much heartache.

With a shuddering breath, Jake turned on his feet and hurried back to his car, fleeing from memories that would never stop haunting him.

"Oh my god," Meg said loudly. Julie pulled her phone away with a wince. "I still can't believe Jake Reynolds, *the* Jake Reynolds, was in your store."

"I know," Julie said as she walked into her bathroom to finish getting ready. She was supposed to be meeting Jake in a half hour. "The past few days have been crazy. Between the reporters and his fans calling, my phone hasn't stopped ringing. I'm sorry I didn't get a chance to call you before now."

"Never mind that," Meg said. "What did he say? How did he smell?"

Julie laughed. "He said he was there to accept my challenge. And he smelled like *every female fantasy* mixed with the familiar scent of *way out of my league.*"

"So…he took a selfie and disappeared into the night?"

"Well…"

"What? There's more? What aren't you telling me?"

"I'm actually about to meet him for dinner. I sent your mom a text earlier letting her know I couldn't make it to her place tonight."

"Wait…are you freaking serious?" Meg shrieked.

Julie could hear Meg's fiancé in the background. "What happened?"

"Sh," Meg said before shouting to Julie, "You're GOING OUT WITH JAKE?"

"Damn," Lucas said. "Ask her if any of the other Holiday Boys are in town."

"Lucas, will you please stop eavesdropping and call my mom? Tell her we're on our way for dinner," Meg said before turning the conversation back to Julie. "Why didn't you tell me about this when we were texting this week?"

"I'm sorry," Julie said. "Honestly, I can't even believe it. One minute I was yelling at Harris Farmington, the next Jake Reynolds was standing in front of me."

"Hold up. Farmington was in Holiday Bay?"

"Yeah."

Meg went quiet before she said, "Why didn't you tell me any of this sooner?"

Julie picked up the hurt in Meg's voice. "I'm sorry. The past few days have seriously been crazy. I've been putting in extra time at the store and not getting home until close to midnight."

"I get that, but still…" There was a tension in Meg's voice. Guilt swarmed Julie.

"I'm sorry," she repeated. "Look, this dinner I'm having. It's a business meeting. Jake wanted to discuss some ideas to help Holiday Bay. It's not a date or anything."

"But you're still having dinner with Jake Reynolds."

"Yeah." A mix of nerves and guilt assailed her. "Listen, I should probably get going. But I promise I'll call you with all the details in the morning, okay?"

"Yeah, fine," Meg said, her tone short. "I should get going, too. Lucas is waiting. Have fun tonight."

Meg ended the call, and Julie stared at her phone before putting it carefully in her purse. She hated that Meg was mad at her. The whole video had been her idea to begin with, but Julie hadn't been lying when she said she'd been swamped. People had called nonstop, wanting to know if Jake would be back, if she wanted to do interviews for the local news. She even had a few national news reporters contact her.

Not to mention that her online sales had shot through the roof. Her normal workload quadrupled in the span of a few hours, leaving her running around the store, getting things ready for shipment, in addition to answering the phone every other minute. She hadn't had time to call Meg, but she felt awful about it.

With a tired sigh, she walked over to the bathroom mirror and took in the dark circles under her eyes. She grabbed her concealer and tried to cover them as much as possible. Still not satisfied with her appearance, she redid her topknot, while ignoring the growing anxiety twisting her stomach.

She shouldn't be getting so nervous. As she'd told Meg, this wasn't a date, though her brief meeting with Jake reminded her why she'd had a crush on him all those years ago. Unlike the rumors that he was an arrogant jerk who treated women like crap, Jake had shown kindness to her when he really didn't need to. He'd done what he could to put her at ease and seemed genuinely interested in her store and the fate of Holiday Bay. She had always hoped that deep down he was still the same humble guy she'd known when she was younger, and he hadn't disappointed.

Twisting one more errant strand of hair back, she viewed her reflection in the mirror. She hoped she was dressed professionally enough. Summer was just around the corner, but the air was still cool. She wore a navy-colored dress with long sleeves, a high neckline, and a tight waistline that turned loose at the hips and flowed down to her knees. She paired the dress with navy tights and fashionable brown boots that would keep her legs warm. Taking a deep breath, she grabbed her light blue trench coat and left.

"It's not a date, it's not a date," Julie chanted as she drove.

Stepping inside the Italian restaurant, she breathed in the fresh scent of garlic. She made her way across the brown-tiled floor to the hostess stand.

"Hi, Ms. Alleen!" the hostess said. There was a flush to her cheeks and she had an exuberant air to her. Julie had a feeling that meant Jake was already here.

"Hi, Isabella," Julie said. Isabella's family owned several establishments in town, including the restaurant they were standing in. "How's your dad doing?"

"He's good, thanks. The cast should come off his leg soon."

"That's great. I bet your mom's relieved."

"She is, though she's still mad that he tried to shingle the roof on his own. She told him to hire a professional," she said with a snicker before asking, "So, are you waiting for your party to arrive?"

"I'm actually meeting someone. Jake Reynolds?"

Isabella's eyes widened as she looked Julie over. "Oh! Your date's already here."

The younger woman's excitement level shot up as she spoke, and Julie was quick to reassure her. "It's not a date."

"But you're having dinner with Jake Reynolds. I mean, *Jake Reynolds*, right?"

"We went to high school together. We're just catching up."

Isabella ignored this. "I'm totally Team Julake, by the way. I know some people think Jori is a thing, but I'm not buying it."

Julie's face flamed at the Julake reference.

"Jori?" she asked curiously before she could stop herself.

Isabella rolled her eyes. "People have been rooting for him and his manager to come out publically for years. I personally don't see it. Whenever you see pictures of the two together, I swear, it doesn't look like Jake can stand her. And besides, she's super old. She's got to be forty at the very least—"

"Well, as I said," Julie interrupted, not wanting to hear any more about Jake's potential love interest, though when did forty become "old"? She was thirty-four. Did that make her middle-aged in Isabella's eyes? "Jake and I are just having a business dinner. It's completely platonic."

"Sure, Ms. Alleen, sure." Isabella grinned before saying, "This way. We gave you our most private table."

Julie barely stopped herself from walking back out the exit. If Jake requested a table that offered privacy, Isabella and Lord knew who else in the restaurant would jump to conclusions. This would be all over town before Julie even left the building.

She followed Isabella past several booths packed with people. The lighting in the restaurant was dim. Candle-lit lanterns sat on each table, creating a romantic setting. Isabella led Julie to a wooden table in the back.

Julie's breath caught in her throat when she saw Jake. For a second, his profile looked grim before he noticed her and his expression lightened. He stood, buttoning the dark gray dinner jacket he wore. It was paired with a crisp white open-collared shirt and black dress pants. His stylish dark hair looked soft to the touch. His blue eyes reflected the candlelight coming from the lantern, and Julie's breath caught. He was so ridiculously attractive.

"Your server will be right with you," Isabella said.

"Thank you," he said politely but dismissively. Isabella winked at Julie and moved away from the table. After she left, Jake turned his attention to Julie. "You look beautiful."

"Ah, thanks," Julie said as she placed her coat on the back of her chair. Jake strode to her side and helped her into her seat.

Julie glanced toward the hostess area. Isabella was talking to a waitress, both whispering while looking in their direction. The waitress finally left the stand and walked over to them, an exaggerated sway to her hips that reminded Julie of a supermodel sauntering down the runway.

"Hello, I'm Paige," the brunette said when she arrived at their table. "I'll be your server tonight." She didn't acknowledge Julie as she spoke, her full attention locked on the superstar. Julie half expected the younger girl to start drooling. "What can I start you off with?"

"Do you like wine?" Jake asked Julie.

Julie nodded. "Red."

Jake smiled. "A bottle of your finest merlot, please."

"Of course," Paige said. She lingered for a second, but Jake didn't look away from Julie once, and the waitress left with a droop to her shoulders.

Julie shifted awkwardly in her seat before meeting Jake's gaze. He had an air of exhaustion to him.

"Everything okay?" she asked. "You seem a little tired."

Jake gave a half smile. "Just been a long day."

Her stomach sank slightly, but she made herself say, "Do you need to reschedule?"

"Absolutely not. I've been looking forward to this dinner for days." Julie bit her lip, not sure what to say to that. Jake smirked. "Tell me what you've been doing with your life since high school. I think the last time I saw you, besides the other day, was back when you were a freshman."

Julie fiddled with the base of the fork in front of her. "I'm surprised you remember me from back then."

His mouth tipped upward. "I don't mean to point out the obvious, but your hair is a unique shade of red. You always stood out in a crowd."

Julie touched it self-consciously. "I hated my hair when I was a kid. My classmates used to make fun of it. Their favorite insult was calling me Gingerbread."

"They were idiots. Your hair is stunning."

Julie's cheeks heated. "Thanks."

"Besides it makes you, *you*."

"Oh, I got over it." The old hurt drifted away at his compliment. "Your hit 'Enchanted' helped me feel proud of my hair. There's a lyric in it about—"

"The redheaded girl, she leaves me enchanted. Oh, how I want to make her mine," Jake murmured.

Julie looked down at the lantern, watching the flame flicker back and forth in a hypnotizing motion. "I loved that song."

"I'm glad," Jake said softly. Julie met his eyes and couldn't look away.

"What—uh—what inspired it? Your wife?"

Julie immediately wanted to kick herself as Jake stiffened.

"No, Angelika has brown hair." Jake picked up the menu and started looking over it. "And she's my ex."

"Oh, right." Julie grabbed her own menu before putting it back down. Florentina's was one of only a few restaurants left in Holiday Bay. It was expensive, so she didn't eat there often, but she had a favorite meal she ordered whenever she could splurge. She peeked at Jake's face and noticed that it was still tense.

"I'm sorry," she said. "I shouldn't have brought her up."

Jake sighed before putting down the menu. "No, I'm sorry. You didn't ask anything that I haven't been asked before. Everyone wants to know who inspired 'Enchanted.'" His shoulders lost some of their rigidness. He scanned the area around them to make sure no one could overhear before he said in a quiet voice, "Angelika's a bit of a sore spot for me. We…didn't part on good terms."

"I'm sorry," Julie said again, not knowing what else to say.

Jake tilted his head as he observed her. "What about you? Ever get married?"

Julie almost laughed at that, remembering her bitter parting from Charlie. "No. Marriage isn't for me."

"Why? I can't believe no one has ever been interested."

"Maybe I was the one who wasn't interested." Her defenses shot up. How many times in her life had she had this conversation? "There's more to life than getting married and having a ton of kids. That might be what some people want out of life, but it's not what every woman wants."

Her mind drifted to the wedding dress Meg had made her try on, and something inside ached. It was easier to pretend—even to herself—that marriage and a happy-ever-after wasn't for her, rather than explain how no man wanted her once they found out she was asexual.

Sure, there were aces out there who had healthy marriages and children, even bringing them into the world the good old-fashioned way. But Julie never wanted to have that conversation, the *Hey, do you want to have sex so I can get pregnant but then I don't want you ever touching me sexually again* kind of discussion. Just confessing she was ace was enough of a deal-breaker for most men.

Paige returned with their wine. "Would you like to sample it?"

Jake motioned toward Julie. "Please."

The waitress poured a small amount in the glass in front of Julie.

Julie took a sip, enjoying the burst of flavor on her tongue. "It's delicious."

"That'll do," Jake murmured.

Paige poured them both a glass before asking, "Do you need more time to look at the menu?"

"I know what I want." Julie handed the waitress her menu. She lifted an eyebrow at Jake, who nodded. Looking at Paige, she said, "Can I get the eggplant parmesan?"

"Sure." Paige turned to Jake and said in a flirtatious voice, "And what can I serve you?"

"I'll have the chicken marsala." He handed the menu to her and didn't look at her again. A pout formed on her face but she left to put in their order. An awkward silence fell on the table.

Jake finally said, "I feel like I'm the one who owes you an apology now." She met his eyes. "How about this. We leave all talk about exes and happily-ever-afters off the table for now."

Julie smiled tentatively. "Okay."

Jake leaned back in his chair. "We used to hang out when we were kids, didn't we?"

Julie's eyebrows shot up. "I can't believe you remember that."

"To be honest, I don't remember much about that time in my life. Things were...distracting...at home. But I have a vague memory of you sitting on Tyler's porch with your nose in a book while the rest of us played baseball on the front lawn."

Julie laughed lightly. "That sounds about right. My best friend, Meg, was Tyler's neighbor. He once told her when they were kids that she couldn't play sports as well as him because she was a girl. After that, she was determined to beat him in every sports game he organized in the neighborhood. She got pretty good at it."

Jake smirked. "Oh yeah, she broke his nose once when she

accidentally hit him in the face with a baseball. He complained for weeks." His forehead scrunched. "Did you ever join us?"

Julie shook her head. "No, I got smacked in the head with a soccer ball when I was in third grade. I avoided sports like the plague after that."

"That'd make sense." Jake took a sip of wine before putting his glass back down. "So, books were more your thing. Was there a particular book or author you liked?"

Julie grinned. "I loved the *Anne of Green Gables* series. I still reread it whenever I have time."

Julie identified with Anne more than she realized back then. People in the fictional town of Avonlea labeled Anne as an outsider and freak, but no matter what life threw at her, she still held her head up high. Julie certainly understood the feeling of not belonging while trying to find your place in the world.

"Tell me about your business," Jake said. "What made you decide to start it?"

"I tried working for a Fortune 500 company right out of college, but that only lasted a couple of years. This might sound terrible, but I hated answering to others and wanted to be my own boss. When I saw that the pharmacy was for sale, I decided to open my own store. Meg and I used to travel around Michigan, hitting different boutiques in our free time—antique shops, art stores, places that offered home goods. I decided that's what I wanted to do. Open a store that sold one-of-a-kind items people could only get in Holiday Bay." Julie smiled self-consciously. "The store did great when it first opened, but as you know, business has really slowed recently."

Jake folded his hands over his chest. "And how's your sister doing?"

"My sister?" Julie startled before remembering that Veronica and Jake had been in the same grade. "She's fine. She lives in California now and has two kids."

"You must miss her."

Julie shrugged. "Veronica and I have never been super close, but I wish she lived nearby. Especially with everything going on with my mo—"

"Excuse me, Mr. Reynolds." An eleven-year-old girl stood next to the table, holding a phone to her chest with hands that shook. "Um, could I get a picture?"

Jake gave her a professional smile. "Sure."

The girl stepped next to him and put the phone on selfie mode. She looked like she won a million dollars as she took the picture and murmured a quiet thank-you before hurrying back over to her parents, who waved at them. On the other side of the restaurant, a group of women of various ages were looking at Jake and Julie and whispering to each other. One held her phone, taking pictures of them.

Julie felt like she was in a fishbowl. "Does that happen a lot?"

"You mean people asking me for my picture all the time, or photographing me without my permission?"

His back was to the table of women, and Julie's eyebrows lifted. "How did you know they were taking pictures of you?"

"You develop a sixth sense for these things, but to answer your question, yes, it happens all the time. Thankfully, it isn't as bad in Michigan as it is in California. Paparazzi stalk you wherever you go there. My son hates it."

"Oh, you have a son." Julie knew that he'd had a child at some point, but she'd been in college around the time Jake had gotten married and his wife had had their baby. Exams took all her time and she'd paid little attention to the personal life of her teenage celebrity crush. "How old is he?"

"Fifteen," Jake said. He looked lost in thought, a hint of sadness to him. "He doesn't really understand all of this." Jake moved his head toward the other patrons who were eyeing them. "I was on the road a lot when he was little, and Angelika never liked to travel with me so they stayed home. He was kept pretty sheltered from my lifestyle. The few times he's been around it…well, let's just say it didn't go well."

Julie wanted to reach across the table and squeeze his hand, to offer him some kind of comfort because in that moment, he looked like he could use some.

"Do you get to see him much now?"

Jake moved the napkin on the table to his lap. "Not as much as I want to, but I'm trying to spend more time with him. He actually doesn't live that far from here."

Julie's face lit up. "That's why you said you were in the neighborhood."

Jake nodded. "I'd appreciate if you kept that just between us."

"Yeah, of course."

Jake eyed her, taking in her sincere expression before relaxing. "Thanks. I really value my privacy."

Paige returned with their meals. She didn't try flirting this time, apparently accepting that it was a lost cause, and after confirming they didn't need anything else, she left again.

Julie took a bite of her food, practically moaning as it melted in her mouth.

Jake took a few bites of food. "This is good."

"Mmm-hmm," Julie responded. "I love their food."

"So," he said when they were halfway through their meal. "You were saying something before we got interrupted. About your sister and your mom, I believe."

"Oh." Julie picked up her cloth napkin and dabbed at her mouth. "My mom was diagnosed with early-onset Alzheimer's a few years ago. Veronica was always super close to her, and I think it was hard on her, seeing our mom so helpless. She left town shortly after we got the diagnosis."

"Leaving you to deal with it on your own?" Julie didn't quite meet his eyes, silently confirming what she didn't want to admit aloud. He shook his head. "You really do have a lot on your plate."

"It's fine."

"It isn't, though." Jake grabbed his wine, swirling the red liquid around in the glass before swallowing it down. "Did you know Veronica used to date my cousin James?"

Julie laughed. "Oh yeah. When I was at the height of my Holiday Boys obsession as a teen, Veronica loved to taunt me about the fact that James had been her first boyfriend."

Jake's lips quirked. "Of course, at the time, James hadn't told anyone he was gay. It wasn't exactly encouraged back then to come out."

"That must have been really hard for him." Julie knew it had taken her years to come out as asexual to the few people she'd told.

"It was," Jake agreed.

Julie brightened. "But it all worked out for him. I read that he married a wonderful man and they're rehabbing houses together."

Jake nodded. "Mason. It was pretty much love at first sight for James, and thankfully, Mason seemed to return his feelings."

Julie looked at him carefully, taking in the way his forehead furrowed. "You sound like you have some doubts."

Jake's face cleared instantly. "No, he makes James happy and that's all I care about. They're good for each other. Paul wants to do a reality show about their rehab work."

"That's amazing!" Julie said. "Do you still keep in touch with all the Holiday Boys?"

"Yeah, we never lost contact with each other. Our falling-out had more to do with our record company at the time, not each other."

"That's good to hear," Julie said, just as Paige came back to their table and picked up their finished plates.

"Can I interest either of you in dessert?" she asked.

"I honestly couldn't eat another bite," Julie said.

"We'll take the bill, please," Jake told the waitress.

"And will this be on one check or two?"

Before Julie could respond, Jake said, "One, thank you."

Once Paige left, Julie said, "I wasn't expecting you to pay for me. This was a business dinner, right?"

One corner of his mouth tilted up. "And yet, there was a serious lack of business discussion."

Julie laughed. "I guess you're right."

Paige came back with their bill. Jake gave it a mere glance before pulling out a couple of hundred-dollar bills. "Keep the change."

The waitress's eyes bugged out of her head. "Th-thank you. Have a great night."

Julie stood up and grabbed her coat from the back of her chair. Jake came over and helped her into it. They made their way outside. A group of fans were waiting by the exit, holding posters for him to sign. News had clearly traveled fast that Jake was there. Julie recognized them as the same ones who came to her store the day Jake posted their picture.

"Sorry, give me a second, will you?" Jake muttered.

"Sure, I'll wait by my car."

Julie pulled her coat closer to her chest as a breeze wrapped around her. She leaned against her SUV and watched as the ombré-haired girl put her hand on Jake's arm. Julie wondered how often women threw themselves at him like that.

The woman whispered something in his ear and the professional smile dropped from Jake's face. He took several steps away from her.

"Not interested," he said firmly before nodding to the others. "Have a good night, ladies."

He left them to walk over to Julie, tightness evident on his face. "I'm sorry about that."

"It's part of the business, right?"

"Like I said, I enjoy my privacy. More importantly, I enjoy my personal space." He shoved his hands into his pants pockets, his expression serious. "Look, I meant it when I said I had some ideas to help promote your shop. I have to attend a meeting tomorrow morning, but do you think you'd have time to meet me again in the afternoon?"

"I'll be at the shop until five p.m."

"Okay, I'll meet you there and we can talk some more, if that's all right?"

Julie blinked twice before nodding. "That sounds like a plan." She turned to open her car door before she looked back at him. "Thanks again for dinner. It was really nice catching up with you."

"You too," Jake said. "I'll see you tomorrow."

He made it sound like a promise. Julie shivered as she watched him walk away. Some murmured voices caught her attention and she glanced at the group of fans who'd been waiting for Jake. They were glaring at her while whispering to each other. Julie couldn't imagine what they were saying reflected well on her.

As she got in her car and started the engine, she thought of how it easy it was for the one woman who had interacted with Jake, confident in her ability to flirt with him. Sure, he'd turned her down, but he could have easily said yes.

He apparently had a lot of experience handling situations like that, and she couldn't imagine he always said no. He had a reputation for being a womanizer for a reason. And womanizers liked sex. A lot.

"Don't you forget that either," Julie muttered to herself before putting the car in Drive.

Chapter Six

Jake stepped out of his closet and buttoned the gray flannel shirt, his mind preoccupied with Julie and the night before.

It had been by far one of the best evenings he'd had in a long time. There were a couple of awkward moments between them, but other than that, Jake really enjoyed himself. Julie was bright, caring, and considerate. More importantly, he felt like he could trust her. He'd been more open with her than with any woman he'd encountered over the past few years, telling her about Dylan, a topic he never spoke about…not to someone he barely knew.

And Julie handled his celebrity with a grain of salt, which he appreciated. She'd been more curious than annoyed when people stared at them in the restaurant, or when that little girl asked for his picture. He remembered when a group of school kids had come up to him when he'd been on a rare dinner date with Angelika, and she had yelled at them. It wasn't too long after that incident that they divorced, Angelika mentally worn down and exhausted by his lifestyle by then.

Glancing at the clock on the nightstand, he saw that he had enough time to grab some breakfast before he needed to leave. He was supposed to meet his bandmates to start recording some new songs. Hopefully, they'd be able to get the vocals for at least two knocked off. While Jake loved the creative process of making music, doing take after take could be a huge pain.

He was pulling on a pair of black boots when he heard

Dylan's moped coming down the drive. Jake left his bedroom and walked into the guest room across the hall, which overlooked the driveway, and watched Dylan draw closer to the house. He half expected him to turn toward the workshop, like he always did, but Dylan headed toward the front of the mansion.

Jake's brows drew together. Normally, Dylan didn't come to the main part of the house, though he was more than welcome. Jake even had a room set up for him in case he ever wanted to spend the night. But that would have required Dylan spending time with his dad, and he usually tried to avoid that as much as possible unless they were working on a wood project.

Jake left the room and headed down the stairs just as Dylan entered the grand hallway. His eyes darted around before settling on his father, his face angry.

"Dylan, hey. Is everything al—"

"What were you doing with Ms. Alleen?"

Jake startled, staring at his son in confusion. "What?"

"It's all over the internet." Dylan pulled his phone out of his pocket and opened up a gossip site, showing it to his dad. Jake didn't bother to look. If you've seen one gutter rag, you've seen them all.

"I thought you weren't allowed on sites like that," Jake said. Angelika was adamant that Dylan stay off the internet so he wouldn't be exposed to Jake's "depraved" lifestyle, as she called it.

"I overheard Mom and Carl talking about it this morning." Dylan pointed at the headline. "Is it true?"

Jake winced as he finally read Dylan's phone.

Is Julie Alleen the Latest Notch on Jake Reynold's Bedpost?

There was the picture Jake had posted of himself and Julie at her shop, and then another one of Julie looking breathtaking in the restaurant as she stared at Jake and the little girl taking a picture together, a soft smile on her face. It only showed Jake's profile, but there was no mistaking it was him.

Jake folded his arms over his chest. "Julie and I went to high school together. She asked me to stop by her shop to give the place a publicity boost. We went out to dinner last night so we could catch up."

"I thought you wanted to stay out of the spotlight. Isn't that why you bought this place?" Dylan waved his hand around the hallway.

"I moved here to be closer to you," Jake responded quietly. He dropped his arms and put his hands in his pockets. "And just because I want privacy doesn't mean I'm going to turn myself into a hermit. Holiday Bay is my home. People are going to see me out in public on occasion."

Jake could almost hear Dylan's teeth grinding. "Holiday Bay doesn't need to be like California. It's nice here."

Jake internally winced as he thought about the few times Dylan came out to visit him in LA. His son wasn't wrong. LA. could get loud, with people screaming Jake's name whenever he walked down a street, or paparazzi shouting obscenities in front of Dylan to get a reaction from Jake.

"Holiday Bay won't be like California." He tried to sound more confident than he felt. His shoulders started tensing. God, he hated the sound of anger.

"But what if it does?" Dylan asked. "How will you be helping Ms. A.'s business when it's just groupies and drug dealers hanging out at her store, chasing off customers who really want to buy something?"

"Drug dealers and groupies? Son, my life's really not as exciting as your imagination seems to think it is."

"That's not what Mom said," Dylan countered. "She said she could never see you when you were on tour because there were too many toxic people around."

Of course she said that. Angelika excelled at creating a slanted narrative about Jake's life, one that she was always so eager to share with their son. Similar to Jake's childhood, Angelika had grown up in a broken home. She had told him more than once that Jake was just like her father. In her mind, they were the same type of person—someone who couldn't be trusted.

"Dylan, you forget this is my hometown. I'm not going to do anything to hurt people here."

"Mom says you hate it here."

"I don't have the greatest memories of this town, that's true," Jake said. "But that doesn't mean I want to destroy people's livelihoods. Julie asked for my help, and I gave it to her."

"She doesn't need your kind of help," Dylan said stubbornly.

Confusion began to set in. Jake felt like he was missing something here. "Where is this coming from? From what I can tell, Julie got the publicity she wanted. Why does this even matter to you? It's not like you know her."

"It's a small town," Dylan argued. "And she deserves to be more than some woman you sleep with and then ditch."

Jake's spine stiffened. "Watch your tone."

Dylan's face turned red with fury. "She deserves better. Just…just stay away from her and her store."

He ran out the entrance.

Jake stood rigid in place, trying to comprehend Dylan's reaction before his feet started moving, chasing after his son. "Dylan!"

Dylan was already on his moped by the time Jake stepped outside. He started it with a roar and took off down the driveway without looking back at his father.

Jake watched him go, his face grim. "What in the hell?"

He rubbed at the side of his face as memories from the past started to pounce inside his brain—the sound of his father shouting and his mom crying. His skin felt prickly. When he looked at his hands, they were shaking. God, he hated fighting.

He truly didn't get what was wrong with him. First Angelika, and now Dylan. Why was it that the two people who should have trusted him without hesitation always thought he had the worst intentions when it came to women? Jake grew up witnessing firsthand the kind of damage a man could do to his wife with his cruelty, not to mention the devastating effects it left on the children. Jake had always vowed that he would never act like his father. Because if he did, what kind of role model would he be for Dylan?

Then again, what kind of role model was he now if that's how Dylan truly viewed him? As some sleaze who couldn't keep it in his pants?

Closing his eyes, Jake took several deep breaths.

His phone buzzed in his pocket and he pulled it out. James had sent him a text reminder not to be late to their recording session. Swearing, Jake went back inside and grabbed his jacket before running to the garage.

He'd give Dylan some time to calm down and then try to talk to him again. He'd assure him that he would always treat Julie with respect, but he didn't see why two consenting adults should have to stay away from each other if they enjoyed one another's company. And Jake *did* enjoy Julie's company. Very much.

As he drove to the studio, a thought manifested inside his head, which continued to grow and formulate. By the time he made it to the studio, he barely remembered to put his car in Park before he jumped out and ran inside.

He waved at Trevor and the audio engineer, and was about to step into the live room when Lori walked into the control booth. She wore her hair pulled into a high ponytail, and dark pants paired with black stiletto heels.

She paused when she saw him, then walked over to him. "You'll be happy to know that the record company really likes the rough recording for 'Starry-Eyed.' They want to release it as the album's first single."

"Great," he asked. "Are the guys here?"

"Yeah." Lori stepped closer to him and brushed her fingers against his cheek.

Jake stepped away from her automatically.

Her turquoise blue eyes narrowed, but she still said, "I wanted to see if you'd like to get some dinner after we wrap today."

"Lori." Jake lowered his voice so the audio engineer and Trevor wouldn't hear them. "I know we spent time together once—"

"An incredible night together," she murmured, her fingers lifting to trace the part of his collarbone that his button-up didn't cover.

Jake grabbed her hand, and gently but firmly pushed it away.

"It was a long time ago," he reminded her. "You and I aren't going to happen again. I respect you as a manager, but that's all there is between us."

"Does this have to do with that woman you had dinner with last night?" When Jake lifted an eyebrow at her, she scoffed. "Did you really think you could go out to dinner in public with some woman and not have it trend all over social media?"

"Who I have dinner with is none of your business. You and I have a professional relationship and that's it. Nothing more."

Lori's lips pursed together before she moved back. "Then as your manager, I think I should remind you that you're wasting our time here. We should be in California in a professional studio."

"Um, ouch," Trevor said, overhearing them since Lori hadn't bothered to keep her voice down. "You do know that I've had the Stones and Rihanna record here, right?"

"Don't take it personal, Trev," Jake said. "Lori and I are just clearing up a misunderstanding between us. Right, Lori?"

Lori narrowed her eyes. "You know, contrary to what your

ego might think, I wanted to have dinner with you for business reasons, not personal."

"Then the next time the entire band goes out to eat, we'll make sure to invite you. That's the only business you and I have, business or personal."

Not bothering to say anything else to her, Jake walked into the live room. Paul and Zan sat on the leather couch, while James and Tyler looked over some sheets of music.

"Hey," Jake said.

"Hey, man," Tyler said. "I think we're ready to record 'Starry-Eyed.' You good with starting with that one?"

"Yeah, but before we start, there's something I wanted to discuss with you guys."

"What's on your mind?" James asked.

"What would you say about announcing our reunion by having a concert in Holiday Bay?"

Lori forcibly pushed the door open between the two rooms, ignoring Trevor's "Heh!"

"What the hell are you talking about?" she snapped.

Jake kept his eyes on his bandmates. "We had our first concert in Holiday Bay. We named the band after the town. The town's been on the decline for years now. What do you think if we held a charity concert, with proceeds going to small businesses in the area?"

"It's ridiculous," Lori said, folding her arms over her chest.

"Why is it ridiculous?" James asked. "I think it's a great idea. We're giving back to the community that supported us right from the beginning. People love nostalgia. Mix that in with the fact that we're doing it for charity, and you have a great PR story."

"When were you thinking?" Tyler asked.

"Next month."

"Next month!" Lori yelled. "We can't organize a concert in that small amount of time. Not to mention we're in the middle of recording your new album! Did you forget about the contracts you signed with the record company stating you would do nothing within your power to delay this album's release date?"

"I hate to agree with Lori," Tyler said, "but that really doesn't give us any time to plan a concert and do the record."

"I know." Jake ran a hand through his hair. "But you haven't been back to Holiday Bay in a while. So much has changed. Half the businesses we knew have closed. Do you remember how the pharmacist sponsored our first concert? Well, he lost his business. He couldn't compete with a chain store that moved into Clarington. I know that because it's where Julie's store is now located. People have to drive a half hour just to get their meds. And he's not the only one that suffered. There are a lot of places we used to hang out at that are gone, and a lot of businesses all over town are for sale." Jake thought back to the strain set in Julie's face before muttering, "How many more people have to lose their livelihoods when we have the power to do something? The town can't wait."

Paul stood up from the couch and pulled out his phone. He began to type something rapidly "I've got the publicity handled."

Jake looked at his friend gratefully. "I'll look for a venue."

A smile formed on his lips. He knew just the person to help him with the project.

"What about the record?" Lori countered. "Some of us do have lives in LA that we'd like to get back to."

"So get back to it," Jake snapped, no longer smiling.

"Seriously," James said. "You don't need to be here, Lori. We're in good hands with Trevor. You can head home and work on getting things done for the concert."

Lori looked between the band members, taking in their determined faces, and accepted defeat. "Fine. You guys want to burn yourselves out so Jake can bed some local hick, you do that."

Jake opened his mouth to unleash his frustration on her, but James put a hand on his arm.

"Like I said—" James's voice was calm "—you don't need to be here anymore. We'll let you know if anything pops up that needs your attention."

Lori looked like her head was about to explode. Jake felt the familiar locking of his muscles as tension radiated through his body. She thankfully didn't say anything else before she pivoted on her stilettos and left the room. She snapped something at Trevor and the audio engineer before stomping out of the control room, slamming the door behind her.

James came over and gave him a pat on the shoulder, and Jake smiled at him gratefully. His cousin understood better than anyone about Jake's childhood trauma and his reaction to arguments. He'd witnessed it enough whenever he'd hung out with Jake and his dad.

"Damn, Jake," Trevor said over the speaker. "Your effect on women should be studied by scientists."

Jake ignored him. "So, are we starting with 'Starry-Eyed'?"

Tyler stared at Jake. "Are you sure about this concert, Jake?"

Jake thought back to the empty stores in town, the worry on Julie's face. "I'm sure. I don't think the town can hold out for too much longer. Maybe this will save a few shops from closing."

Tyler nodded. "Okay then. And to answer your question, yeah, let's start with 'Starry-Eyed.' If we can nail this down, maybe we can play it at the concert."

Jake grinned before making his way over to the sound booth in the corner of the room, thankful for his friends.

He hoped again that they could get through this session without having to do too many takes. Because he couldn't wait to see Julie and tell her his news.

Chapter Seven

"And then what happened?" Meg's voice asked over the car speakers as Julie pulled into a parking spot.

"Nothing, really. Some of his fans were outside the restaurant so he signed some autographs. There was this really flirty girl all over him but he walked away from her—"

"Oh, *that's* interesting."

"Not really."

"Yet you brought it up."

Julie put the gearshift into Park. "Anyway, he told me he still wanted to talk to me about helping the town. He's supposed to get a hold of me sometime today."

"Two days in a row? You sure this is just business?"

Julie laughed bitterly. "I'm not going there. You should have seen the women waiting for him last night. He could have asked anyone of them to sleep with him and they wouldn't have hesitated."

"But he didn't ask them," Meg said. "He came back to you."

"Meg, come on. He wouldn't want me in the long run."

"I hate when you talk like that. He'd be lucky to have you. Besides, there are ways men can be satisfied without actual intercourse. That's why God invented masturbation."

"How long do you think a guy would be satisfied with his hand?"

"Then buy him a sex toy." Meg paused before letting out a giggle. "I can picture it now. A carefully packaged box under the Christmas tree. Jake reaches for it and pulls out...a fake vagina. Get him one of the rubber ones that includes a butt he can slap."

"And on that note, I should really—"

"Wait! If you get him a blow up doll, can you please make sure I'm there to record his reaction?"

"So anyway, I'm at the store." Julie tried to sound serious, but she couldn't keep the amusement out of her voice. She was too used to Meg's antics by now. "I have to get going."

"Deflection," Meg grumbled. "Fine, we'll talk more later, all right?"

"Sure, talk to you later."

Julie opened her car door, a smile on her face. Her best friend was in a much better mood than she'd been the night before, much to Julie's relief. She hated fighting with Meg, and she hadn't liked the tension between them.

As Julie walked down the cracked sidewalk toward her store, nervous anticipation fluttered inside her. She was going to see Jake today. He'd mentioned a meeting in the morning, but that he'd stop by afterward.

It still seemed surreal that she had dinner with him last night. Even though it was supposed to be a business dinner— and despite what she'd told herself—it had *felt* like a date.

Don't go there.

The last thing she needed was to feel any kind of hope. She was serious when she told Meg that Jake could have his choice of people to sleep with. He wouldn't want her.

As she reached her store, she heard bells chime as someone exited the knit shop across the street. Glancing over her shoulder, she felt her anticipation turn to dread as Harris Farmington walked away from the shop. He paused when he saw her before giving a mocking nod. He slid into the back seat of the Mercedes-Benz parked by the curb. As it drove away, Julie ran across the road and burst into Kyleigh's Knits.

Kyleigh, the shop's owner, stood behind the counter, her posture stiff as she stared at a slip of paper in her hand. Julie knew what it was.

"Please don't do it," she said.

Kyleigh jerked her head up. "Oh, hey, Julie."

A couple of elderly women came out of the craft room at the back of the store.

Julie plastered a smile on her face. "Hi, Leona. Bernice."

"Julie, how are you?" Leona asked.

"I'm good, thanks."

"How's your mom doing?" Bernice asked.

Julie's smile was painful at this point as she forced herself to continue with it. "She's doing fine, thanks. She has her good days and bad days."

"We miss her at bridge," Leona said. "Tell her we said hello."

"I will." She would, though it was doubtful her mom would remember either woman, despite the fact that they were in the PTA together for years.

Bernice turned to Kyleigh. "Same time next week?"

"You bet," Kyleigh said. "Be prepared to work on your featherstitch."

Julie waited until the women left before she dropped her smile. Turning to Kyleigh, she pleaded, "There's very little standing in Farmington's way from taking over the entire town. He'll tear this building down. Do you remember the stories of this place when it used to be the town's dance hall? My grandparents went on their first date here. We celebrated your sixteenth birthday in the craft room. I felt so cool that you invited me because I was only thirteen at the time. And do you remember how much fun we had that night?"

Kyleigh held up the paper. "Look, I don't want to sell, but what he's offering could help me with some of the debt the shop's incurred over the past few years."

"At what cost?" Julie implored. "He's going to destroy this town. He plans on tearing down all of our history—everything that makes Holiday Bay what it is—so he can build some ugly warehouse."

Kyleigh folded the paper and put it in her pocket. "We don't all have the luxury of being best friends with famous people. Sales have been slow. Quite frankly, I don't know how much longer I can hold on without going completely bankrupt. And what he's offering will set up my daughter and me financially for the next few years."

Julie chewed on her lip. "Did you already agree to sell to him?"

She held her breath as she waited for Kyleigh to respond. She relaxed slightly when the other woman shook her head.

"No. I told him I wanted to think about it. I love this town just as much as you do, Julie. I'm well aware that Farmington doesn't give a damn about us. You know my mom started this shop for me. It's my legacy. Something I plan to pass on to Holly someday. I don't want to see it torn down. She took her first steps in the aisle over there. But I don't know what other options I have unless I get some serious cash flow soon."

"Look, I understand where you're coming from," Julie replied. She thought back to Jake's invitation to meet up. Hopefully, he could work that miracle she needed. "Give me forty-eight hours before you get back to Farmington. Okay?"

"Fine," Kyleigh said. As Julie turned to leave, she added, "Julie, look, I don't want to give you false hope. I'm probably going to have to sell."

"Forty-eight hours," Julie repeated before leaving the shop. She opened her store and spent the majority of her morning processing internet sales and researching different types of small-business grants that she and Kyleigh might qualify for.

Around noon, the chime above her door dinged. She glanced up from her laptop, half expecting Jake. Instead, she saw Dylan. She started to smile but the gesture quickly diminished when she noticed how upset he looked.

Julie jumped off her stool and hurried around the counter so she could stand next to him. "Dylan, is everything okay?"

"Ms. A., please don't get involved with Jake Reynolds."

She stepped back in surprise. "What are you talking about?"

"You went out to dinner with him, right?"

She tilted her head. "Dylan, I mean this in the kindest way possible, but how is that your business?"

Dylan's hands clenched at his side. "I… I've heard bad things about him. He likes women…a lot. He's not someone who knows how to be faithful. I don't want to see you get hurt."

Julie took in the teen's earnest expression. "You act like you know him personally."

"I… I've just heard a lot of stories about him."

"And where there's smoke there's fire, right?"

Dylan's tight frame relaxed. "Exactly."

She reached out and squeezed his shoulder. "I appreciate you looking out for me, I do, but I'm a big girl. I can look out for myself."

Dylan's face showed his disappointment. "Will he be coming to the shop a lot then?"

"I… I don't know. I don't see why he would keep coming here."

Dylan opened his mouth as if to say something else before shaking his head sadly. He left the store without another word. Julie stared blankly after him. Even Dylan, who was just a baby when Holiday Boys were around, knew of Jake's reputation.

She tried to shrug off the conversation as she went back to looking up different ways to save her town.

As the day rolled on, her earlier nerves came back and she found herself continuously glancing at the clock on the wall.

Was Jake still coming? When it finally hit five, Julie walked over to her door, trying not to feel too crestfallen as she turned the open sign to Closed. She cashed out her daily sales and walked into the bathroom to touch up her hair.

When she'd fussed with it enough, Julie went back to the front of the store and peeked at the clock again. It was now five forty-five. She meandered around the shop, straightening items on display while strategizing how she was going to set things up for the Christmas season. It might be her store's last, and if that was the case, she wanted to make it as memorable as possible for her vendors and customers. One of her vendors made homemade cloth garlands that would look great strung along the front counter.

After walking through the store several more times, Julie accepted defeat. Jake wasn't coming. Either he got hung up on something or he'd forgotten that he said he was going to meet her. She checked her phone and saw that she had no messages from him.

Maybe he had changed his mind and wasn't going to help her. Maybe he didn't want to be bothered by her again. Dylan's words whispered inside her head, reminding her that people didn't view Jake as a good guy.

Pushing that thought aside, Julie grabbed her purse, ready to leave. It had been a long, mentally draining day and her stomach was starting to growl. She wanted nothing more than to go home, change into her comfortable sweats, and binge on some chocolate cherry ice cream.

She exited the building and turned to lock the shop door. A voice behind her said, "Hey."

Julie shrieked and dropped her keys, swinging around with her hand on her heart.

Jake bent down and grabbed the keys, then handed them back to her. "Sorry I'm so late. I was worried I might have missed you."

"You almost did," Julie said just as her stomach growled again. She finished locking the door before facing him. "I should probably—"

"Can I—"

They stopped speaking at the same time. Julie waved for him to continue.

"Can I take you out to dinner?"

A part of her wanted to immediately answer yes. The other part of her wanted to run for the hills before her celebrity crush turned into something real.

"I… I should get home," Julie finally said. "I have some things I need to do."

She didn't, but she couldn't shake off Dylan's earnest expression when he warned her about the singer's reputation. Jake stood in front of her, handsome and perfect. It was better to nip this in the bud now before feelings happened.

"Just a quick bite?" Jake implored. "I have something I want to talk to you about."

Julie noticed for the first time that there was an excited energy to him.

"I…"

"Please."

Curiosity getting the better of her, she said, "How about we go to Franki's Pasty Shop?"

Jake grinned and Julie's heart sped up.

"That sounds good," he said. "I haven't had a pasty in years."

Pasties were a type of pastry folded in a half-moon shape and filled with vegetables and meats. Over the years, the dish had become a Northern Michigan staple. Though the Upper Peninsula claimed to sell the best in the state, Julie's classmate, Franki Nichols, could give the UP a run for its money.

They entered the small restaurant, the scent of fresh dough in the air. Pictures of Michigan lighthouses hung from sterile white walls. Only a few red tables and matching plastic chairs stood on large white tiles. Most people ordered their food to-go, so seating wasn't really necessary.

"Julie, hey," Franki said when he saw her.

"Hi, Franki. How's it going?"

"Good, business could be better, but you know how it is."

"I do." Julie tried not to sound discouraged. "How's your family?"

"They're doing good. Ava lost another tooth."

Julie smiled, thinking of his young daughter. "Does she have any teeth left at this point?"

"Not many," Franki laughed. "You want your usual?"

"Yes, please," Julie said. While she couldn't afford places like Florentina's very often, Franki's had some of the most affordable food in the area. It was her go-to place when she didn't have time or felt too lazy to cook a meal.

Franki's eyebrows shot up when he finally noticed who was with her. "Jake, hey. It's been a minute."

"Franki, good to see you again."

"You two know each other?" Julie asked.

Jake nodded. "We had some classes together in high school, if I remember right."

"That we did." Franki grinned before asking him, "What can I get you?"

Jake turned to Julie. "What's your usual?"

"There's three pasties you can choose from. Chicken and beef are two. I always order the vegetable option with an iced tea."

"I'll take that, too," he told Franki.

"For here or to-go?" the restaurant owner asked.

"Here's fine," Julie said.

"Okay, have a seat and I'll bring it right out to you."

They sat at one of the small tables, Jake leaning back in his chair as he observed her. "Did you have a long day?"

"I look that bad, huh?" she said with a light laugh.

"I don't think that's possible," Jake replied and Julie flushed. "But you do look like you've got a lot on your mind."

Julie shrugged. "It *was* a long day. I saw Harris Farmington leaving one of the stores across the street from my shop today. He made the shop owner an offer she's probably not going to refuse. I spent most of my afternoon looking for ways to bring an influx of cash to the shops in town, but there aren't many options."

"Well, I might have some new—"

"Here you are," Franki said as he walked up to them. He placed their iced teas in front of them, followed by two pasty-filled paper plates. After giving them some disposable wooden cutlery wrapped in paper napkins, he said, "Let me know if you need anything else."

"Thanks, Franki," Julie said.

She unwrapped her cutlery and cut into the flaky crust. Steam and fresh vegetables baked in spices and gravy oozed from the center. Julie's mouth watered before she shoveled a bite in. She probably didn't look that attractive, but she was so hungry she didn't care. She closed her eyes, enjoying the flavorful concoction of veggies and fresh piecrust.

Jake cleared his throat and Julie's eyes flew open as she remembered the celebrity's presence. He was staring at her mouth. She quickly brought up the napkin to dab at it, mortified that she might have crust on her lips.

Pulling his gaze away, he cut into his pasty and took a bite. He looked pleasantly surprised as he chewed. "This is *really* good," he said after several more bites.

"Right? Franki has the best pasties around." Julie took a sip of her sweetened iced tea. "So, what did you want to talk to me about?"

Jake glanced toward the kitchen area where Franki was before he leaned toward her. The gesture caused Julie's breath to catch as she took in the light specs of gold in his otherwise pure blue eyes.

"What I'm about to tell you needs to stay between us. Can you give me your word on that?"

"Of course," Julie said.

Jake peered over his shoulder one more time, making sure Franki hadn't moved before he said, "Holiday Boys are getting back together."

"WHAT!" she shouted.

Jake winced at her volume and straightened in his seat.

"Everything okay, Julie?" Franki asked, hurrying out from the back.

"Sorry, Franki," she replied, her eyes not leaving Jake. "Everything's fine." Once Franki disappeared again, she whispered, "Are you serious?"

"Yeah, that's where I was this morning. We're recording an album in Charlevoix."

Julie started bouncing her leg up and down, barely able to contain her excitement. "Oh my god, all the Holiday Boys are in Michigan. Even Tyler?"

"Um, ow," Jake joked. "I thought I was your favorite."

Julie grinned. "Don't worry, you are. Tyler was Meg's favorite, though I don't think she'd ever admit that aloud. Probably because they were sworn enemies growing up. Oh…" Some of her excitement diminished for a second. "Not that I'll tell her."

"I know," Jake said. "I trust you."

Happiness soared inside Julie, and she tried not to look as pleased as she felt at that announcement.

"When does the album come out?" she asked. "Wait…how did it even happen? I never thought you guys would reunite."

"We try to get together at least once a year, you know, just to hang out and catch up. Tyler started talking about a song he'd written several months ago. He said he couldn't imagine anyone else singing it but us. One conversation led to another and here we are."

Julie continued to sit there, letting the news flow over her.

"I never knew why you guys decided to call it quits after such a short time together. You were really magic, and oh my god, I'm completely fangirling right now, aren't I?"

Jake chuckled. "It's okay, I'm glad you enjoy our music."

"But…why did you…"

"Break up?" Jake swirled the leftover gravy around on his plate with his knife. "Let's just say, I got pissed at the record company for reasons that aren't really my story to tell, so I walked."

"But things are okay now?"

"Things are different now. Times are different. And we really do love each other. We're brothers. It was never about each other."

Julie brightened. "Well, if you ever decide to go on tour again, I'll make sure to get tickets."

Jake smirked. "Speaking of that…"

"You guys are going on tour?"

"Not a full tour. Not for a while anyway. But I did speak with the guys and we've decided to do a charity concert."

Julie reached over and briefly squeezed his hand. "That's so great. Where are you doing the concert? Central Park? LA?"

"Here."

Julie was in the middle of dragging her hand back but froze, staring unblinking at him. "Come again?"

"We're doing a concert here next month, with proceeds going to small businesses."

Julie continued to sit stock-still. "Are you serious?"

"Yeah. We're working on getting the permits now. With the money our concerts raise, you and the rest of the shops in town should be taken care of for a while. Not to mention, it'll bringing a ton of people and publicity to the area."

Julie jumped from her seat, ran around the table, and threw her arms around Jake. "Thank you. Thank you so much."

Jake placed his hands on her waist, giving her a couple of small squeezes. "You're welcome."

Julie realized she was practically plastered against the superstar. She took a quick step back before sitting in her chair again. Grabbing her drink, she took a couple of sips for something to do. She finally asked, "So, um, where are you going to be holding the concert?"

"Well, that's what I was hoping you could help me with."

"Me?"

"Yeah, I really want to do everything in our power to make sure businesses in Holiday Bay benefit from this. I was hoping you'd be able to help out with that. Everything from helping me scout for locations to any other ideas you might have. What do you say?"

Julie realized her mouth was hanging open, and she closed it. Jake wanted her input. They'd get to spend more time together, while doing what they could to save the town from Farmington. She tried to remember her earlier reservation about spending time with Jake, but in that moment she didn't remember the reason, nor did she care to. Tears of relief formed in her eyes.

Knowing he was waiting on her answer, she gave him the only one he was looking for.

"I say yes."

Chapter Eight

Julie sat in the administrator's office of her mom's assisted-living facility, her stomach aching with dread. "Can you please repeat that?"

Aubry's face was cool and impatient. "Your mother's repetitiveness has gotten much worse over the past few months. In addition to that, she almost lost her balance the other day—"

"Almost, but didn't."

"We still have to factor in if her equilibrium is going to be a concern. Which means more staff will have to take time out of their schedules to check on her. Between this and a decrease in overall cognitive abilities, we are increasing her care by three points."

Julie wrapped her arms around her waist. Red Oaks had a point system. The more points the resident had, the more expensive their care was.

"So, where does that put us financially?"

Aubry named the figure and bile rose in Julie's throat. Her mom's bill was going to cost an extra five hundred a month.

"That's a lot," she whispered.

"You can always apply for financial assistance."

"She doesn't qualify for it."

Her mom not only received a pension from her years of working at the local utility company, she also still received a pension from the employer of Julie's dad. Combined, they put her mom over the financial cap to get government assistance, but it didn't pay enough to cover her mom's monthly rent in full. Her mom was also too young to qualify for Medicare. Even if she was older, she needed to be at a certain financial threshold, and thanks to the amount of her life insurance policy, she would never meet the requirement. Julie paid the rest of her mom's rent with Veronica chipping in a little here and there.

"I... I don't know if we can afford that amount." Julie hated to admit it. "Is it possible to do a smaller increment?"

She knew the answer would be no, but she hoped that Aubry might be willing to be a little bit flexible.

She wasn't. "I can give you the number of a few other facilities that might be more in your price point."

Julie stared at the younger women as anger built inside her. She understood assisted living was a business, but wasn't there any level of empathy toward their residents? All that mattered to Aubry was sucking as much money out of her mom as possible.

Julie stood up on shaking legs. "I'll let you know."

"I do need you to sign the agreement for the new pricing." Aubry slid a document across the table. A ballpoint pen rested on top of it.

With her body tight with tension, Julie bent down and scribbled her name. As she turned to leave, Aubry added, "If you decide to move your mother out, don't forget that we require you to give us thirty days' notice, or there's a three-thousand dollar fee."

Julie gave a short nod before leaving the room, her hands trembling. As soon as she was far enough away from the administrator's office, she leaned against the wall and drew in a shaky breath. How was she going to manage the new increase?

Julie dragged a hand across her face before straightening her shoulders. She would have to find a way to make this work.

As much as she hated the heartlessness of Red Oaks, her mom was comfortable there and was friends with the other residents. Julie didn't want to take her out of there. Especially since the next closest facility had multiple complaints against it.

She was going to have to call Veronica again. She was already dreading that conversation.

Trying not to let her bitterness surface, Julie made her way to her mom's room. Her mom was in her favorite brown chair, working on another puzzle.

"Hey, Mom," Julie said with forced cheer as she stepped into the living room.

Her mom jerked her head up, her graying red hair perfectly styled. Julie held her breath, waiting for her reaction.

"Julie!"

Her mom set her puzzle book on the table next to her and stood up, walking over to Julie without showing any problems with her balance. Equilibrium issues, her ass.

"Hey," Julie said again, wrapping her mom in a close hug. Her mom smelled like fresh soap, which meant she showered recently.

"Where have you been?" her mom said, pulling back to frown at her daughter. "You haven't been to see me in months."

Julie had been there last week, but she wasn't about to argue with her mom. It would do no good and was pointless anyway.

"I'm sorry," she said instead. "Things have been kind of crazy at the store."

"You know, I'm not going to be around forever. You should visit more."

Julie swallowed hard. "I'll try better."

Her mom nodded before returning to her chair. She waved her hand at the love seat and Julie promptly sat down.

"So, why haven't you been to see me lately?"

Julie's hand gripped her cushion until her knuckles turned

white. She repeated, "Sorry, Mom. Things have been busy at the store."

"You spend too much time at that store. When are you going to provide me with some grandbabies? You aren't getting any younger, you know."

Julie tried her best not to let old anger rise inside her. This wasn't the first time she and her mom had had this conversation. Her mom used to say this to her even before she got sick.

Instead of yelling *I'm not going to get married or provide you with a bunch of grandkids,* she said, "I'll give that some consideration."

Her mom nodded, looking slightly mollified. "And when do I get to meet the man in your life?"

"What man?" Julie said, picking at a loose thread on the love seat.

"A woman always looks a certain way when there's a man in their life. So, who is the lucky guy?"

"That's such an antiquated idea," Julie responded. Her mom only gave her a knowing look. Throwing her hands in the air, she said, "Fine, there is someone that I've been hanging out with recently, but nothing's going to happen between us."

"And why not?" her mom asked.

"Because he's so far out of my league there's no chance of us becoming anything else."

"Pfft," her mom said. "Any man would be lucky to have you."

Julie smiled at that. Her phone buzzed in her purse and she pulled it out, seeing that she had a text from Jake. He wanted to meet in a half hour to start scouting spots for the concert. Julie still couldn't believe that Holiday Boys was reuniting.

"Listen, Mom, I need to go, but I'll be back later this week to spend more time with you, okay?"

"Okay," her mom replied. Julie got up and walked over to her mom, then kissed her cheek.

As Julie crossed the room, her mom said, "Julie."

She turned back. "Yes?"

"You know, I'm not going to be around forever. You should visit more," she said, her eyes starting to go blank as her Alzheimer's took over.

"I'm sorry, Mom," Julie whispered. "I'll do better."

Her mom picked up her puzzle book and opened it again, forgetting that Julie was there.

Julie let out a quiet sigh before leaving Red Oaks and heading for her shop. It was Monday, the one day off she gave herself each week. She parked outside of Pieces of Home and sat in her car, listening to the radio play pop hits from the early 2000s. A song from Holiday Boys came on and she smiled, quietly humming along as she waited for Jake to show up. Her phone began to ring and Meg's name appeared on her car's touch screen.

Hitting the button on her steering wheel, Julie answered, "Hey Meg."

"Hey." Meg sniffed, instantly alerting Julie that something was off.

"What's wrong?"

"Nothing."

"Meg." Julie waited patiently.

"Fine, Lucas and I got into a huge fight this morning."

"Oh no," Julie said sympathetically. "What happened?"

"Clarice talked to our caterer and changed our whole menu for the reception. Lucas and I spent hours on that, tasting different options and deciding what to pick. What Clarice picked out is horrible. She got rid of all the vegan options, despite knowing that I don't eat meat."

"Meg, I'm so sorry," Julie replied. "What are you going to do?"

"I told Lucas that he needed to speak with his mom and remind her that this was our wedding, not hers. He said his mom was only trying to help and wanted to feel included. As you can imagine, that didn't go over well with me."

Julie winced. Meg, for the most part, was a calm, happy-go-lucky individual. It took a lot to make her mad, but when she did, people needed to duck for cover.

"I know you probably don't want to hear this right now," Julie said. "But good for you. You can't let Clarice keep interfering with your lives."

"Yeah," Meg said quietly. "What are you doing right now? Do you want to hang out?"

"I really wish I could, but I'm meeting Jake."

"Again?" Meg perked up. "Is this another 'not a date, but totally a date' thing?"

"It's not a date," Julie said firmly. "He's got a plan to help Holiday Bay's small businesses and he wants my input, that's all."

"What kind of plan?"

"I…" Julie didn't want to lie to Meg, but she had promised Jake she wouldn't mention that Holiday Boys was reuniting. "I think he wants to use his celebrity to raise awareness. I don't have all the details yet."

"If you say so." Meg's voice was light, but Julie could still hear the sadness in her tone.

"Why don't you and I meet tomorrow after I'm done at the shop?" Julie said. "We can go get Chinese, hang out at my place, and rewatch *Bridgerton*."

"Yeah, that sounds like a plan."

"Okay. Love you lots, Meg."

"Love you, too, Jules," Meg said before disconnecting the call.

Julie glared at the steering wheel, thinking of the many things she'd like to say to Clarice. A knock on her window made her jump, but she relaxed when she saw Jake standing there. He wore aviator sunglasses and a beat-up hoodie jacket, the hood covering his head.

Grabbing her purse and stepping out of the car, she said, "Hi."

"Hi." Jake gave a crooked little grin that caused Julie's stomach to flutter. "Everything all right? You were looking a little fierce there."

"Yeah." They began to walk toward the town's fairgrounds. "It's just been a morning. I normally see my mom on Mondays. I mentioned before that she has Alzheimer's, right?" When Jake nodded, Julie admitted, "Sometimes it's really hard to see her go through it."

"I'm sorry."

"It's okay." Julie pushed a strand of her red hair behind her ear. "I'm a little worried about Meg, too. She's getting married soon. To be honest, her future mother-in-law isn't the most pleasant person. Meg doesn't deserve half of what Clarice throws at her."

"Clarice… I remember a Clarice. She was the mayor's wife when I was in high school."

"She still is the mayor's wife. Not much has changed there since you've been gone."

Jake whistled. "I remember singing for a talent show my freshman year of high school. She was one of the judges." Jake smirked. "She said that I should stick to earning an education because my voice wouldn't get me anywhere."

"Yeah, that sounds like Clarice," Julie muttered.

"Marriage is an ugly enough business without having a meddling mother-in-law in the mix."

Julie glanced at Jake. "You think marriage is ugly?"

"I think people go into it with all these romantic notions about things, but marriages rarely last. Don't get me wrong, I enjoyed certain aspects of marriage…building a life with someone, but you don't need a legally binding piece of paper to do that. Especially if you're having problems right from the beginning. It's better to end a relationship instead of doing something you regret down the road. Trust me."

Julie nibbled on her lip. She didn't say anything else. She wasn't an expert in the department of love, let alone marriage, and she didn't want to sour the day any further by asking Jake to break down his marriage to her. But something deep inside Julie ached at the idea that Jake thought marriage was pointless.

"So," Jake said as they continued to walk. "Why didn't we just meet at the fairgrounds?"

"Too much exercise for you?" she joked, her mood lightening. She eyed the light hoodie he wore and how the fabric strained around his muscled arms. He was in better shape than she was.

"Fresh air makes me twitchy." He smirked at her.

"Um." Julie quickly looked across the street and missed the branch lying on the sidewalk in front of her. Her foot tripped on it and she started to fall. Jake grabbed her by the waist and pulled her to him. She hit his chest hard, and the air was knocked out of her.

"You okay?" he asked softly.

"Yeah," she said when she caught her breath. "Slightly horrified and the ground is welcome to swallow me up at any time, but I'm okay."

Jake laughed, the motion causing his chest to vibrate... which she was still clinging to, her hands clutching his hoodie. He hadn't let go of her waist either. This close to him, she could breathe in the fresh scent of his ocean-breeze cologne. His heart beat strongly against her fingers, and she flattened her palm against him. Her eyes drifted to the firm lines of his mouth, and she felt his pulse speed up underneath her touch. It made her feel powerful.

Someone across the street let out a catcall and they jumped apart.

Julie's face heated. "Thanks, uh, thanks for the save."

"Anytime." Jake's voice was barely a whisper. She could feel his eyes on her from behind his aviators.

She forced herself to start moving, doing her best to ignore what had just happened. "To answer your question as to why we're walking, I wanted to show you some of the shops in town. I wondered if there was a way we could feature them at your concert. Maybe on a screen before the show starts, or something."

Jake nodded. "That's a good idea. I'll see if Paul can put something together. We can feature it on our social media accounts, too. Of course, Paul will probably go completely Hollywood and make it a two-hour production."

She smiled and felt his gaze on her again.

An awkward silence fell between them. Julie tried to think of something clever to say, but her mind kept snapping back to what almost took place moments ago. Would Jake have kissed her if they hadn't been interrupted? Would she have let him? *Yes.*

A bright burst of white caught her eye. The cherry trees along Main Street were in full bloom, the flowers filling the air with their sweet scent.

"It's beautiful this time of year," she said. When he looked at her questioningly, she pointed at the trees. "I love Michigan in the spring."

"That's one thing I've really missed about living here. Spring's always been my favorite season. It's peaceful, you know?"

Julie started to nod in agreement when something dawned on her. She inspected the street more thoroughly and frowned.

"What?" Jake asked.

"I was just thinking it's weird to be out walking with you and not have a crowd of people chasing us."

Jake smirked. "That's why I pay my publicist well. As far as the world knows, I was only in town for a few days and now I'm somewhere in Europe."

"Smart," she said as they arrived at the fairgrounds. Julie waved her hand around the expansive space. "So, what do you think?"

Directly in front of them was a large field, which usually hosted the demolition derby and town fair. To the left was an area where food trucks typically set up. To the right were several barns, which the town used to judge livestock and produce.

"You can probably get a few hundred fans in here legally, which I know isn't the normal size Holiday Boys would get, especially when you consider you'll be doing your first concert in years. But you have bathrooms and electricity." Julie tried to inspect the place through Jake's eyes. "I know it's not what you're used to. Unfortunately, Holiday Bay never built any huge venues in the years you were gone, and anywhere else in town won't be able to offer you the necessities you'll need, like public bathrooms and crowd control. The only other option I could think of was the campground Meg's parents own. It's just outside of town, and the space is large, but you're having the concert around the same time that they start hitting their busy season. Greta—Meg's mom—said that many of the lots have already been rented out."

"This is perfect," Jake said, nodding toward the fairgrounds. His mouth twisted up as he looked at the field in front of him. "This place has a lot of nostalgia for me. The first time I ever performed, I played on that field. I think I was eight. I sung 'Dream a Little Dream of Me,' while James played the ukulele behind me. It's where I got my first taste of what I wanted to do for the rest of my life."

Julie briefly glanced at him. "Sometimes it's hard to remember you started your career here. I mean, I know you're from here—I went to Holiday Boys' first concert at the high school—but it's hard to picture you as a kid singing on that cheap wooden stage they have."

Jake lifted an eyebrow. "Why?"

Julie shrugged. "Because you've come so far. You're one of the biggest names in the world."

"We all start somewhere. And yeah, I've had a career that's been more successful than I ever anticipated, but I'm still me. I'm still the same person who sung on that stage while Eddie Harley threw up a corn dog in the front row..." Julie laughed and Jake smiled in response. "I met Paul and Zan here for the first time. Tyler had joined James and me by then. We had just finished our set when these two guys from Clarington came out on the stage and blew the crowd away with their talent. That field is where Holiday Boys was born." His face went from fond to serious. "For better or worse, Holiday Bay is my roots."

Julie stared at him hesitantly before blurting, "That's the second time you've said something like that about Holiday Bay. Are you...are you not happy to be back?"

Jake furrowed his forehead as he shoved his hands in the front pocket of his hoodie. "I'm sure you heard the gossip about my family."

Julie bit her lip. She did know—most people who grew up in Holiday Bay knew that Jake's family life was dysfunctional—but she didn't put too much stock into a bunch of spineless gossip, especially the jealous talk that ramped up after Jake hit it big.

She shrugged. "I heard things here and there. I assumed most of it was made up."

"Most of it probably wasn't," Jake muttered before giving her a tight smile. "I don't really like to talk about it."

Julie nodded before changing the subject. She inclined her head toward the barns. "I thought we could have different busi-

nesses set up booths in there so they could sell their products…
if you don't think that would be tacky or anything."

"Why would that be tacky?" Jake put a hand on her shoulder, giving it a light squeeze. Julie found herself leaning into the touch and missed the warmth of his palm when it dropped back to his side.

"I think it's a great idea," he said. "Showcase everything that Holiday Bay has to offer while announcing to the world that Holiday Boys is back together." Jake grinned at her warmly before pulling his phone out. He took a few pictures of the place. "Let me send this to my manager."

A few seconds later, his phone began to ring. The name *Lori* appeared on the screen before Jake hit ignore.

"Do you need to answer that?" Julie asked. Isabella had mentioned the ship name *Jori* and that people thought Jake was involved with his manager. Julie wondered what role Lori actually played in Jake's life.

"No, Lori can wait. She's a competent enough manager. She'll figure it out."

"Oh, she's your manager?" Julie tried not to sound as interested as she was.

Jake looked at Julie, taking in the sudden stillness of her frame. "Yeah, just my manager."

Her face softened before her gaze drifted back toward the barns.

Jake was half tempted to grasp her chin and make her look at him. She'd barely met his eyes since that moment on the sidewalk. He wondered what would have happened if that person hadn't whistled at them. Would Julie have kissed him? He had wanted—badly—to feel her lips against his. He was even more tempted to undo the messy bun on top of her head so he could feel the shiny waves of her hair in his hands, like he'd wanted to since that day in high school. He wondered what her hair smelled like up close. Sometimes he could pick up the scent of roses from her. Did she use a rose shampoo? Did she spray a rose-scented perfume all over her body? The urge to bury his face against her to find the source of that smell grew every time he caught it on her.

Reining his mind away from that path, he asked, "Do you want to walk around town some more? You can point out the businesses we should invite to have a booth."

"Invite all of them." Julie's lips curved upward. "But yeah, let's do that."

They spent the rest of the afternoon together, Julie showing him the different shops and giving a little history of when the stores opened. The longer they talked, the more she seemed to relax around him—their earlier awkwardness almost gone.

"McFarley's is still here," Jake said, nodding toward the hardware store.

"Scott took over for his dad about ten years ago," Julie said. "Do you remember Scott? I think he was in your grade or the year before." Jake shrugged. "He married Lana Highland, who was in my grade. They have twin boys and a little girl. Lana and I started the Holiday Bay Christmas Committee a few years ago. You should have seen the tree-lighting ceremony we had last year at town hall…"

As Julie continued to speak, Jake started to realize something. Julie wasn't just interested in saving the history of the buildings in Holiday Bay. This community was family to her. From what he learned of her so far, her mother was in assisted living, her father passed away years ago, her sister was on the other side of the country, and her best friend was about to get married, beginning a new chapter of her life that may exclude Julie. Jake knew he and Tyler had drifted apart after Jake married Angelika…but that might have also been because Tyler never liked her.

This community was one of the few things Julie had left.

His heart ached for her and he became even more determined than ever to save Holiday Bay.

As it grew later in the day, they made their way to Franki's for more pasties. Julie entered first, only to come to an abrupt halt. Jake peaked over her shoulder and saw a couple sitting at one of the tables. The man was tall and had floppy blond hair. The woman looked pale and miserable as she pushed a salad listlessly on the plate in front of her.

She perked up when she saw Julie. "Hey!"

"Hey, Meg. Lucas."

Lucas nodded but otherwise didn't say anything. He barely looked in their direction as he focused on the pasty in front of him, his face expressionless.

Jake looked at the woman again. He hadn't recognized Tyler's former neighbor at first, since the last time he saw her she was a young teen. She had grown up to be a lovely woman. He was half tempted to call Tyler and tell him who he'd run into. He would bet money that Tyler would love to get caught up with his childhood archrival.

"Do you want to join us?" Meg asked before her gaze drifted over Julie's shoulder and she made eye contact with him. "Oh…"

Jake could tell she wanted to freak out at seeing him by the way she shifted in her seat, as though she barely restrained herself from jumping out of her chair. But she kept her composure, which Jake appreciated.

"That's okay," Julie said. "We're actually ordering ours to-go." Franki came out from the back kitchen area, wiping his hands on a rag he was holding. "Hi, Franki. Can I get my usual, please?"

"You bet," Franki said before looking at Jake.

"Same."

"Be right back with your food."

Jake watched as Julie observed Meg's meal of a salad and

glass of water. She frowned. "Do you want me to get you anything? Sweet tea?"

"She's on a diet for the wedding," Lucas said.

Julie stiffened. "She doesn't need to diet."

Lucas held up his hands defensively. "That's what I told her," he said before looking at Meg. "Unless you changed your mind?"

"No, I haven't changed my mind." She gave Jake an embarrassed look. "Hi, Jake. I know you don't remember me, but—"

"Of course I remember you, Meg," Jake said, walking over to the couple. "Didn't you once challenge Tyler to a hot dog–eating contest? From what I remember, you had him beat until you threw up."

Meg face-palmed. "Of all the memories you have of me…"

Jake laughed. "We had some good times when we were younger. Tyler still brings up when you 'accidentally' kicked him during that one football game. He says he can feel phantom pain on a rainy day."

"I'm surprised he remembers my name," Meg replied just as Lucas said, "You kicked someone?"

"I was eight." Meg nodded toward Jake. "Lucas, you remember Jake Reynolds, I'm sure."

Lucas's eyes grew wide before he hopped to his feet and offered his hand to Jake. "Hello! Welcome back to Holiday Bay."

"Thanks," Jake said, briefly shaking the other man's hand.

"Will you be in town long?" Lucas looked over Jake's shoulder. "Will any of the other Holiday Boys be around?"

"Just me."

Lucas's face flickered with disappointment—clearly Jake wasn't his favorite Holiday Boy—before he said in a tone that was almost resigned, "I'm sure my father would love a chance to connect with you at his office."

The last thing Jake wanted to do was be seen with Mayor Beaumont. People might think he was endorsing the guy, and from what Jake remembered, the mayor was as small-minded as his wife.

"To be honest," Jake replied. "My schedule is pretty tight at the moment. Maybe some other time."

Franki came out with two bags. "Here's your order."

Julie grabbed the food. "Thanks, Franki. You're the best!"

As she started to reach for her purse, Jake said, "I've got it."

Julie murmured her thanks. As Jake paid, he could hear Meg and Julie whispering to each other.

Julie leaned down and gave Meg a brief hug. "I'll call you tomorrow, okay?"

"Are we still getting together for dinner?" Meg asked.

"Yes. Do you want to meet at my store after closing?"

"Sure."

With a wave, Julie exited the building, Jake following behind.

Her expression was grim as they headed toward the bay.

"You okay?" he asked.

"Yeah. Lucas and I have a tendency to rub each other the wrong way. I keep telling myself the important thing is that Meg's happy. That's all I can ask for."

"She didn't look happy to me."

"No, she didn't." Julie bit her lip. "Honestly, neither of them did."

Jake gave her arm a comforting squeeze before they turned toward the bay. They reached the beach, the stones underneath their feet crunching as Julie led them over to a long log that rested twenty feet from the water. Jake sat beside her, shoving his aviators into his hoodie pocket and pulling the hood off. He opened his container of food and ate quickly before the late spring air stole the heat.

"I'm going to order some of these for the road next time I go on tour," he said between bites.

"When do you think that'll be?" Julie asked.

"Probably sometime next year. It depends on how quickly we finish this album. Knowing our manager, I'm sure we'll be on a world tour before it's even available for download."

Julie gave him a brief smile and continued her meal. After they finished eating, they sat in silence, watching the water develop an orange hue as it reflected the setting sun. Julie shifted beside him and he leaned closer to her.

Their shoulders touched.

Neither moved away.

"This is my favorite place in all of Holiday Bay," Julie murmured, her head tipped up, the waning light caressing the gentle curves of her face. "It breaks my heart to imagine Farmington's ships docking here, dredging up the bay and disturbing the peace."

"The price of commerce." Jake saw the anger in her eyes and held up a hand in a passive gesture. "Hey, I agree with you. I don't think we have to develop every single piece of land out there."

"Farmington will, too." Julie nodded toward a small boating dock meant for pontoons and paddleboats. "There's no way he'll be able to get larger ships in the bay without digging it out. People won't be able to fish or swim here anymore. Not with those ships around. I don't understand why people don't realize how much we'll lose if he gets his way."

"I'm surprised he can get away with it, given that there has to be some environmental restrictions."

"I thought about that, so I did some research in hopes I could stop it that way. Per Holiday Bay regulations, all Farmington needs to do is get the blessing of city council." Julie waved her hand toward town. "You saw Lucas in there. His dad would do anything for a photo op with famous people. I think he has ambitions to run for state senate or some other higher government position, and it's been years since he had that scandal. If Farmington donated just enough money to his campaign and maybe took a picture with him, that could give Mayor Beaumont the boost he wants."

They sat in silence for several minutes, each lost in thought, before Julie bent down and picked up a stone, a smile breaking out on her face. "Look, a Petoskey stone." She showed it to Jake before pocketing it. "I have a vendor who likes to use them for different projects."

Jake's mind went to his son, and his good mood dimmed slightly. Dylan loved using the stones in his own work as well. He wondered if Dylan would ever return to finish the table he'd been working on. His son hadn't spoken to him since the day of their disagreement. Jake was going to give him a little more time to cool off before he tried reaching out to him again.

For the life of him, he still couldn't figure out what had set Dylan off so badly. It wasn't like he knew Julie, and Jake and Julie were consenting adults. Neither needed permission from a teenager.

"You okay?" Julie asked.

Jake looked over at her. "Yeah, why?"

"You have this line between your eyes, like you just thought of something unpleasant."

She reached out and traced the area with her finger. An electric jolt shot through Jake's body. She started to move her hand away, but he grabbed it, moving it until the palm of her hand clasped his cheek. He held his hand over hers, soaking in the warmth of her touch.

"Your cheek is cold," Julie whispered.

Jake stroked his knuckles against hers.

"So is yours." His voice was low and soft.

His fingers drifted down to her jaw before caressing her ear, continuing to the back of her neck. He pulled her toward him, and brushed his lips gently against hers. Sparks flew across his skin and he deepened the kiss. Her lips parted, molding to his, and his arms encircled her, pulling her against him.

Julie stiffened in his arms. She pulled back and looked at Jake with something akin to horror.

"Wha—" he started to ask but she turned her face.

"I'm sorry." She wouldn't meet his eyes.

"Julie." He reached out to touch her cheek again, but she jerked away. Jake felt something twist inside his stomach. "Look, I'm really sorry if I stepped out of line here."

"No." She briefly looked at him before glancing away again. "It's not you. I... I have to go."

She jumped up from the log, her movements skittish.

"Let me walk you to your car," Jake offered.

"No, it's okay. Thank you for the evening and everything and I just... I'll talk to you later, okay?"

"But—"

Jake didn't get to finish what he was about to say. Julie stumbled her way across the stone beach, hurrying down a path that cut between two tall maple trees. Jake ran a hand through his hair and stared back at the water.

What the hell happened? One minute, it felt like he was touching fire, needing its warmth to survive. The next, the light was gone and he was left with nothing but numbing coldness.

Chapter Nine

Julie tried to push down the overwhelming anxiety she felt as she walked into her mom's apartment. She'd woken up that morning exhausted from a restless sleep, her neck aching with tension, which soon shifted to her head and turned into a full-blown headache.

Her mom slept peacefully in her recliner, so Julie sat down in the love seat, placing her purse beside her. For the first time since it had happened, she allowed herself to think about the previous evening.

The moment on the beach had been perfect. The way their shoulders pressed together as they watched the setting sun. The way Jake's fingers traveled over her skin, causing goose bumps to break out that had little to do with the cooler air.

And that kiss.

Wow.

Julie always enjoyed a good kiss and the spark of heat it was capable of creating inside her. When she was in college, she attended a few parties and kissed several guys. For the most part, kissing did nothing for her. Just two people exchanging drool. But she remembered a couple guys who left her breathless. Her college boyfriend, Charlie, had. That's what a good kiss could do.

Jake Reynolds was an *excellent* kisser.

It was when a guy asked to go further that the small bit

of passion she could conjure disappeared as quick as lightning. When she'd felt Jake's arms wrap around her, pulling her closer to the strong muscled wall of his chest, desire ignited inside her. But just as soon as it happened, the arousal fizzled. Like it always did.

Embarrassment replaced want and she'd fled, leaving him looking confused and hurt. She felt heartsick.

Her mom shifted in her chair, slowly opening her eyes.

"Hi," Julie said as brightly as she could muster.

Her mom startled, her eyes frantically going to the door leading to the hallway. "What are you doing in my room?"

"It's me, Mom, Julie."

"You're a liar, Julie's at preschool." Her mom gripped the arms of her chair. She started yelling, "Help! Help! There's an intruder! Don!"

The pain in Julie's head increased at the mention of her dad's name. "Mom, please calm down before you hurt yourself."

"Help!" she shouted again.

The nurse and one of the caretakers ran into the room, surveying the scene.

"Jane," the nurse said. "I need you to take a deep breath and calm down."

Her mom pointed to Julie. "There's an intruder!"

"I'll leave," Julie offered. She grabbed her purse and ran out of the room, her mom's angry voice following her.

Once she was a few rooms down, Julie leaned against the wall and ran a shaky hand over her face. The pain in her head intensified. More than anything, she wanted to curl in a ball and cry.

No...

What she wanted was to see her mom like she'd been when Julie was a child. Healthy and someone Julie could talk to. They might not have always seen eye to eye when Julie was young, but she was always willing to listen when Julie needed to unload her problems. Her mom would have done a happy dance if she knew that Julie was having guy problems for the first time in years.

"Are you okay?"

Julie opened her eyes. The nurse stood in front of her with a concerned expression.

"Not really." Julie sighed tiredly. "I know she has more bad days than good lately, but I was really hoping today would be a good day."

The nurse was sympathetic. "I'm going to give her something to help her settle down. Maybe come back in a few hours."

Julie knew she wouldn't be able to because she had to be at the store, but she nodded anyway and left the facility. Hopping in her car, she grabbed some pain relievers from her purse and swallowed them dry. She drove to Pieces of Home with the windows cracked, hoping the air would help clear her head.

To her surprise, Dylan was waiting outside the store with a beautiful Craftsman nightstand by his side.

"Hi," he said. He frowned at the dark circles under her eyes. "You don't look good. Are you sick?"

Julie laughed at his bluntness, despite her pain. "Hello to you, too."

She opened the door and entered the store. Dylan followed, carrying the nightstand.

"But are you sick?" he asked.

"I woke up with a bit of a headache." Julie moved around the counter to put her purse away. She glanced at the table with its delicate drawer. "That's beautiful."

"Thanks." Dylan tapped his finger nervously against the table surface. "Do you still want to sell my, uh, my dad's stuff?"

"Of course. Why wouldn't I?" she asked in a confused tone.

"Because of how I acted the last time I was here. About, you know, Jake Reynolds."

"Oh." That was a reminder she didn't need. Against her will, her mind briefly went to the way Jake's lips molded to hers, but she quickly pushed the memory aside. She walked over to Dylan instead. "You've made it no secret that you don't like the man."

"I just think you could do better than him."

Julie let out a choked laugh. It was either that or cry. "He's a good man. He's trying his best to help me save this town from—"

She stopped talking. There was no reason to burden a teenager with her problems, no matter how much she liked Dylan.

"From?" he asked anyway.

"It's nothing." Julie tried to brush it off. "There's someone interested in buying properties in the area, mine included."

"But you wouldn't sell Pieces of Home, would you?"

"No, not if I can avoid it."

"And Jake is helping you."

"Yeah." Though Julie had no idea if Jake would still help her after last night. "He's looking at ways to raise money for small businesses in Holiday Bay, my store included."

Dylan stared at her. "I see."

Forcing a smile to her lips, she touched the surface of the smooth nightstand. "Is that something you wanted to sell, or are you just carrying furniture around town for fun?"

Dylan glanced down at it blankly. "Oh, yeah. It's for sale."

Julie took the table and placed it next to the counter. She'd have to find a good spot for it in the store. "Your father's work is beautiful."

"Actually...we, um, we did this one together."

"Really? Well, you did a great job." Julie examined the perfection of the piece, her mouth turning upward when she saw

Petoskey stones embedded on either side of the table's small drawer handle. "That reminds me…"

She grabbed her purse and removed the Petoskey stone she found on the beach.

"This is for you." Julie handed it to Dylan. "I thought your dad could use it in some of his work. It's good quality. It just needs to be polished."

"Thanks, Ms. A." Dylan took the stone in his palm, running his thumb over the surface. "And I'm sorry again for how I acted."

"It's okay," Julie assured him. "Seriously, don't give it a second thought."

Dylan chewed on his inner cheek as he glanced at Jake's poster. "You think he can really help your store?"

"He said he wanted to try."

Dylan nodded before peering back at her. "I hope the table helps, too."

"I know it will."

He smiled. "I'll see if I can get anything else to you sooner."

"Thanks Dylan. And thank your father, as well."

He seemed to startle before saying slowly, "Yeah, I'll do that."

After he left, Julie grabbed the nightstand and found a place for it in the back corner of the store where most of the furniture vendors sold their items. She felt jumpy throughout her day and kept looking at the door, half expecting Jake to turn up. Just as she was getting ready to close for the evening, Meg walked in.

"Hey." Julie eyed her friend, who brimmed with happiness. It wasn't what Julie had expected, considering how Meg had looked at Franki's. "You seem like you're in a much better mood than the last time I saw you."

"Lucas told his mother off!" Meg practically shouted. "He let her know that she had no right changing our wedding menu, and if she pulled a stunt like that again, she would be uninvited to the wedding."

"Really?" Julie was impressed. She didn't think Lucas had it in him.

"Yeah." Meg grabbed Julie's hands. "Look, I know you and I made plans tonight, and I really appreciate you wanting to cheer me up, but Lucas asked if he could take me out to talk. I think we really need this. Things were really tense between us last night. With all the wedding planning and his mother's antics, I think we could use some time to decompress and—"

"Meg, you don't have to explain it to me." Julie squeezed her friend's hands before letting them go. "Have a great time tonight. You and I can get caught up a different time."

"Thanks." Meg started to leave, but paused when she examined Julie's face. "Are you okay?"

"Yeah." Julie didn't want to burden her friend, especially when she knew Meg wanted to get to Lucas. "I woke up with a bit of a headache and it's been a long day."

"Did you take anything?"

Julie lifted a shoulder. "I took some Tylenol a little while ago. Seriously, I'm okay. Go see Lucas."

"Okay, thanks Julie." Meg gave her a hug. She headed for the exit but abruptly stopped. "Oh, I forgot to tell you. Jake's not the only Holiday Boy in town."

"What do you mean?"

"My mom saw Tyler visiting his parents last night. I can't remember the last time he came to town. Isn't it funny how Jake and Tyler are back in the Bay at the same time after all these years? I wonder if it means anything. Maybe a Holiday Boys reunion."

Julie plastered on a smile. "That'd be something."

After Meg left, Julie finished closing the store. Once she locked the door behind her, she turned and almost jumped out of her skin when she saw Jake standing beside her.

"I wish you'd stop doing that," she said. "You'll give me a heart attack one of these days."

"Sorry," he said.

He wore thick-rimmed black-framed glasses. His dark hair was a mess, as though he'd run his fingers through it several times. For the first time since she'd reunited with him, he didn't look effortlessly put together. That didn't mean he still didn't look devastating in dark jeans, black biker boots, and a thick cream-colored wool sweater.

"I didn't know you wore glasses," she said.

"I normally wear contacts, but my eyes were tired." Jake shoved his hands in his jeans pockets. "Can we talk?"

Even though her stomach filled with dread, she said, "Yeah."

He led them over to a bench in front of Baxter's. What she wouldn't do for one of their mocha lattes right now. But they'd already closed up shop and were in the process of selling all their equipment. If she could've afforded it, she would have loved to buy their espresso machine for Pieces of Home.

Sitting down on the bench next to Jake, Julie began to fiddle with the strap of her purse. She could feel Jake's eyes on her, but couldn't find the courage to meet his gaze.

He finally sighed. "Are you uncomfortable with me now?"

Julie briefly met his eyes before she looked away again. "No, of course not."

"I know I crossed a line last night."

Julie hated the misery in his tone. "It wasn't you. It's not your fault."

"Is that why you've been avoiding looking at me since I showed up?"

Julie took a deep breath before angling herself so she had no choice but to face him.

"You didn't do anything wrong," she said. "I… I wanted you to kiss me."

"Are you sure? Because I thought…" Jake ran a hand through his hair, causing it to stick up even more than it already was. Julie ached to smooth it back in place.

"The thing is, Julie," he said. "I like spending time with you. You see *me*, not Jake Reynolds, superstar—"

"Well—"

"Okay, you don't see me like that all the time." His tense demeanor relaxed and his lips briefly ticked up. "I thought there may have been something developing between us, but I guess I read it wrong, and I'm so sorry for taking advantage of you last night."

"Stop, please." Julie couldn't take it anymore. "I keep trying to tell you that you don't have anything to be sorry for. Like I said, it's not you."

"But—"

"Jake, it's me, okay?"

"Oh." The lines around Jake's mouth deepened. It was his turn to avoid her gaze. "You're not into me."

Julie let out a derisive laugh. "You really do need glasses." She grabbed his hand, giving it a gentle squeeze. "I like you, too."

Jake moved his fingers so that they interlaced with hers.

"I don't understand then," he said. "You say you like me, but when I kissed you last night, you looked at me as if I had grown an extra head."

Julie pulled on her hand to remove it from his. He let her go and she immediately missed his warmth as she settled her palm in her lap. It was time to tell him everything. She wasn't ashamed of being ace. She had accepted that about herself a long time ago. But she didn't want to lose him and she knew she was about to.

Taking a steely breath, Julie said, "Jake, I'm ace."

When his only response was the wrinkling of his forehead, she added, "I'm asexual. I'm not into sex. As in, ever."

Jake blinked twice before saying, "Oh."

"Yeah, as much as I like you and enjoy being with you, I know that you and I would never work out." She gave him a small, sad smile. "Even though it's surprisingly easy to forget you're Jake Reynolds, megastar, considering you're my all-time favorite singer, the fact is, you *are* a huge celebrity. You can have your choice of any woman on this earth, and she'll be able to give you *everything* you need. I can't."

Jake shook his head, his face growing dark. "You don't know that. You don't know what I want."

Julie let out a huff of air before standing up, gripping her purse tightly to her. "I've been down this road before. I dated a guy back in college, fell in love with him, had him say he loved me too. And you know what happened? As soon as I said no to sex, he said 'see ya later'."

"That doesn't mean I would do that." Jake also stood up.

"Be realistic. You'll be on tour with women in every city who would kill to have sex with you. Hell, I just watched that girl at the restaurant practically offer herself to you on a platter. And you're telling me that in a world where you literally sell sex appeal for a living, that you'd be truly happy never having sex again?" Julie's heart *ached* as she took in the confusion on his face. "Because that's what you get with me. Someone who might cuddle with you on the couch or who'd be happy holding your hand, but who will never initiate sex. Think about that. Is that really what you want in a relationship? Would that really make you happy long-term? Long talks and romantic walks on the beach, and nothing else?"

Jake didn't say anything, but he didn't have to. His silence was answer enough.

Julie nodded wearily. She took several hurried steps toward her car, her movement uncoordinated as she walked on legs that shook.

She opened the door with a jerk. Before she got in, she made herself look at Jake.

"I wish things could be different." Her throat ached. "But this is the way I am. I hope you'll still do the benefit concert because the town needs this, but I—I'll understand if you don't want to work with me anymore. There are some great people in Holiday Bay who are more than qualified to help you organize your concert. I…"

She couldn't speak anymore. Her heart shattered at his continued silence. Jake didn't try to stop her as she got into her car.

He remained unmoving as she pulled out of the parking space and drove away.

Chapter Ten

Jake found himself driving around the next day. He knew he probably shouldn't be behind the wheel. He was too distracted to focus.

He couldn't get over what Julie told him. Truthfully, he couldn't even comprehend what she'd said. Who the hell didn't like sex? Unless…something had happened to her. Had someone hurt her?

Blind rage raced through him at the idea of someone putting their hands on her without her consent. His heart ached at the idea of her going through that, and he certainly understood why she'd want to avoid intimacy.

If that's what had happened to her, he felt even sicker with himself for kissing her on the beach. He remembered how good Julie felt in his arms, and he'd pulled her tighter against him on instinct. Her response had been instant, her rejection clear. Had he brought up bad memories for her? He wouldn't be able to forgive himself if he'd cause her pain.

But if his theory was wrong and she simply didn't want sex…yeah, he didn't understand. Sex was as natural to him as breathing. He'd been enjoying it since he was sixteen years old. How could someone not want it? To not feel the rush of being with someone like that. To not want to be close and intimately connected to someone. It didn't make sense.

And God, he *wanted* it to make sense. He hated that he let

Julie walk away from him yesterday. He hated the weary acceptance on her face as he stood there like a statue.

But to not want to ever have sex? He couldn't let that go.

Before he knew it, Jake found himself parked outside of Patti's Diner again. He stared at the building, the pain of the past a welcome distraction for once. His thoughts went to his father and the final act of cruelty he'd shown Jake's mom that fateful day.

His fingers tightened on the steering wheel as he thought about his crassness with Julie on the beach; the lack of understanding he'd shown her when she'd told him the truth. Jesus, was he turning into his father?

Bile rose in his throat and he swallowed it down. He couldn't go down that path. He wouldn't let himself. Taking a shaking breath, he pulled his cell phone out of his pants pocket and called his attorney.

"You realize it's five a.m. in California, right?" Marcy grumbled into the phone after a few rings.

"Don't pretend you weren't already awake," he said, smiling despite his sour mood. He'd work with Marcy enough over the years to know when she was really pissed, and this wasn't it.

"As a matter of fact," she said waspishly, "my wife and I were just sitting down to a well-earned breakfast."

"I'll apologize to Sasha next time I see her," Jake replied as he stared at the faded for-sale sign next to the diner. "I need you to do something for me."

"This can't wait?"

"No," Jake insisted.

Marcy let out an obnoxious sigh, but he knew she'd take care of whatever he needed. The reason she had a penthouse in one of the best apartment buildings in LA was because of the salary Jake paid her to keep her on retainer.

"What do you need?" she asked.

"I want to buy a piece of property in Michigan. It's an old

diner in my hometown. I don't care what it costs. Get past any legalities you come across and make sure it's mine by the end of the business day." He rattled off the number on the sign.

"What are you going to do with a diner?"

Jake stared at the building, a muscle in his jaw twitching. No matter how long ago it was since he had last seen his father, the man still held too much power over him. Jake needed to let go of the past. For Dylan's sake. For Julie's.

For his own.

"Jake?" Marcy prompted when Jake continued to remain silent. "What are you going to do with a diner?"

"I'm going to burn it to the ground."

Julie held her iPad in her hand as she walked through the store doing inventory. She didn't need to. She had done inventory the other day. But if she didn't do something to keep herself busy, she'd go crazy.

She hadn't heard from Jake since she drove off last night. She knew he was a busy man, but part of her hoped he'd be at the store when she got there that morning.

A miserable, foolish part.

Now that he knew everything, she'd probably never see him again.

It was for the best. Getting involved with someone like Jake—one of the most famous men in the world—would only lead to heartbreak. Hadn't she been telling herself that from the moment she had agreed to meet him for a "business" dinner?

"You're so freaking ridiculous," she muttered as she picked up a crocheted owl and moved it to a different shelf.

The chimes to the door went off and she sighed in relief, welcoming the distraction.

"Julie?" a tearful voice called out.

Julie, instantly alarmed, hurried to the front of the store.

Meg stood there, looking lost. She wore a crumpled yellow sweatshirt paired with black yoga pants. Her brown hair was unkempt, her blue eyes puffy.

Julie ran to her side. "What's wrong?"

"We called it off."

"What?" Julie asked in shock.

Meg held up her hand to show her ring finger. The engagement ring that was normally there was absent.

"I don't understand. What happened?" Julie asked.

"What do you think? Clarice happened." Meg wiped at a tear streaking down her cheek. "Lucas and I went out to eat. Things were fine, and then he ordered something that his mom had chosen for our wedding dinner, and he said, 'This is good, maybe my mom was right and we should have ordered it.'" Which of course led to another argument. Then he looked at me—" Meg put a hand to her chest and sucked in a harsh breath "—and he said he couldn't do this anymore. He doesn't think we'll work out."

"You two have been dating since high school, and he decides *now* you aren't going to work out?" Julie was irate. "If I ever see Lucas on the street, I'm going to create such a scene, it'll be besmirch the Beaumont name for generations. *Besmirch*!."

Meg let out a laugh, which quickly turned into a sob. "I don't know what I'm going to do. I've been with Lucas since I was sixteen. He was my first everything. First love, first person I had sex with. He's been a part of me for half my life."

Julie pulled Meg into a tight hug.

"Here's what we're going to do." She stepped back and brushed away several more tears now fully streaming down her best friend's face. "I'm going to close the store early, and you and I are going to get Chinese and binge-watch something on Netflix."

"No *Bridgerton*," Meg muttered.

"No, we don't need romance right now." Julie ignored the pang in her heart as she thought of Jake.

She left her friend's side to grab her purse before guiding Meg out to her car. They stopped by their favorite restaurant, ordered their food, and headed back to Julie's.

"There's a good murder mystery on," Julie said.

"Fine." Meg flopped down on the plump couch cushion.

Julie had designed the entire living room with a soothing Zen vibe in mind. The walls were soft beige, and the room contained matching, cream-colored furniture. In the middle of one wall was a whitewashed fireplace with a dark wood mantle. Over the years, she had collected a few things from her travels with Meg, as well as items that came into her store. Her style was a mix of vintage and farmhouse decor.

Meg began to sniffle, her cheeks turning blotchy—the telltale sign that she was about to cry again. Julie handed her a box of tissues, before heading into the kitchen to grab some plates for their food. When she came back, Meg had her arms wrapped around her stomach. Her breaths were coming out rapid and shallow.

"Are you okay?" Julie asked. "You're breathing weird."

"I…" Meg's voice was raspy. "I can't breathe."

Julie stared at her friend, unsure what to do. "Are you having a panic attack? Try taking a deep, slow breath."

Meg sucked in a deep, shaking breath, but if anything, that seemed to make her worse. She jumped from the couch and started frantically pacing around the room, her movements jittery.

Julie put the two plates down on one of the tables next to the couch. She glanced toward where she'd left her purse and car keys. "Do you need to go see a doctor?"

Meg grabbed the remote control for the TV and pressed the on button. She turned the volume so loud that Julie winced as the title credits began to blare.

"I just need a distraction," Meg said. "There's too much going on in here." She tapped the side of her head. "I need to block out the noise in my brain."

Julie stared at her friend, feeling uneasy. She'd never seen Meg like this, not in all the years they'd known each other. Meg was confident and collected. She wasn't like this. "What do you need me to do?"

Meg shook her head. "I—I'll be okay." She sat back down on the couch, her body strung tight. "I'm just feeling off. Give me a few minutes."

"Are you sur—"

"Julie, stop. I appreciate it. But I need to f-focus on something other than myself right now."

Julie bit her lip before nodding. "You need to eat something. Here." She handed Meg her plate. "Do you want anything to drink?"

"Water, thanks."

Julie got Meg her water and sat beside her on the couch. Meg stared at the glass as though she'd never seen water before. Her breathing grew shallow again before she put the glass on the side table closest to her. Julie wanted to press her, but decided to respect Meg's wishes. She'd give her a few minutes longer to work through her panic attack, and if she couldn't pull herself out of it, Julie would take her to the doctor whether she liked it or not.

Grabbing the remote from where Meg had placed it on the couch, she turned the volume down slightly. She found the murder mystery she'd mentioned and hit Play. As the program began, Julie took a bite of her food, but as the actors on screen reenacted a grisly murder, she found her mind wandering.

"What is it?" Meg asked after a while, her voice stronger than it had been a short time ago.

"Hmm?"

"You've been sitting there for ten minutes, twirling the same lo mein noodles on your fork."

Julie glanced down at the mangled noodles and put the plate on her side table with a sigh.

"It's nothing. Just me being me." She reached over and patted Meg on the arm. "Today's about cheering *you* up."

Meg put her untouched plate on the table beside her. "I told you I need a distraction. What's going on?"

"Are you sure? I don't want to bring up any sensitive subjects." Meg waved for her to continue, and Julie said, "Well… Jake kissed me."

Meg sat up straight. "What! When?"

"A couple of nights ago."

"Why didn't you tell me when I came into the shop yesterday?"

"I was going to tell you, I swear, but you had to get to—"

"Lucas, right." Meg's face became unnaturally bitter before turning downcast. "I still wish you would have told me. You seem to be keeping so much from me lately."

"I'm sorry," Julie said. "I don't mean to make you feel that way. You've just had so much going on—"

"Yeah, well. I've got plenty of time now." Meg slouched down on the couch. "So what does this mean? The kiss, that is."

"Absolutely nothing." Julie stood up and grabbed her plate, taking it into the kitchen and putting it in the sink with a shaky hand.

"Okay, but you don't go around kissing guys," Meg called out from the other room. "This is a big deal."

"No, it really isn't." Julie walked back into the living room and plopped back down on the couch. "And I kissed several guys in college, thank you."

"A few strangers at the occasional party who you had no emotional connection with."

Julie shook her head. "It doesn't matter. Nothing is going to happen between Jake and me."

"But—"

"I told him I'm ace."

Meg's eyes widened. "What'd he say?"

"He didn't say anything. He literally stood there looking like he'd just been petrified by Medusa. So, I left. I haven't seen or spoken to him since."

Meg scanned Julie's face before handing her the box of tissues.

Julie laughed despite her misery. "Thanks. It's nothing to get upset about. It's not like we were really a thing."

Meg's expression was sad. "Does it help? Telling yourself that?"

Julie stared blankly in front of her. "No."

"Yeah." Meg grabbed another tissue and blew her nose.

Around dinnertime, Meg decided it was time to head home.

As Julie parked outside of Meg's apartment, she looked worriedly at her friend. "Are you sure you don't want to stay at my house tonight? The guest room is always available. I know it's the size of a closet, but you're welcome to it as long as you want."

Meg stared somberly out the window toward her building. "Thanks, but I need to get up early and start canceling everything for the wedding."

"I hate leaving you like this."

"I'll be okay." Meg gave a pained smile. "I'm sorry I freaked out earlier."

"You don't have anything to apologize for."

Meg nodded absently. She let out a deep sigh as she looked at the apartment again. "He never wanted to move in here. I told him so many times that we could find a different place, somewhere that we could live together. He always said no... that he had to set an example as the mayor's son."

Julie grabbed Meg's hand and squeezed it. "Meg, I'm so sorry you're going through this."

"I wonder if he ever planned on marrying me," Meg said listlessly. "Things have felt off between us for a while. He's been growing more and more distant ever since we agreed on a wedding date. Did he ever love me?"

"He wouldn't have asked you to marry him if he hadn't."

"We've been together for sixteen years—almost half my life—and he *just* proposed." Meg let out a laugh that turned into a hiccupping sob. "God, he was such a huge part of my life...in every plan I made for myself. What am I going to do now?"

"You're going to find your way." Julie leaned over and hugged Meg. "You'll get through this. I know you will."

Meg pulled away, looking depressed. "I should go in. Thanks for everything today."

"You bet," Julie said. "Call me tomorrow if you need anything or you want to talk."

Meg nodded and got out of the car. Julie waited until her friend was safely inside before she put the gearshift into Drive. Her heart hurt so much for Meg, and there was a part of her that was feeling pretty sorry for herself as well. The idea of going back to her quiet, empty house made her feel lonelier than ever. Needing something to preoccupy her mind, she drove to the store to finish her inventory.

As she turned into the parking space in front of Baxter's, her car lights lit on a lone figure sitting on the bench outside the shop. Her mouth dropped open and she could only stare at the familiar face in disbelief. She put the car in Park, got out, and slammed the door.

She stomped over to the man hunched on the bench. "What are you doing here?"

"I guess you've spoken with Meg," Lucas said listlessly, not making eye contact with her.

Julie wanted to scream at him, make him hurt as bad as he had hurt Meg. Instead, she said, "I have nothing to say to you."

"I just wanted to make sure she was okay," Lucas muttered.

Julie and Lucas had never been close, but they'd hung out multiple times over the years. She never took him for being foolish. Pretentious, oblivious, yes, but never foolish.

"How the hell do you think she's doing? You strung her along for years, and now you're going to sit here as calm as can be and spew all that garbage?"

Lucas looked up at her then and Julie gasped. For as long as she'd known Lucas, he'd always put too much stock in his appearance. Hair styled to perfection, clean-shaven, looking every bit like the politician's son.

As he sat in front of her, she hardly recognized him. His eyes were red-rimmed as though he hadn't slept an hour since he broke Meg's heart. There was a day's worth of scruff on his face, and he looked deathly pale under the streetlight.

"It was for the best," Lucas said, his voice barely a whisper. "I couldn't put her through it anymore. She deserves better."

"I don't understand," Julie said. "You let your mom treat Meg like trash for years. You broke it off with Meg, destroying her. And yet you have the audacity to sit here, looking like you actually give a damn."

"Of course I give a damn," Lucas snapped. "She's my best friend. But she deserves better."

"You keep saying that," Julie said. "All she wanted was you."

Lucas laughed then, but there was no humor to it. In fact, he sounded completely devastated. He stood up but wavered on his feet. Julie wondered if he might be drunk.

"I'm sorry I bothered you," he said. "I just wanted to make sure she was okay. I couldn't get a hold of her by phone and she wasn't at her place when I went there earlier. I figured she was with you."

Julie's eyes narrowed. It wasn't exactly a warm evening. "How long have you been sitting out here?"

Lucas lifted a shoulder. "Don't know. A few hours, I guess? I'll leave you alone now." He started to walk away but paused. Without looking at her, he said, "Don't tell Meg I was here."

"Did you ever love her?" Julie murmured to his retreating back. She didn't think she had said it loud enough for him to hear, but he stopped nonetheless.

Lucas tilted his head up and stared at the overcast night sky. "I wouldn't have broken up with her if I didn't love her."

"That doesn't make sense."

"It doesn't have to. Not to you."

He left before she could say anything else. As she watched him go, she heard a car pull into one of the other empty spots. Turning to see who it was, she felt her second shock of the night as Jake stepped out of a black Camaro.

"Hey," he said, looking achingly handsome in dark jeans and his long-sleeved Henley.

"Hi," she whispered back.

He glanced toward Lucas in the distance. "Is this a bad time?"

"I...no, it's okay." Julie would think about her weird conversation with Lucas another time. She had to gear herself up for whatever Jake came here to say.

He pointed to the closed sign on her door. "I stopped by earlier. I thought I might have missed you."

"Meg and Lucas broke off their engagement last night. I decided to close the shop today so she and I could spend the day together."

"I'm sorry," Jake replied.

Julie glanced in the direction Lucas had gone. "I'm only

here now because I wanted to do some inventory." She paused. "How'd you know I'd be here?"

Jake shoved his hands in his jeans pockets. "I drive around a lot when I have things on my mind." His lips twisted upward. "I've been driving all day. It was a coincidence that I saw you. I was actually on my way home."

"Oh." Julie pressed her lips together before asking, "Do you want to come in?"

"Yeah, thanks."

Julie unlocked the shop door and went inside, Jake following her. His eyes skimmed the shop, landing on his poster. She was more tempted than ever to tear it down.

He finally looked back at her. Uncomfortable silence descended between them.

"What are you doing here?" Julie asked.

"I… I didn't like how we left things yesterday."

"I don't know what else there is to say," Julie replied. She took off her spring jacket and purse and laid them on the counter. Leaning over the gray laminate, she grabbed her iPad and booted it up.

"I wanted to talk about what you told me."

She continued to focus on the tablet, opening the CRM— customer relationship management—app that she needed as she waited for him to continue.

"I'm trying to understand," Jake said. "I've never met someone who's—"

"Asexual?" Julie swung around to face him, clutching the iPad to her chest.

"Yeah. I mean, who doesn't like sex?" Jake winced as soon as he said it, but the fire that had been burning inside Julie since their last meeting erupted.

"I know. I'm a regular freak, aren't I? That's what my college professor called asexuals. He was talking about society norms and he told the class, 'There's nothing wrong with being gay. If you want to look at freaks, look at the asexuals.' Everyone in class laughed. Everyone but me. I didn't even understand I was asexual at the time. I just knew I didn't find it funny." She walked over to one of the shelves and picked up a wood acorn. "I mean, I've always known something was different about me. When I was a teen, my friend had a slumber party and the topic turned to masturbation. When the girls found out I didn't touch myself, they taunted me. It was horrifying and humiliating." Julie put the acorn back and turned toward Jake, lifting her chin. "So to answer your question about who doesn't like sex...me, I don't."

"I'm sorry, I'm not trying to make this worse. I..." Jake ran his hand through his hair. "Did something hap—"

"Happen to me?" She didn't need him to finish that sentence to know where his mind had already headed. Usually, when she told people about her sexual orientation, either they assumed she was on a medication that killed her sex drive or she'd survived some horrific trauma. "No, I'm fortunate enough to say that nothing like what you're thinking ever happened to me. You don't become asexual because of some outside influence. You're born asexual. Like people are born gay, straight, bi..."

Jake nodded in understanding, but she wondered how much he actually comprehended. As she'd told him yesterday, he came from an environment where the mantra was *sex sells*. It was in everything he touched, from his lyrics to his image to his groupies.

Silence once again fell between them.

Jake shifted on his feet. "Where does that leave us? Because I think there might be something between us. I'm not ready to let us go yet. Unless you don't want this."

Julie's eyebrows shot up. She knew he wasn't getting it— what a relationship with her meant. She grabbed his arm and dragged him to the storage room at the back of the store, out of sight from people who might be passing by the large shop windows. She let go of him once they were inside the small space so she could clasp her hands together, twisting them as she tried to think of how to get her point across.

"I consider myself graysexual," she told him. "For the most part, I don't experience sexual attraction. Romantic attraction, definitely, but what I want in a relationship is going to be a lot different from what you want. What I find sexy are big romantic gestures and the little things like holding my hand." She picked up his hand and brought it to her neck. "Kissing me here? I find that very sexy. It makes me shiver all over when a guy kisses my neck. It's a huge turn-on for me. And when you touch me here…" She moved his hand to her wrist and manually moved his thumb back and forth across the pulse point. "You can feel how you affect me—feel my heart racing. But this…" She placed his hand over her breast, pressing it so that his fingers cupped her. "This does nothing for me."

He stared at where his palm touched her before jerking his hand away. "Why are you letting me touch you then?"

"Because it doesn't mean to me what it does to you." She took a step back from him. "Do you understand? I really enjoyed your kiss, and there are things we can do together if you truly want a relationship with me. I'd even be willing to have sex with you on occasion if that's something you wanted to discuss. I mean, I can have sex—"

"Can?" His face darkened. "Like you *can* do the dishes or laundry or some other chore."

She smiled sadly at him then, because he finally understood. He was starting to get what a relationship with her would be like.

He seemed to realize it too as he slowly nodded. "Okay."

"I…" Julie had to swallow over the painful lump that had formed in her throat before she could continue. "I'll send you the names of the people I think might be a good fit to help you with the concert."

"Hold up. Just…give me a second here, okay?" Jake started to pace in front of her. "You dropped a bit of a bombshell in my lap."

"But it's really not."

"Are you serious?" He stopped pacing so he could stand right in front of her. "You're acting like I should shove these feelings I have for you to the side—" Julie's heart leaped at his admission that he felt something toward her "—without giving me any time to process everything."

"Jake, I know how this ends. I told you, I've been through this before."

"Well, you haven't been through it with me!" he snapped before moving again. He came to an abrupt halt in front of one of the shelves that lined a wall in the room. Various seasonal items were stored there, waiting for the right time of the year. He picked up a stained glass heart-shaped frame meant for Valentine's Day. He turned it from one angle to another, the ruby-colored glass catching the overhead lights in the room.

"Do you have feelings for me?" he asked, his voice determined.

"I don't see why that—"

Jake put the frame back and swung around to face her. "Just answer the question. Do you have feelings for me? Me, not Jake Reynolds, the guy on your poster."

"I…yes," Julie whispered.

"Okay. Then give me some time to process what you told me. Can you do that?"

Julie nodded. Jake looked like he wanted to kiss her. She really wished he would, but he turned on his foot and left the store without another word.

Chapter Eleven

Jake sat at the piano of the recording studio, absently playing the keys. It had been a week since he last saw Julie, even longer since he'd spoken with Dylan, and he didn't know how to fix either situation.

"Hey, man," Tyler said as he entered the live room, James following closely behind. "You're early."

Jake shrugged. "Couldn't sleep."

"New song?" James asked.

Jake glanced down and realized he was still playing the piano. The tune was melancholy, which fit his mood perfectly. He pulled his hands away and placed them in his lap.

"No, just messing around."

Tyler leaned against the piano. "What's with you lately?"

Jake stared at his friend blankly. "What do you mean?"

"Well for one thing, you've been the first one here all week and you're always notoriously late."

"Maybe I didn't want to waste everyone's time," Jake muttered. "You guys are doing me a favor recording here."

The teasing expression that had been on Tyler's face faded and he turned serious. "And you've been quiet this week. I mean, it's always hard to get a word out when Paul's around, but you've been unnaturally silent."

"I have a lot on my mind."

James sat on the room's couch. "You want to tell us about it? You know you can trust us."

"I know that," Jake said. Tyler and James weren't just his best friend and cousin. They were like brothers to him. They'd been close since they were kids. Hell, he'd spent more time in their homes growing up than he had his own. Jake glanced around, making sure they were alone. "What do you think of asexuality?"

"What about it?" James asked.

"Do you know anyone who's asexual?"

"I live in California." Tyler lifted his shoulders. "You meet people from every spectrum of life there."

"There's usually a group of aces who march in the pride parade," James said. "We're all part of the LGBTQIA community. Why?"

Jake touched his fingertips along the cool keys of the piano, not putting any pressure down so they remained silent. "If, hypothetically speaking, you were interested in someone and they told you they were asexual, what would you do?"

"I guess it would depend on how deeply I felt for the person," Tyler said. "But to be honest, I don't know if I could live the celibate life."

Jake ran a hand over his face, his fingers brushing against the few days' old beard that had grown because he'd been too preoccupied to bother shaving.

Tyler sat down on the piano bench next to him. "Does this have to do with Julie?"

Jake didn't say anything. He trusted Tyler and James with his life, but was Julie even out? He couldn't remember if she mentioned that or not.

James walked over to them and leaned against the piano. "Let's say we're talking in hypotheticals. So, hypothetically, let's say Julie told you she was ace. How did you react?"

"Hypothetically speaking..." Jake sighed. "I stood there like a damned statue, and then when I went to see her again, I didn't react any better." He remembered the soft curve of her breast in his hand; the complete blankness on her face as she pressed his palm intimately against her body.

"That's rough," Tyler said. "What are you going to do?"

"I don't know," Jake admitted. "I asked for time to think things over."

"When was the last time you talked to her?" James asked.

Jake winced. "Last week." Tyler gave him a disgusted shake of his head and James looked like he wanted to smack him. He added weakly, "I sent her a text."

Julie's only response was a list of people in town who could help him with the event.

"Damn, man," Tyler said. "And I thought I was bad at communication."

Jake stared up at the ceiling, trying to gather his thoughts. "The fact is, I like sex. It's not even so much about the act itself, but more about the emotional connection you get with someone, you know?"

"For you, maybe," Tyler said. "Personally, I love sex. I love finding pleasure when and where I can. It's a fun way to blow off steam. But you're a one-and-done kind of guy. You've always been like that, wanting to be in a relationship versus having meaningless sex. Even if that relationship is a train wreck, like what you had with Angelika."

"Angelika and I weren't so bad together."

"She accused you of cheating on her all the time," Tyler reminded him.

"You know what her childhood was like. Her dad was straight-up garbage. He didn't exactly instill trust in men with her."

"So was your dad," Tyler argued. "You didn't go around accusing her of cheating."

Jake stared at his friends miserably. "I wasn't around long enough to accuse her of anything."

Even though Jake wouldn't admit it at the time, Angelika

asking for a divorce had been the right call for both of them. Despite what he told the guys, he and Angelika had never been right for each other, and she'd been brave enough to accept it before he had. Hell, they probably wouldn't have even gotten married if Angelika hadn't gotten pregnant.

He pushed that thought away as he focused on what else Tyler had said. "You think if I got in a relationship with Julie, it'd be a train wreck?"

"I didn't say that." Tyler gave him a squeeze on the shoulder. "I've always thought deep down you've been trying to prove to everyone—even to yourself—that you aren't like your dad. That's why you stayed faithful to Angelika, no matter how bad things got, and I figure that's why you stayed married to her no matter how miserable you made each other." Jake didn't say anything to that, so Tyler continued. "You've been looking for someone you can have a real connection with for as long as I've known you. To be with someone who sees you for *you* and not for who you've become. You didn't find that connection with Angelika, but you can't tell me that's not what you want."

Jake pressed one finger down on a piano key and it hummed loudly in the silence. As the sound faded away and his friends didn't say anything else, he looked at them angrily. "What do you want me to say? That I want a relationship like what both your parents had? That I want to find a true partner, one who doesn't care that the person behind the fame is messed up?"

"You're not a mess," Tyler said.

"Angelika and Dylan would disagree with that."

"Dylan loves you," James said. "You two just need to work on your communication. And there's nothing wrong with wanting to be in a healthy, committed relationship."

"But to never have sex again..."

"Did you not listen to what Tyler said?" James asked. "Having an emotional connection to someone is more important to you than having a physical one. Since you've reconnected with Julie, you've been happier than I've ever seen you. Why are you fighting this?"

Jake let out a frustrated breath. "You guys are acting like I'm about to propose or something. Julie and I haven't even gone on an official date yet. She basically told me to find someone else who could meet my physical needs as well as that ridiculous emotional connection you guys keep mentioning. She wouldn't suggest that if either of us had deep feelings for one another."

"That's bull," James said. "You've liked her for years. We were there when you came up with the idea for 'Enchanted.' We know who that song is about."

"That doesn't mean anything," Jake said, trying to reason.

"You remember what I said about being in too deep?" Tyler clasped Jake on the shoulder. "You, my friend, are in too deep."

"That's not true."

James snorted. "Oh really? So you didn't post a picture of yourself with her online, despite how much you value your privacy. And you haven't bent over backward to get this concert organized in an absurd amount of time for her."

"That was to help Holiday Bay."

"Keep telling yourself that," James said, "when we all know that if it wasn't for Dylan, you wouldn't be in Michigan, let alone living back in the Bay."

The door from the control room opened and Lori walked through, a satisfied air to her that had Jake narrowing his eyes.

"What are you doing here?" he asked. "I thought you were working on the concert from California."

"Good to see you too, Jake," she said with exaggerated pleasantness. "I wanted to tell you in person I got the permits for that hellhole you picked out. I also wanted to tell you that

I've booked all of you for *America, Good Morning.* You're announcing your reunion as well as the concert."

"You could have told us all this from California," he said.

Lori's eyes narrowed. "Do you know how much work needs to be done here to make this concert a success? I need to talk to the different shops who will be involved, make sure ticket sales are running smoothly—"

"Fine," Jake muttered just as Zan and Paul walked in.

"Excellent," Lori said. "You won't even know I'm here."

He didn't like the way Lori looked, like she had just won the lotto on Christmas Day. As she walked back inside the control booth to speak to Trevor, who'd just arrived, Jake turned back to Tyler and James. James had pulled his phone out and was texting something, his forehead scrunched into lines.

"By the way," Jake said to Tyler, changing the subject now that he knew Lori was around, "I forgot to tell you I ran into Meg Archer."

"Yeah?" Tyler's face lit into a smile. "How's she doing?"

"Honestly, I don't think too good. She and her fiancé just broke up."

Tyler's eyes snapped to his. He had a weird expression on his face that Jake couldn't label if he tried.

"My mom mentioned she'd gotten engaged," Tyler said slowly before his features shifted to something almost like fondness. "It's crazy. It's hard to think of Meg ever getting married. Whenever I picture her, she's still that bratty kid next door who let the air out of my brand-new bike tires all because I set her Barbie's hair on fire."

"Why would you do that?" James asked.

Tyler squinted. "I think I was playing G.I. Joe at the time. He was rescuing Barbie from a mission. It didn't go well."

Jake rolled his eyes. "'Cause clearly Meg was the one who had issues in your weird relationship."

Tyler snorted before asking, "Who was the guy she got engaged to again?"

"You remember the mayor's son, Lucas Beaumont?"

A loud clattering crash resounded through the quiet room, causing Jake and Tyler to look over with a start.

"Damn," James said. He bent down to pick up his phone where he'd dropped it on the floor.

"You okay over there?" Paul asked from across the room.

"Just lost my grip," he replied.

Tyler shook his head as he continued his conversation with Jake. "I can't believe she got engaged to Lucas. My mom told me they were dating years ago, but I had no idea they were still together." His expression turned reflective "The Beaumonts were such pretentious jerks."

"Lucas wasn't bad," James said, looking up briefly from his phone.

"Did you know him in high school?" Jake asked. He thought he knew all of James's friends in school because they were also Jake's friends.

His cousin shrugged. "We were on the track team together."

"All right, guys," Trevor said over the speakers. "Let's get to work."

After Jake finished laying down the vocals for the song they'd worked on, he headed home. He thought about what Tyler and James had said.

They were right. They usually were, though Jake would never let them know that.

Jake was in too deep already with Julie.

The fact that their brief kiss on the beach meant more to him than sleeping with countless women should have been enough of a warning sign. The first time he recognized her in that video, he should have known it was too late.

Of course, he'd blown it to hell and back with her, and there was still so much he was unsure about. But the one thing he did know was that he wanted to be with her.

He just needed to convince her of that.

Glancing at his watch, he saw that it was 3:00 p.m. Julie would be at work until six, so he'd wait until then to go to the store.

After parking outside of his house, Jake headed to his study. The room's decor hadn't changed much since the home was built. Mahogany-wood walls lined two parts of the room. The wall to the left of the entrance contained floor-to-ceiling bookcases, filled with books that Jake had collected and read on his different tours over the years. The remaining wall featured large windows that let in natural light, bathing the room in the afternoon sun. Plush green carpet and dark leather furniture filled the rest of the space.

Jake pulled his cell phone out from his pocket and checked to see if Dylan had sent him a message. Still radio silence from his son. He typed a short message asking if they could talk. When there was no response after several minutes, Jake let out a weary sigh and threw his phone onto a nearby chair.

Sitting down in the luxury executive chair behind his desk, Jake hit the power on his laptop and waited for it to boot up. He stared at the screen, trying to figure out what he was seeking.

He slowly began to type *How to date an asexual*.

Multiple website links popped up and he clicked on the first one. It gave a breakdown of asexuality, listing the different spectrums that asexuals fell under. Biromantic, aromantic, heteroromantic, homoromantic...

When he saw the term *graysexual*, he opened up the page, remembering that Julie had called herself that. The article said that people who were gray rarely experienced sexual attraction.

What did *rarely* mean?

Jake sat back in his chair as he thought about it. Julie said she could have sex with him, but she made it sound as pleasant as having a root canal. He wouldn't put pressure on her to have sex, and he certainly didn't want her to feel like she had to. But were there things she was open to?

Resting his hands against the keyboard once more, he typed *How to be in a relationship with an asexual*. Several websites popped up and he clicked on one at random. This site gave suggestions on how to create intimacy without sex.

Remember that asexuals are human. Some crave human contact as long as it's consensual. Exchange an intimate moment by kissing in the rain, going for walks on the beach, snuggling on the couch under a warm blanket on a cool fall day. Buy something for your ace partner that'll warm their hearts.

Jake glanced around the room, thinking of presents he could give Julie. He certainly had the means to buy her anything she wanted. A trip to Paris? No problem. A new Porsche? Just tell him the color. But he didn't think Julie would be into any of that.

He thought of her store. He could always pay off any debt she might have...but he could just imagine her reaction to that. She'd fought for everything she had. She would probably punch him in the face if he offered any handouts.

Jake pushed his chair back from the desk and walked over to his book collection. He ran his fingers across the different bindings. An image of Julie filtered through his mind. He remembered her as a little girl, sitting on Tyler's porch, her bright red hair in pigtails and her nose in a book.

A smile lit his face. He grabbed his phone from the chair and began to type a short message to someone he knew in California. After he was through, he went into the kitchen and made himself a sandwich. Looking at the clock on his microwave, he saw that he still had a little over an hour before Pieces of Home closed for the day.

Needing to burn some energy but not in the mood to work out, he headed into his workshop. He hadn't been inside it since his argument with Dylan.

Jake scraped his hand against the bristles on his chin.

He still didn't know what he was going to do about Dylan.

He moved to Michigan so they could bond, but Jake felt more distant from him than when he'd been in California. Dylan must have stopped by at some point in the past week. The Craftsman nightstand he'd been working on was gone. It hurt that he came by at a time when he knew Jake would be at the studio.

Jake got some cherrywood from his storage area, piled everything on top of his worktable, and tried to envision what he would make. When he was younger, he could take a piece of wood and turn it into any project that popped in his brain. It never came out quite like how he pictured—a talent his son possessed that he lacked—but Jake needed something distracting to do until he could go see Julie.

He grabbed his tape measure and began marking the wood for where he wanted to cut. He remembered a lesson his grandfather taught him years ago. If he couldn't think of something to make, build a box. It was quick, simple, and something people could always use. His heart ached for the older man who'd been gone almost ten years. He'd been good to Jake and his sister, taking them in for a while after Jake's mom had her nervous breakdown.

As Jake began to saw, he heard the workshop door open. Quickly switching off the machine, he turned to see who was there. Dylan stood behind him, staring at the floor.

"Dylan, hey," Jake said.

"Hey."

"I'm glad you came over. I've been trying to get a hold of you. I sent you several texts."

"Yeah, I know."

Jake cocked his head. "How'd you know I'd be home?"

"I called the studio." Dylan walked over to the table where Jake had placed the wood. He picked up a piece, running a hand over the edge. "I ran into Ms. A. earlier this week. She said there was someone buying up all the properties in Holiday Bay, and they were pressuring her to sell her shop, too."

"She told you that, huh?" Jake was a little surprised Julie had been so open with Dylan. He didn't realize they knew each other that well.

"Not in those exact words, but I read between the lines," Dylan said. "It's that Harris Farmington guy, right? I've seen him around town. I thought it was weird. Aren't billionaires like him too busy launching themselves into space to be bothering with towns like Holiday Bay?"

Jake nodded. "You're pretty observant."

Dylan returned the wood to the pile. "Do you really think you can help Ms. A. save her store?"

"I hope so. The guys in the band agreed to do a charity concert in Holiday Bay next month. We're donating all proceeds to small businesses in town, and stores have been invited to host booths where they can sell their stuff. That's all confidential, though. We're going to be doing a formal announcement in the coming week."

Dylan chewed on his inner cheek before saying, "It's really cool that you're willing to help the town. I know how you feel about it."

"It's still my history. It's a part of what made me who I am. Besides, it's important to Julie."

Dylan observed his dad intently. "I see." He shifted from one foot to the other. "I'm sorry for how I acted last time I was here. You were right. It's none of my business if you want to date Ms. A."

Something inside Jake shifted and a bit of his tension bled away at hearing his son's apology. "It's okay."

Dylan's shoulders slumped and his face turned sad. "That day I came over, I got into a fight with Mom about going to college again. All I want to do is focus on wood making, and she doesn't get that. Then when I saw the pictures of you and Ms. A. at the restaurant…" Dylan grimaced. "She's a really good person. She was one of the first people in town to welcome me. Dad, I don't want her to get bitter like Mom is sometimes." Jake winced. "And her store has all this awesome stuff in it, and I just—I didn't think it was a good idea for you to be around her or Pieces of Home. I still don't, to be honest. But I don't want her to lose her store either."

Jake brushed some sawdust off his hands as he walked over to his son. He placed a hand on Dylan's shoulder and gave it a squeeze. "Son, if you really want a career in woodwork, do it."

"Yeah?"

"Of course, but like I told you before, you should at least get a few business classes in."

"But…what about Mom?"

"I'll talk to her. Dylan, this is your life. If you don't want to be a lawyer, that's your call. Just know that I'll support you no matter what you decide."

The tiniest lift of Dylan's mouth appeared on his face before he looked at the saw Jake had abandoned. "What are you working on?"

"Nothing really important." Jake walked back to the machine. "I was going to make a box."

"Stuck, huh?"

Jake laughed for what felt like the first time in ages. "Yeah."

Dylan eyed the wood again. "You could always make something for Ms. A.'s booth. I bet if people knew it was from you, she'd be able to sell it for a huge cost."

"That's not a bad idea," Jake said. If anything, it might get Julie to talk to him. He mentally kicked himself for not reaching out to her earlier. Looking at Dylan, he said, "Do you want to help me? I could use your artistic input."

This time, Dylan didn't try to dampen his smile as he said, "Yeah, that'd be cool."

As he and his son discussed ideas for what they could make, Jake watched the excitement on his son's face.

He knew Angelika would be furious with him for not pushing Dylan to attend law school, but he didn't care. This was Dylan's passion. He could make a living from it if that's what he wanted.

He didn't regret telling his son to follow his heart. And as they worked on their project together, Jake realized something.

He needed to follow his own advice.

He needed to follow his heart.

And his heart was leading him right to Julie.

Chapter Twelve

When Meg's mom, Greta, walked into Pieces of Home that morning, both Meg and Julie were in midst of a full-blown mope session. Julie stood behind her counter, listlessly going through online orders. Meg sat on the stool next to her, chin in hand, eating her way through a bag of Swedish Fish.

"All right, enough," Greta said. "You two have been miserable this entire week."

"Pretty sure I'm allowed to be miserable," Meg grumbled just as Julie said, "No, we haven't."

"Meg, shouldn't you be at work?" her mom asked.

"I'm using the time I saved up for my honeymoon to have a little me time," Meg replied, her tone defensive.

"In that case..." Greta walked over to the counter and slapped two gift certificates down on the counter. "I've booked you both an appointment at that spa in Traverse City. Facial, manicure, and back massage. You better get going too because—" she pulled out her phone and tapped something "—the facials are scheduled to start in forty-five minutes."

"Greta, thank you," Julie said. "But I can't close the store."

Greta walked behind the counter and eyed the iPad next to Julie's hand. She touched the screen and looked at the store's point-of-sale program. "It looks like the same POS we use at the campground. I've got this. You girls get going."

"I can't ask you to stay at the store all day," Julie protested.

"You didn't ask. I volunteered." Greta stepped closer to Julie so Meg wouldn't hear. "Meg needs this. So do you. I hate seeing you both so miserable. Do it for her if not for yourself. Spending the day with her best friend will do her wonders."

Julie's eyes narrowed. "Now I see where Meg gets her ability in emotionally blackmailing someone."

"It's a talent, I know." Greta reached up and patted her cheek.

"What are you two whispering about?" Meg asked.

A reluctant smile popped on Julie's face as she picked up one of the certificates. "We were just discussing who should drive. Me or you?"

"I'm glad we did this," Meg said five hours later. "We need to treat ourselves to a spa day more often."

"Agreed," Julie replied. She took a deep breath in, enjoying the scent of lavender on her skin.

Pulling up outside Meg's apartment building, Julie noticed her friend scanning the area. "I don't think Lucas is going to randomly show up again."

Julie hadn't wanted to lie to Meg, so she'd given her a brief overview of her encounter with Lucas. Ever since, Meg kept looking for her ex whenever she went out in public these days, which was rare.

Meg blushed. "I just think it's weird that he would show up at your store all concerned, but he hasn't had the balls to follow up with me directly."

"Maybe Clarice locked him in his room or something. He was acting off."

"I wouldn't put it past her," Meg muttered before she sighed. "I just hope he's okay."

Julie leaned across the console and gave her friend a hug. "You're a good person. Much better than he ever deserved."

"You deserve better, too," Meg replied.

Pulling back, Julie decided not to say anything about that. "You need anything, you call me. No matter what time it is."

"I will."

As Julie drove to the store, her mind went to Jake. She hadn't heard from him for the past week, other than a single text letting her know he was in the recording studio. No calls or other contact, which spoke volumes as to what his stance was regarding a relationship with her.

Her asexuality was clearly a deal-breaker. She didn't blame him, even though her heart ached at the loss of what could have been. Jake was everything she wanted in a romantic partner: kind, considerate, funny. But she obviously wasn't what he wanted in return.

When she walked into the store, Greta was behind the counter, looking at something on the store's laptop.

"Hi," Greta greeted. "Where's Meg?"

"I dropped her off at her apartment," Julie explained. "Everything go okay?"

"Everything is fine. I enjoyed myself. In fact, I sold that antique table set you had in the back."

"That's great!" Julie said as she removed her jacket. "Thank you!"

Greta closed down the computer. Walking around the counter, she asked, "What about you two? Did you both have a relaxing time?"

"It was wonderful. Meg really needed it."

Greta hugged Julie. "So did you. You've been unhappy."

"I just have a lot going on."

Greta looked at her. "You know I'm here to talk if you need me."

"I know."

Greta looked around the store. "You know, if you ever decide to hire some extra help, let me know. I'd be interested."

Julie laughed before she took in the seriousness on Greta's face. "Oh… I'd love to hire some extra help, but unfortunately, it's not in the budget right now." She nudged Greta with her elbow. "Besides, wouldn't Harry miss your help at the campground?"

A flutter of emotion crossed Greta's face at the sound of her husband's name, an expression that made Julie pause, and then it was gone as though it had never been there.

Before Julie could ask if there was anything wrong, Greta said, "I suppose he would. But if you do need a break again, let me know."

"I will."

After Greta left, Julie opened her laptop and answered some inquiries she'd received from online customers. She'd just finished answering one when the bell above her shop door rang. As she looked up, the relaxation she'd been feeling since her spa appointment disappeared instantly.

"Back again, Mr. Farmington?"

"I wanted to check if you've reconsidered our deal."

"We have no deal," Julie countered. "I'm not selling my store to you."

"Do you really think this concert is going to change anything?"

"How do you—"

"I make it my business to know everything that goes on in a potential business transaction."

Julie lifted her chin. "Then you should know that you're wasting your time here."

Farmington smiled cruelly. "What do you think this concert will accomplish? All you're doing is wasting energy and buying yourself a few months' time, if that. Take the deal I've offered you. My next one won't be as generous."

"Goodbye, Mr. Farmington," Julie said firmly.

The cold derision on his face sent shivers down her spine, but he thankfully stepped outside and slid into the back seat of a waiting Mercedes-Benz. The car left without a noise, which was more chilling than if it had roared away.

Julie thumped down on the stool behind her counter and checked her store's website for any transactions. It looked like the person who'd sent her an inquiry earlier decided to buy the jelly cupboard she'd listed. Forcing herself to focus on the job, she grabbed her dolly and moved the item to her storage room so she could get it ready for shipping later.

After returning to the front, she finished checking her email. There was one with the subject line "Join Us for a Charity Concert." Julie clicked open the email and realized it was the official invite to have a booth at the event. It didn't mention the Holiday Boys' name and Julie wondered if Jake had changed his mind after all.

But it *did* say that there would be a concert and it was expected to draw a huge crowd. Maybe they found another big name to do it, and Jake was probably already back in California, having sex with some young woman who'd only be too happy to do anything and *everything* he liked in the bedroom.

Don't go there.

Julie filled out the reply for the concert to reserve her booth and then called a potential vendor who'd been waiting to have a space in her store. One of her current clients needed to end his contract because he'd gotten a job promotion across the state. While she was happy to get new clients, as it helped keep the store looking fresh, it did hurt that her longtime client was moving away from Holiday Bay.

At the end of the business day, Julie closed the store and had started heading toward her car when she heard someone call her name. Glancing over at the bench in front of Baxter's, she saw Jake sitting there. He was still in town. Relief washed over her, though she kept her face impassive.

Today, he wore a thin beige corduroy jacket and his aviator glasses. He'd grown a short beard since she saw him last. It looked good on him. *Really good.* Jake stood up and walked over to her, removing the glasses and tucking them into his coat.

"Hey," he said.

Julie's stomach knotted with nerves. "Hi."

He looked even more handsome than he normally did, despite the air of exhaustion to him.

"How'd it go at the studio?" she asked.

"Good, just time-consuming." Jake shoved his hands in his pants pockets. "Listen, I—"

"Did you get—" she started to say at the same time. They paused and Julie wanted to cry at how awkward everything felt between them.

"Go ahead," he said.

"Did you get the list I sent you regarding people who could help you with the concert? Is that why you're here?"

"Partly." Jake shifted on the back of his heels before straightening. "Are you hungry?"

"A little."

"I've been craving Franki's pasties all week. Do you want to get one?"

She stared at him in misery. Why did he have to draw this out? He had a list of people he could call for help with the concert. He could disappear from her life again, and she could go back to admiring the celebrity, while wishing she could forget how wonderful the man was.

"Please," he said softly when she didn't say anything.

"Okay," she said.

His shoulders relaxed. "Do you mind if we walk? After being in the studio all week, I could use the fresh air."

"That's fine," she said. "How's the album going?"

"Good." They made their way toward the restaurant several blocks away. "I think we're making good progress. In fact, I'm pretty sure we'll be able to do one of the new songs at the concert."

Julie nodded, but didn't say anything else as Franki's came into view.

As they walked toward the entrance, a husband and wife walked out. Julie recognized them as Sam and Melanie Drake. They were both ten years younger than Julie so she didn't know them well, though Sam's family had owned an orchard down the road for generations. They took one look at Jake and promptly freaked out. Melanie actually shrieked.

"I've been a huge fan of yours for years," she said, patting his arm like she had the right to.

"She made us dance to 'Come Back to You' at our wedding," Sam said, wrapping his arm around his wife, trying to keep a cool facade when Julie could tell by the way he rocked on his feet that he wanted to freak out, too.

"Technically, my cousin, James, wrote that one."

He was unfailingly polite as he interacted with the pair, every bit the charismatic celebrity that he was. Julie felt awkward standing there. What the hell was she doing, agreeing to have dinner with him? They hadn't encountered too many fans since his publicist put out a false story regarding his whereabouts. But standing there, watching Jake with his fans, reminded her all over again how different their worlds were.

"Will you excuse us?" Jake finally said after a few minutes.

The couple looked at Julie, noticing her for the first time since they ran into each other. The pair thanked Jake for his time and left. Jake held the restaurant door open for Julie and they walked in.

After ordering their food, they sat at one of the tables.

"Sorry about outside," Jake said.

"It's fine," Julie assured him. It was fine, too. It was a good, healthy dose of reality she needed. Franki delivered their food and Julie took a couple of bites of her pasty. She finally said,

"Thank you for not canceling the show. Even if… I really appreciate that you're still willing to help."

"Julie, I…" Jake frowned as he stared down at his half-eaten meal. "I wouldn't do that. I told you we'd do the concert. I always keep my word."

He looked at her more intently than she thought the conversation warranted. She gave him a small smile and took another bite of her food.

Jake let out a quiet breath. "Look, I know I should have acted better when you told me about being asexual."

Julie kept her eyes on her plate. "It's not like a lot of people identify as asexual. Some statistics say only one percent of the world's population identifies as ace. There's not a ton of us out there, so your reaction wasn't unusual."

"You still told me something very personal and I should have handled it better. It shouldn't be considered 'unusual' to be asexual. You didn't deserve the reaction I gave you." Jake pushed the remainder of his pasty aside and put his forearms on the table in front of him. "I asked for time to think about us and you gave it to me."

Julie held her breath. This was it. Jake was going to wish her the best and send her on her way. He was going to tell her that he accepted her for who she was, but being with an ace wasn't for him. She was so convinced of it that she could only stare at him when he said, "Would you like to go on a date with me?"

Her jaw dropped. "I… I'm sorry?"

"Would you like to go on a date with me?" he repeated, his voice sincere.

"But why?" Julie started to fiddle with her fork. "I told you how it is with me."

"I know." Jake reached across the table and covered her hand with his. "Julie, the thing is, I like you. I really want to see where this goes between us."

"I told you where this goes. It means—"

"I know what you mean," he interrupted. He let go of her hand and folded his fingers together in front of him. His eyebrows pulled together as he gathered his thoughts. "The fact is, I haven't been able to stop thinking about you this past week. And believe me, I heard what you said. I thought of little since."

"Then why…?"

"Why would I want this?" he asked, and she nodded. "Why *wouldn't* I want this? Julie, you're amazing and brave and beautiful inside and out. I do understand you have fears. I have them, too. People tend to view me as this untouchable being, but the spotlight only shines so bright for so long. Once people get past the awe of dating someone famous, and they have to deal with the real person behind the glitz, they're typically very disappointed."

"Do you think I'm only talking to you because you're famous?" Julie couldn't hide the hurt in her voice. If anything, Jake being famous—and everything that came along with his fame—was her main source of trepidation.

"No, not you," Jake answered. "Maybe other women, but not you." He ran a hand over the beard. "I'm not explaining this well." Looking into her eyes, he said, "I didn't have a very stable homelife growing up. You may have heard the stories around town. My family was a popular topic of ridicule for years. My father was an emotionally manipulative bastard who constantly cheated on my mom. He made our family life a living hell. It was a blessing when he was finally out of our lives. But the gossip was unbearable. It's one of the reasons I left Holiday Bay and didn't come back for so long."

"I'm so sorry," Julie said, her voice thick with emotion. Julie had heard rumors when she was younger about his dad, but the adults in her inner circles always shut up about the topic whenever she and Meg were around as teens.

"It's not something I share." He looked at her intently. "The truth is, my parents' marriage had lasting effects on me. I'm always worried that I'll repeat their pattern of mistakes. I already did once. I neglected Angelika and didn't put our marriage first." He briefly closed his eyes before looking at her again. "What I'm trying to say is I worry that once you really get to know me, you won't like what you see."

Julie fiddled with a napkin Franki had placed on the table. "I guess we both have baggage we're bringing to the table."

Jake smiled grimly at her. "I guess we do."

Julie's eyebrows drew together into a frown. "Why on earth would you want to help Holiday Bay if it has such terrible memories for you?"

His eyes crinkled. "Because of you. This town means a lot to you. I don't want you to lose what you love because of Harris Farmington."

Julie's mouth dropped open. "You're doing this for me? Why?"

"I told you. I like you. I'm really hoping you'll give us a chance."

"Even with sex off the table?" He hesitated for only a second, but it was enough to raise all Julie's red flags. "See. This is a bad idea. You like sex."

Jake let out a sharp, impatient breath. "I do like sex. Very much. I'm not going to deny that. But that's not what I'm looking for in a relationship. I'm tired of having sex just for the sake of it."

"What are you saying?"

"I'm saying I'll take whatever conditions you want to give me. I meant it when I told you I've been distracted all week. I wanted to call you a thousand times, but I didn't think you'd speak to me. I think the guys in the band are ready to kick me out. Paul seriously threatened to lock me in the recording booth this afternoon unless I came and spoke with you." He gave her a determined look. "Julie, I don't know what the future holds. I can't give you any guarantees. I know it won't be easy being with me, but I promise I'll always treat you with the absolute respect you deserve. If you need time to think about it, I'll understand, but I hope you truly consider it—consider us." His lips quirked suddenly. "So, what do you say? Will you accept *my* challenge and go on a date with me?"

Julie smiled briefly at his chosen wording. Her heart shouted for her to say yes. Her brain said to run as far away from this man as she could. He wouldn't be happy in a sexless relationship forever. She knew that logically no matter what he said. It didn't matter if it was five months from now or five years. Eventually, he'd tell her that an emotional connection wasn't enough.

Did she want to risk devastating heartache for a brief moment of happiness?

"I… I need to think about it," she said after a moment of wary silence.

Jake's expression showed his disappointment, but he didn't try to change her mind.

Instead, he said, "Take your time. I'm not going anywhere."

Chapter Thirteen

Jake leaned against a tree in his backyard. He stared at the lapping water of the bay where it touched the rocky shoreline of his property. The air was wet from a heavy fog that had rolled in earlier, dampening his clothes with its mist. The cloudiness still lingered across the water, shrouding the bay from visitors who might want to see its wonder.

Jake ran a hand over his face. He didn't know what to do about Julie.

Now that he knew how much he wanted to be with her, Jake was impatient to see her again. He was excited to start a relationship with her.

The problem was… Julie wasn't ready. Not yet anyway.

So, he was going to play it as cool and bide his time. He would give her space to think about why they would work.

But how much space was too much? For one brief second in their conversation the night before, he thought she would say yes. Instead, she asked for time.

Time for what?

To think about all the A-list celebrities he'd dated in the past five years? To imagine all the opportunities he'd have to supposedly cheat on her? To wonder about his alleged history of being a womanizer?

That's how Angelika used to spend her time when she wanted to "think."

His phone buzzed inside his pants pocket and he grabbed it, welcoming the break from his torturous thoughts.

He saw it was a text message from his lawyer, Marcy. The fire department accepted your anonymous donation to use the diner for a practice burn. When would you like it to happen?

As soon as possible, he typed back. Make sure you send me the date.

He couldn't wait to watch that place burn. He'd just hit Send when his phone rang. Jake's eyebrows shot up when he saw the call was from Dylan.

"Dylan, hi." He couldn't keep the surprise out of his voice. His son rarely called him.

"Hi...um, I was wondering if you were doing anything today?"

"I'm staying at the house, working on a couple of songs for the new album."

"Oh, so you're busy?" Dylan sounded unsure.

"Not too busy, no." Jake's curiosity was piqued as to why Dylan was willingly calling him.

After a pause, Dylan said, "I was thinking about the chest you're going to build for Ms. A.'s booth."

"Yeah?"

"I think you should buy more expensive wood...if you want. Something that'll get a higher price."

Jake turned toward the house and started walking. "What did you have in mind?"

"Rosewood."

Jake smiled, despite the worry he had over Julie. "That'd look really good. It's not the easiest to come by."

"There's a slab of it for sale at a store in Clarington right now. I looked it up on their website. We could go get it, if you want."

Jake's eyebrows shot up at the *we*. "You want to go right now?"

"If you're not too busy."

Jake hated that Dylan even felt he needed to ask that. "I'm on my way."

An hour later, Dylan and Jake pulled into the store's parking lot. Jake took in the large gray barn that someone had converted into a business.

"This is really nice," Jake said. "How'd you hear of this place?"

"We pass it on our way to see Aunt Shelby," Dylan said, mentioning Angelika's sister. "Carl's taken me here a few times while the women bond. That's what he calls it."

Jake tried to push aside the stupid burst of useless jealousy he felt at the mention of Jake's stepdad.

"That's great." Jake reached into his pocket and pulled out his credit card. "Here, buy the nicest wood you can find. I don't care what it cost."

Dylan stared at the card. "You're not coming in?"

Jake's eyes widened. "I didn't think you'd want me to."

The last time they'd gone shopping together, Jake had taken Dylan to a mall in LA to buy school clothes. Jake disguised himself by wearing a baseball cap and aviator glasses, but that hadn't stopped people from recognizing him. Father and son were soon swarmed by paparazzi, who rarely saw the pair together. One ardent photographer accidentally elbowed Dylan in the face in his haste to get to Jake. Dylan didn't speak to him for the rest of their trip.

Dylan chewed on his inner cheek before shrugging. "Like you've said, Michigan isn't LA."

Jake wasn't going to argue with that. They got out of Jake's silver pickup truck and headed inside the barn. Jake pulled on the edge of the beanie he wore as he looked around. It was much bigger inside than it appeared. Large slabs of pine, piles of barnwood, and various other woods filled up aisle after aisle.

"It's this way," Dylan said, knowing exactly where he was going.

When they reached it, Jake ran his hand over the spectrum of red and brown colors in the wood. It would make a beautiful chest.

"This is perfect," he murmured.

"Can I help you?" a man said from behind him.

"How much is this piece?" Dylan asked.

"Isn't it a beaut? We have it on sale this week for $750."

"We'll take it," Jake said, keeping his back to the man.

"Oh...sure," the guy said. "Is there anything else?"

"Would you mind bringing it up to the register so we can look around some more?" Dylan asked.

"You bet," the guy said. "I'll just go grab a cart."

After he left, Jake said, "You got your eye on something?"

"I want to build Charlotte a toy box for her birthday," Dylan replied, mentioning his little sister.

"It's her third, right?" Jake asked.

Jake and Angelika had talked about giving Dylan a younger sibling, but with Jake's chaotic lifestyle, Angelika had put it off when they were together. She found the family life she wanted with Carl. Boring, safe, reliable Carl.

"Yeah," Dylan replied. "Her toys are all over the place. Figured she could use something cool to stuff her things in."

Jake swallowed over the unexpected lump in his throat. "You're a good big brother."

Dylan shrugged, his cheeks tinting red, but Jake could tell he was pleased by the compliment.

After Dylan found what he was looking for, they made their way to the front of the store. When Jake went to pay for Dylan's, Dylan shook his head.

"I can pay for my own." He whipped out a wad of cash from his wallet. There had to have easily been one hundred dollars.

"Where'd you get that kind of money?" Jake asked. There

was no way Angelika would let their son walk around with that much cash. She would've put it in a savings account for him, for sure.

Dylan played with the edge of his wallet as he waited for his change. "I've been saving for a while. Doing chores around the house and helping Aunt Shelby work on that fixer-upper she bought."

Jake eyed the money suspiciously. "You need to talk to your mom about opening a bank account."

"I already have one. That's where this came from." His shoulders hunched.

Before Jake could say anything else, the elderly man behind the counter said, "And how will you be paying for the rosewood?" After Jake pulled out his credit card and paid for his purchase, the man yelled out, "Billy!"

The man craned his neck, looking for someone. Then he shook his head. "That grandson of mine. He'd lose his head if it wasn't attached to his body."

"I'm right here, Gramps." The same guy who'd helped them earlier came up to them. He froze when he saw Jake, but he didn't say anything, much to Jake's relief. He loved his fans, but he wanted this day to be about Dylan.

"Help these two load up their car," the man said.

"Sure thing."

Once they got the oak and rosewood loaded into the truck, Billy hovered beside them, looking like he wanted to say something. Dylan rolled his eyes and hopped into the vehicle.

Billy finally spurted, "I'm a big fan. You were my first huge celebrity crush."

Jake gave a professional smile. "Thanks. I'm honored." He stuck out his hand, and Billy shook it, looking like a kid on Christmas. "And thanks for your help today. I appreciate it."

"No problem." Billy waved and walked away with a huge grin on his face.

When Jake settled behind the steering wheel, he looked over at Dylan, worried that the encounter with a fan had put him off. His son was very much like his mother in that regard. Dylan merely raised an eyebrow at him.

"What?" Jake finally asked.

"At least I didn't get elbowed in the face this time."

The following Monday, Julie walked out of her mom's assisted-living facility. Her mom was tired during their weekly visit, but the nurse assured her that all was well. Glancing at her phone, she saw she had a new text from Jake.

It had been a few days since she saw him in person. He was giving her space to think, like she had asked. A part of her was grateful to him for that. A bigger part hated the distance. She kept thinking about what he'd said…that maybe she wouldn't like him once she got to know him better. So, she started randomly texting him, asking personal things that he wouldn't mind sharing. Questions like what his favorite color was, or if he had a favorite subject in school. And he started asking her questions in return. He knew that she'd watched *Schitt's Creek* multiple times, and that her favorite non-Holiday Boys song was the '80s classic "In Your Eyes" by Peter Gabriel.

Her phone buzzed and she opened up their text exchange. She smiled when she saw he had sent her an answer of his own. My favorite song? Gotta be "While My Guitar Gently Weeps."

She smiled before replying, Isn't that a George Harrison song? I thought you were the Paul McCartney of boy bands?

He didn't answer right away, but she didn't expect him to. She imagined he was in the recording studio today. As she headed back to town, she saw a large puff of black smoke in the distance. Knowing that was in the direction of the campground Meg's parents owed, Julie turned in that direction and sped down the road.

To her relief, it wasn't the campground. A large crowd of

people stood in its parking lot to stare at the building across the street. It was completely on fire. Julie's heart jolted when she saw it was Patti's Diner. It hurt to see such a landmark burn to the ground.

She parked on the street and joined the crowd, which was kept at a safe distance away by police officers. None of the firefighters seemed in a hurry to save the structure. The sound of breaking glass could be heard in the distance as fire consumed the window frames.

"Josh," Julie called out to one of the police officers she knew.

"Hi, Julie," he said. "Came to see the show?"

Julie pointed toward the campground with her head. "I was worried that it was Archer's Campground."

"Nope." Josh crossed his arms over his chest. "Someone bought Patti's and donated it to the fire department so they could practice a controlled burn. Thankfully, we don't get too many real fires around here, so it's good the newbies get some real experience. But it's a shame to see Patti's go. I went on my first date there."

"Do you know who donated it?" she asked, starting to get a tingling sensation at the back of her neck.

"Nah, person was anonymous."

She nodded before saying her goodbyes. She could feel the heat of the blaze on her skin, even though she was safely away from the fire. Looking away from the scene, Julie began to scan the crowd. She didn't see what she was looking for until she noticed a black Camaro parked down the road. Pushing her way through the crowd, she walked down the sidewalk to the passenger's side door. Bending down, she saw Jake behind the wheel. He didn't even notice her, his eyes transfixed on the inferno. When she rapped on the window, he jumped. Seeing who it was, he unlocked the door and reached over to push it open, an invite for Julie to jump in.

"Hey," he said.

"Hey."

They sat in silence, a weird energy in the air. Gone was the man who asked her to give him a chance. Gone was the man who sent her flirty texts since they had parted. There was absolutely no trace of the adored celebrity that millions of people loved around the world.

Jake looked like death. His face was pallid, his eyes red and strained. He sat with his hands in his lap, his gaze unable to move away from the fire.

"I take it this is your doing?" she asked gently.

He nodded sharply. "Bought it from Patti for over double what she wanted and donated it to the fire department."

Her mouth dropped. He might as well have taken a pile of cash and set it on fire instead of burning it down.

"Why would you do that?" she asked. "Why didn't you try to restore it or something?"

Jake was quiet for a long time, so much that she considered repeating her question, but she knew he had heard her.

"My mom..." he finally said. "My mom had to work three jobs to support us. And when she came home at the end of her day, exhausted from being on her feet all day, my father would be waiting for her, shouting at her that she was nothing, that she wasn't enough of a woman for him." Jake swallowed hard. "I tried to protect her and my sister from him. So he'd turn his crap on me, telling me I'd never amount to anything and that I was worthless."

Julie wanted to reach for him, to comfort him in some way, but his body was so tense she didn't think he'd even feel her touch.

"Shortly after I turned eighteen, things were finally starting to look up. Holiday Boys had just signed a contract with Big Poppa. He was our first manager. He promised he could make us stars as long as we gave everyone this squeaky clean image that would have moms running to buy our albums for their kids." Jake leaned his head back against the seat. "I got a call from Patti two weeks after I signed my contract. She told me that while she'd run to the bank, my dad came in with his latest girlfriend. Since my mom was the only waitress working, he refused to leave until she waited on him. So she did."

Julie sucked in a horrified breath. Jake pulled his eyes away from the fire to look at her, the dark circles under his eyes prominent. "By the time I arrived at the restaurant, my dad and his girlfriend were groping each other in the booth, while my mom was nowhere to be seen. I found her outdoors, standing next to the dumpster. She looked like a zombie. I went back inside, grabbed my dad by the shirt, and dragged him out of the booth." A bitter smile formed on his face. "I wasn't a little kid anymore that he could push around and intimidate. He tried. He started to say how pathetic I was, that I needed to be a man like him. I punched him as hard as I could. Damn near broke my hand. Definitely broke his jaw. I told him to leave and never come back.

"I'm sorry," Julie whispered. "I had no idea."

Jake looked back at the fire again. "There were always rumors floating around town about my father. But the only ones who really knew the full story were me, my parents, and Patti. Patti wouldn't have told anyone. People knew my dad left town quick with his latest mistress and that was enough to feed the vultures."

"What about your mom?"

Jake blanched as though his memories were too painful. "I found her behind the diner. She was so far gone mentally, we had to hospitalize her. My sister was sent to stay with my maternal grandparents. Big Poppa showed up for me, did his magic to cover any possible scandal, and got me the hell out of town."

"How's your mom doing now?"

He smiled, the first one with real emotion in it since she joined him in the car. "She's good now. Fully recovered and remarried to an amazing man. They live in Florida near my sister and her family."

Julie remembered what Jake had said before, about how he didn't share a lot of information about himself with people. She was touched that he trusted her this much to confide something so personal. Some of the guards she'd placed around her heart crumbled as they sat together in the warmth of his car.

"Did you ever see your dad again?" she asked.

Jake's smile turned brittle. "He showed up a few years after I hit it big. He came to one of my concerts, babbling that he always knew I'd be a big success, and then promptly asked for money. I filed a restraining order against him."

The diner was turning into a shell of what it once was as the fire ate away at it.

"I should have brought marshmallows," Julie murmured, hoping to pull Jake out of his solemn mood. "That's a good fire for s'mores."

Jake barked out a laugh. He laid his hand on the console between them and she placed her own in his.

"George is my favorite Beatle," he said randomly. When Julie looked over at him questioningly, he nodded toward where his phone rested on the car's dashboard. "You texted me about being like Paul McCartney. Don't get me wrong, I love the comparison, but Harrison's music was pure poetry. He didn't contribute as many songs to the Beatles as McCartney and Lennon, but every time he did, he knocked it out of the park. James is a lot like him. I told him once he should be a full-time songwriter because anything he ever wrote for Holiday Boys turned to gold. But he was always content to sit in the background."

The firefighters started to hose down the diner.

"What are you going to do with the property once the diner's demolished?" Julie asked.

Jake laid his head against the headrest. His thumb started

to move absently back and forth across the back of her hand. "My mom always used to garden when I was younger. It was her escape. I thought I'd turn the space into a community flower garden."

"That'd be beautiful," she said softly.

They sat in silence for several minutes, watching the firefighters work. The silence could have been awkward, but it wasn't. Sitting beside Jake felt good. It felt *right*.

As though he could read her mind, Jake asked, "Have you given any more thought to that date?"

Julie copied his posture and laid her head on her seat's headrest. "Honestly? It's all I've thought about, but I can't stop thinking what this means for you."

"I told you, I want to be with you in any way you'll let me."

Julie turned pleading eyes on him. "But what about sex? There must be a hundred women who'd be willing to sleep with you. I know it's not fair, but I can't be in an open relationship."

"Who said I wanted an open relationship?" His expression was sincere. "Despite what you may have heard or read about me, I'm a loyal guy." He waved his free hand at the diner. "After what my dad did to my mom, I could never treat a woman with that level of disrespect. When I'm in a relationship, I'm completely faithful."

Julie looked into Jake's deep blue eyes, taking in the sincerity she saw there.

"Will you go out with me?" he asked.

Despite the conflicted feelings coursing through her, she said, "Yes."

The answering smile she received erased some of her uncertainty. She only hoped that she hadn't just made a huge mistake.

Chapter Fourteen

Julie nervously paced her living room as she waited for Jake to arrive.

He said he wanted to take her for dinner and dancing, so she'd put on a nice black dress that hugged her hips and flared down to the knees. She'd put her hair into a twist; her makeup was done to perfection.

The evil voice inside her head taunted her again. *He doesn't know what he's getting into. He's not going to be with someone for long who won't have sex.*

Julie glanced at the clock on the wall and saw she still had a half hour before Jake was supposed to pick her up. Grabbing her purse, she pulled out her phone and called Meg.

"Tell me I'm not making a mistake," Julie said as soon as she heard her friend's voice.

"You're not making a mistake," Meg assured her. "You deserve this, Julie."

Julie's ears perked up, hearing the sad undertones in her friend's voice. "What about you? What are you going to do tonight?"

"Well, about a half hour ago, I sent a message to everyone I'd invited to the wedding and let them know it was canceled, and now I'm currently sitting on my parents' couch shoving cookie dough ice cream into my mouth."

Julie's heart ached for her friend. "I can always cancel and come over."

"Don't you dare!" Meg said. "You're going on a date with a Holiday Boy. I need to relive all my teen fantasies vicariously through you."

Julie laughed softly. "All right. I'll give you all the dirty details tomorrow."

Meg snorted because they both knew there'd be nothing dirty taking place. "You better. I want a call first thing in the morning. No, but seriously, have fun tonight. Love you."

"I love you, too. Good night."

"Night. I—holy crap!" Meg's voice went up ten notches. "I think I see Tyler walking up to his parents' house."

Julie smirked. "Maybe we're both supposed to spend an evening with a Holiday Boy. Go say hi to him."

"Are you serious? I haven't washed my hair since yesterday, and I'm currently wearing an old pair of sweatpants that I found in my childhood bedroom. Seeing that I'm about twenty-five pounds heavier than I was in high school, it looks like I sprayed them on."

Julie heard a car pull up. "I think Jake is here. I should go. Have fun spying on Tyler."

"As if I would," Meg said. "Night, Jules."

"Good night." Julie ended the call, smiling as she put her phone back in her purse. Hearing Meg's voice brighten for a few minutes made Julie's heart a little lighter. Jake knocked on the door and Julie went to answer it.

"Hi," Jake said, his eyes skimming over her. "You look beautiful."

She wanted to say *So do you*.

Jake wore an white open-collared shirt with a midnight blue blazer and dark jeans. His hair was styled to perfection, high off his forehead and soft looking. Julie fought off the temptation to run her fingers through it. He'd shaved his beard and she quietly mourned the loss. It had given him a rugged look that she really appreciated. She didn't realize beards were a thing for her, but Jake was apparently an exception to the rule. When wasn't he though?

"Thank you," She stepped back so he could enter her house. "Come on in. I just need to grab my jacket."

She led him into her living room.

He looked around. "You have a nice place."

"Thanks," she replied.

Jake helped her with her trench coat, observing her face. "Seriously though, you look really happy. I'd love to think it's because you're excited for our date, but…"

Julie suppressed a laugh. "That, too, but I just got off the phone with Meg."

"How's she doing?" he asked as they made their way out the door.

"She's doing okay," Julie replied. "She thought she saw Tyler."

"Yeah, he told me he planned on seeing his parents this weekend. He liked your video, by the way."

Julie stumbled. "He saw it, too?"

"Well, Paul's the one who first pointed it out," Jake teased.

Julie briefly closed her eyes. "Are you telling me all of the Holiday Boys saw it?"

"Yep." He emphasized the *p* so it popped on his lips.

"Excuse me while I go crawl in a hole somewhere," Julie said. "You know, it was Meg's idea to begin with."

Jake snorted. "Why doesn't that surprise me? From what I can remember, she had a knack for getting in trouble. Tyler got grounded more than a couple of times because of her."

Julie grinned. "That sounds like Meg. She always came up with brilliant ideas that usually led to me getting in trouble. I remember one time she decided we should have a secret hide-out in the attic space above her garage. While we were looking around, she told me to walk on the beams, but I was a kid and didn't know what those were. Next thing I knew, I heard a loud crack and I fell through the ceiling."

Jake halted in the process of opening the passenger door. "Did you get hurt?"

"Miraculously, there was a roll of insulation right next to where I fell. It somehow unrolled and landed perfectly underneath me. I hit that instead of the garage floor."

"You could have been killed."

"Don't I know it. We both ended up grounded for a month."

They got in the car and Jake started the engine.

"I can't believe I didn't pay attention to you when we were young," he said.

"Well, I was just a kid compared to you. I'm not surprised you never noticed me."

"I did notice you in high school."

Julie turned amused eyes on him. "Yeah, right."

"I'm serious."

"Oh, please," Julie said. "I remember you very well from school. You were surrounded by groupies even before you were famous."

Jake stared at her before a smirk appeared on his lips. He began to sing. "The redheaded girl, she leaves me enchanted."

Julie's eyes widened as she recognized the lyrics. "What? Are you saying the redheaded girl in 'Enchanted' was me?"

The grin on his lips widened but he didn't say anything.

"But...you and I ran in completely different circles then. We never even spoke."

"That might be true, but I definitely noticed you. I remember seeing you walking down the hall one day with Meg, and you were laughing at something. I thought you were beautiful. I went to homeroom and wrote out the first draft of the song."

Julie realized her mouth was hanging open, and she snapped it shut. Shaking her head, she said, "I can't believe it. That was one of Holiday Boys' biggest hits. That song meant so much to me because you made being a redhead something beautiful. And you're telling me that song was about me the whole time?"

Jake looked almost proud. "Like I said, I noticed you."

Julie sat in complete shock as he put the car in Drive. How many times had she listened to "Enchanted" over the years? She loved that song so much.

Jake glanced at her as they came to a stop sign. There was a trace of laughter in his voice as he asked, "Did I break you?"

Julie tried to compose herself. "I used to drive my sister nuts when I was a teen. I listened to 'Enchanted' so much I could write the lyrics out by heart."

"I'm glad it meant that much to you." Julie looked at Jake to see him staring at her with an expression she couldn't describe. The romantic in her wanted to call it tender.

"So, um, where are we going?" she asked, and he continued to guide the steering wheel in his strong hands.

"I thought we could have dinner at my place."

"Oh." Julie's nerves kicked in. She trusted Jake, but she'd never gone to a man's house on a first date. At least she didn't have to do the whole *I'm asexual* conversation with him.

"Is that all right?" He looked worried. "If you're not comfortable with that, we can go somewhere else. I just thought it'd be nice to go somewhere we could enjoy dinner without being interrupted."

She thought back to their dinner at the restaurant; the woman who took pictures of them and the crowd of fans waiting outside.

"It's fine," Julie assured him.

"Are you sure? I can tell the caterer he can go home and we can go somewhere public."

She tilted her head as she looked at him. "You hired a caterer?"

Jake nodded, running a hand over his smooth cheek. She again lamented the loss of his beard.

"I hired someone who came highly recommended from Traverse City. He specializes in vegan food." When she looked at him questioningly, he said, "I've noticed you always order vegetarian or vegan meals when we've eaten together."

Her heart warmed. "I didn't realize you noticed."

"I did," Jake said simply.

"We can go to your place. It's fine."

Jake side-eyed her as if to double-check that she was serious, and relaxed when he saw she meant it.

"Okay," Jake said. "There's something I want to show you when we get there."

"What?"

Jake's face lit up. "You'll see."

After driving for ten minutes, he turned down a dark path that she didn't even know existed—and she thought she knew every spot in Holiday Bay. It seemed to go on forever before it finally broke away to a large mansion.

Julie sucked in a breath. "Your house is beautiful."

"Thanks," Jake said, pulling up to a large black entryway door that had frosted glass on either side of it.

"I never knew this was here."

"I think all the previous homeowners did their best to keep this place off people's radar. That was its biggest appeal to me when I bought it. I love the privacy it gives me."

Julie looked at him in awe. "How long have you owned it?"

"A couple of months now."

She shook her head. "I can't believe you've been right down the road from me all this time."

"Hi, neighbor." Merriment made his eyes shine and she was struck again with how attractive he was. Jake got out of the car and walked over to her side, then opened the door for her.

Julie glanced down at her dress. "If I'd known we were going to your house, I would have worn sweats."

His shoulders shook with humor. "Next time, I promise."

Julie's cheeks flushed. He was counting on a next time. She was already looking forward to it.

"Come on, I want to show you my surprise."

Jake grabbed her hand and led her to the garage area. He guided her to a side door and they entered a workshop. There were various wood projects around the shop and every tool imaginable.

"I didn't realize you were into woodwork."

"Something I like to do with my son when we have time." Jake's grip on her hand tightened as he brought her over to a table. "This is what I wanted to show you."

On the surface of the wood table was the base of a box made from a beautiful wood. Next to it was a drawing of the completed box, a music note on the lid.

"This is lovely," Julie ran a finger across the music note.

"I thought you could sell it at your booth. I'll sign it and you can tell people I made it. Maybe you could find a way to auction it off."

Julie jerked her head up to look at him. "Are you serious?"

"Of course," Jake said. "We could even advertise it on Holiday Boys' website when we announce our reuni—"

He didn't finish what he said, because Julie threw herself into his arms, wrapping him in a fierce hug.

"Thank you," she murmured against his chest. "You've already done so much for me. This is too much."

Jake's arms tightened on her. He was quickly realizing that there was very little he wouldn't do for the woman in his arms. Especially when she let him hold her close like this. Something settled inside him that felt like it'd been out of place for years. He knew what it was, because he'd experienced it before.

Being with Julie made him feel like he was home.

She pulled away and he let her go reluctantly. A strand of her beautiful crimson hair had come loose from her twist, and he tucked it behind her ear.

"Are you ready to eat?"

She nodded, and he took her hand in his again, loving the way her fingers clasped his. As they walked by the table where Dylan's latest project was—a rocking chair—Julie came to an abrupt halt.

"What is it?" he asked.

With her free hand, she picked up one of the Petoskey stones from Dylan's collection and stared at it.

She let out a gasp, her gaze swinging to his. "You're my mystery vendor."

Jake's forehead wrinkled in confusion. "What?"

Julie gave him a knowing look. "My vendor—you know the one that always has his son drop off his work because he's too busy. Too busy? That's one way to put it."

Julie grinned at him and his confusion grew.

"I'm sorry," he said. "I don't understand what you're talking about."

Julie picked up a particular stone. "You don't have to pretend. This is the stone I gave Dylan the other day."

Jake let go of her hand so he could face her more fully. "Hold up. Dylan's been giving his projects to you?"

"Like you don't know." Julie tilted her head. "I've been selling your stuff for weeks now. I had no idea it was your work, though."

"Wait..." Jake held up his hand. "Dylan has been bringing things to your store and you've been selling them with the understanding it's my work. What exactly has he been selling?"

Julie's face turned concerned. She seemed to be growing aware that something wasn't right. "There was a crate-size chest that he brought in a couple of weeks ago, and then the other day he came in with a gorgeous Craftsman nightstand. Didn't he have your permission to sell them?"

"I didn't know anything about it."

"But...you signed a contract. He gave me the paperwork."

"What name was on it?"

"I…well, to be honest, it was hard to read. Are you seriously saying you don't know anything about this? He told me that he was simply delivering his dad's work."

"I didn't know," Jake said, running a hand through his hair.

Julie put the stone back on the table. "It says in my vendor contract that all clients have to be at least eighteen years of age. He forged the contract." Julie paled. "I deposited money from his sales into a bank account that I thought was his father's. What if I unwittingly committed bank fraud?"

She looked like she was about to have a panic attack. Jake placed his hands on both her cheeks, forcing her to look at him.

"We'll get this sorted, okay?"

"Why would he lie about it though? Why not just tell the truth?"

"He's been trying to save up money for his own store. His mom's been against the idea and despite our differences, Angelika and I agreed that if Dylan wanted to do something big, we had to run it by each other first. He probably guessed correctly that I would've spoken to his mom before I agreed to sign a contract on his behalf."

"I can't let him sell anything else in my store." Julie pressed the bridge of her nose between two fingers. "If Harris Farmington ever finds out about this, I'm done."

"Look, I'll call my lawyer and we'll get this figured out."

Julie nodded but she wouldn't meet his eyes.

Jake took in the misery on her face and sighed. "Do you want me to take you home?"

"I think that might be best."

With his face grim, Jake led Julie back out to the Camaro.

The tense silence between them was a sharp contrast to the joy that had started their date.

Chapter Fifteen

Julie tapped her pen nervously against the countertop at her store. She'd slept restlessly and the six cups of coffee she'd slammed to get through her day hadn't helped. Jake had texted her that morning stating he wanted to see her today, and she'd agreed.

She felt like kicking herself for not noticing how similar Dylan and Jake were. They had the same hair color and same build.

Dylan's animosity toward his dad certainly made more sense. He'd said repeatedly that Jake wasn't a good guy—something Julie still thought was a ridiculous idea. Jake had mentioned himself that he didn't have an easy relationship with his son, but it was something he was doing his best to change.

She didn't know what she was going to do about Dylan. She liked him, she really did, but in his effort to put some money away for his future, he may have unwittingly jeopardized hers. She felt stupid and naive for not demanding to meet his father first before she deposited any money in his account, but she had never faced this kind of problem before. She'd known most of her vendors all her life. She trusted them. Julie never would have imagined that one of them could potentially destroy Pieces of Home.

She glanced at her phone for what felt like the hundredth time that morning to see if the attorney in town had called her back. There was still nothing from him. Julie's stomach clenched as she wondered again if she'd broken any laws.

When it was close to noon, Jake walked in, carrying a bag of food from Florentina's. "I come bearing gifts."

He placed the bag in front of her, the scent of marinara making her stomach growl.

"I don't know if I can eat," she said, despite her hunger.

"I spoke with my lawyer. You won't get into any trouble." Julie let out a relieved breath. Jake, on the other hand, tensed, grim lines forming around his mouth "She said if you want to file charges against Dylan for fraud, you'd be within your right."

Julie instantly rejected the idea. "I would never do that."

Jake's shoulders relaxed. "Thank you."

She reached across the counter and squeezed his hand. "Thank you for checking with your lawyer."

"I'm just sorry for the whole thing." Jake opened the bag of food and pulled out a couple of containers, pushing one toward Julie. "How do you want to handle the situation? I mean, I know what I'm going to do on my end—I'm going to let Dylan know the workshop is off limits for the next month." He pulled out some plasticware. "Are you going to let him still sell his products if he does it properly this time?"

"I don't know." Julie opened the container, her mouth watering at the sight of spaghetti. "There's a reason I require vendors to be at least eighteen, so I can avoid these types of scares. And I'm not crazy about the lying he did. I have to think about it."

Jake grabbed her hand and kissed her on the wrist. Her heart sped up in response.

"Whatever you decide, I'll support you. I know he went about things the wrong way. I also know what his motivation was for doing it. He doesn't want any handouts from me to start his business."

"That doesn't mean he should be lying to get his way."

"I agree. I wouldn't blame you if you said no. There's no pressure for you to say yes." Jake bit into a meatball, his expression preoccupied. "Can we have a redo on our date? The caterer left me with plenty of delicious food. And my living room is big enough for the dancing I promised you." He smiled. "You can even wear your sweats, if you want. I really don't care, as long as we can spend a little time together."

Julie twirled a noodle on her fork. Her lips perked upward. "I'd like that."

Jake nodded, a look of relief appearing on his face. "Should I pick you up at your place?"

"Why don't I drive to your house?" If things went bad again during their second attempt, she could at least get home without the awkward silence that happened last time.

"That sounds great," Jake said. "How about seven o'clock?"

Julie's smile widened. "It's a date."

Julie wiped her clammy hands on the loose black skirt she wore as she stared up at the giant house before her. Her nerves were in full force tonight. She wanted things to go smoothly since the previous night had ended in disaster. Checking her reflection in the rearview mirror, she redid her ponytail, making sure she smoothed away any bumps.

Julie got out of the car and took a deep breath. She walked past a large Hummer and knocked on the door. A few moments later, the door swung inward.

Julie startled.

A woman with jet-black hair and heavy makeup stared at her with an eyebrow raised. "Yeah?"

"I—I'm Julie." She fidgeted with the strap of her purse. "I'm here to see Jake."

The woman's eyes ran over Julie, her lips pursing. "So *you're* Julie." A smile formed on her lips, but Julie didn't think it was meant to be pleasant. "You're exactly how I pictured you."

Julie lifted her chin, not missing the derision in the other woman's words. "And you are?"

"Leaving. But we'll be in touch soon."

The woman brushed by her. Julie watched as she hopped into the Hummer, revved the engine, and roared down the driveway.

"Julie?" Jake's voice said behind her.

Julie swung around to face him. "Hey, sorry. I just ran into...actually, I didn't catch her name."

"Lori, my manager." Jake didn't look too happy.

Julie remembered something that Isabella said. That fans had been rooting for Jake and his manager for years. Julie tried to brush that aside. She was here with Jake now. Not Lori.

Still, she had to say, "I didn't mean to interrupt. If you have business you need to deal with..."

"No, it's fine." He took a step back so she could enter.

If Julie ever took the time to imagine how the rich and famous lived, this would be what she pictured. The grand hallway was so fancy, she was afraid to walk across the gleaming marble floor in her boots.

"Your home is beautiful," she said.

"Thanks."

Jake took Julie's hand and they began walking down a hallway to their right. They soon entered the kitchen. This area looked a little more lived in and not as opulent as the front entryway. A kitchen island the length of a small school bus took up most of the space. Brown granite countertops, espresso-colored cabinets, and stainless steel appliances ran throughout the rest of the kitchen.

Jake moved over to the refrigerator and began removing plastic containers. "The caterer had prepared Chinese. I hope you like that."

"I love Chinese." Julie wandered to the island. "Is there anything I can do to help?"

"Nope." A smile tugged at his lips, which sent heat over Julie's skin. "So, how was your week?"

"It was good," she answered. "There's a lot of buzz around town right now. People have been stopping by the store, asking if you're the mystery act that'll be playing at the charity concert."

"What'd you tell them?"

"I told them it wasn't you, which is technically true since it's *all* the Holiday Boys."

Jake snorted. He grabbed some spoons and put them in different containers. He next pulled a couple of plates from one of the cupboards, handing one to Julie. "Help yourself."

After reheating their food in the microwave, Jake led her to an alcove off the kitchen, which held a small table in the same dark brown color as the cabinets. He left only to return with a couple of glasses filled with red wine.

"I was half expecting a dining room table the size of an elephant," she joked.

"Oh, I have that, too, and a ballroom." Jake smirked. "But that's for more formal events."

"Got it." Julie forked up the vegetable fried rice and took a bite. "This is delicious."

"I'll let the caterer know," Jake replied.

Throughout the rest of their meal, they'd continued to play twenty questions. Julie knew more about Jake now than she ever had. He told her how he thought about becoming a psychologist if he never made it as a singer, and that he and his ex-wife named Dylan after Bob Dylan. In return, she told him one of her more embarrassing fangirl stories.

"Wait…" Jake looked amused. "You started a Holiday Boys fan club in school?"

Julie face-palmed. "I was fourteen."

"What did you discuss?"

"Um, I think we once had a serious debate over who had the prettiest eyes. We almost disbanded over it."

Jake wiggled his eyebrows. "So who had the best eyes?"

"No comment," she said, and he laughed.

After dinner, he said, "There's an ice-cream place near the recording studio in Charlevoix. It has the best lavender ice cream I've ever tasted. I know it doesn't really go with Chinese, but I bought a container the other day. Would you like some?"

"Yes, please."

"Great." Jake grinned. "It wasn't easy to get home. I forgot to grab a cooler, so I had to drive home with the air conditioning on so it wouldn't melt. It was cooler that day, too. I froze my ass off."

"My hero," Julie joked.

Jake gave her a lopsided grin and left to get the dessert. He returned a short time later and handed her a dish.

The rich lavender flavor burst on Julie's tongue. "Oh my god. Do you always eat like this?"

"No," he admitted. "Usually I'm on the run, so I grab a bagel or whatever I have in the freezer."

Julie took another bite, enjoying the relaxed mood between them. She looked up and saw Jake looking at her, a small smile on his lips.

"What?" she asked.

"You have a little..." He reached over and wiped at some ice cream at the corner of her lips. He brought his thumb to his mouth and licked it off. Julie suddenly felt warm all over.

"So, uh..." She cleared her throat so it didn't sound so breathless. "How's the recording going?"

Jake gave her a knowing look, but didn't comment on her reaction. Instead, he said, "It's going good. Music has changed so much over the past twenty years. It's been fun adding a modern twist to our sound."

Julie swirled her spoon around her bowl. "I can't wait to hear it."

"I'll make sure you get an advanced copy."

Their eyes met. They stared at each other, no words exchanged, before returning to their ice cream. Once they were finished, Julie helped him rinse off their dishes and load them into the dishwasher. Jake took her hand again and led her into another room at the end of the house. It was the size of Julie's Cape Cod home. The shape of the room reminded Julie of a gazebo. The three walls that didn't make up the entryway were made of floor-to-ceiling glass. Plants sprawled throughout the room in planters of all shapes and sizes. Vintage wicker furniture resided wherever there was remaining space.

"Because of course you have a solarium," she muttered. "You're living the stereotypical lifestyle of the rich and famous, you know that, right?"

Jake laughed. "It came with the house. The whole place was built in the 1910s. Very little of the original layout has changed. With the exception of a few minor updates." He walked over to a panel on the wall and pressed a button. The lights in the room dimmed. He hit another switch and soft classical music began to play. He strolled over to her and pressed his chest to her back, his hands skimming lightly down her arms.

Goose bumps broke out on Julie's skin at his touch.

"Look up," he whispered in her ear.

She did so and gasped. With the lights dimmed, she got a clear view of the outside surroundings. The night sky shone through the room's glass ceiling. A million different stars twinkled above.

"It's beautiful," she said in awe.

"This is my favorite room," Jake told her. He gently turned her so that she could get a view out the side window. A short distance away, the bay shimmered in the moonlight.

"I can see why." Her tone was soft. Jake pulled her closer, his hands going to her waist.

"It's a good place to write songs or think." The feel of his breath against her neck caused her to shiver. "Julie?"

"Hmm?" she said, turning so that she could face him.

"Will you dance with me?"

"Now?"

His lips turned upward. "I promised you dinner and dancing the other day, didn't I?"

"You did," she said. She put her hands on his shoulders and he took that as his cue.

As they began to sway to the music, Julie closed her eyes. She moved closer to him so that she could rest her head on his shoulder. Her hands wrapped around his lower neck.

He stiffened for a second before pulling her tighter to him. "Is this okay?"

"Yes," she assured him.

They danced until the song ended. He didn't let go as another one began and she sighed happily.

"Can I ask you something?" he asked.

"Yes," she replied. She breathed in his clean, masculine scent of fresh soap and his cologne.

"What are your boundaries?"

She pulled back to look at him. His face was shadowed in the dim light.

"Boundaries?"

He nodded. "This, for example. You're okay with me holding you?"

"Yes." Julie slid her palm down to where one of his hands rested lightly on her waist. She pushed it more firmly against her. "It's okay for you to touch me. Being asexual doesn't mean I'm not human. Most humans need touch."

"I never want to make you uncomfortable."

The sincerity in his eyes caused a mixture of happiness

and yearning to surge through her. Julie stood on her toes and clasped the base of his neck again with her free hand. She lightly touched her lips to his.

"I enjoy kissing you," she said against his mouth. "I mean *really* enjoy it."

He took that as his cue and pressed their mouths back together. Without hesitation, Julie slid her tongue across the crease of his lips. When he granted her access to his mouth, she licked inside, tasting the lingering lavender. He breathed in sharply through his nose and his hands tightened on her.

She pulled back slightly so that she could slide his hand up her side, letting it brush against her breast before settling it against her neck. "And I told you, kissing me here is a huge yes for me."

A sexy smile appeared on his lips, which sent her blood racing. He leaned down and pressed his mouth to that telling point on her neck. She let out a soft moan, moving her head to give him better access.

He nibbled on her skin and Julie sucked in a breath. She moved so that she straddled his thigh, her loose skirt allowing her to move how she wanted. Jake groaned against her neck, his hands moving to her ass. He gripped it, molding her warm flesh in his palms. She arched and he hardened against her. Wet heat began to form at her core. She ground against his leg, enjoying the building friction. Her breath became rapid as a tingling sensation formed at her core.

And then…it was gone.

The pleasure evaporated. Emptiness invaded and the feeling that she was doing something unnatural took over. Bitter tears filled her eyes.

"Julie?" Jake's voice shook. She could still feel his hardness.

"I'm sorry." She couldn't meet his gaze. "I didn't mean to—my high school boyfriend used to call me a tease. That is…when he wasn't calling me a frigid bitch."

Jake let go of her bottom so that he could grasp her chin. He gently raised it until she met his eyes.

"He's an idiot." Jake leaned down and gave her the softest kiss on the corner of her mouth. "I asked what your boundaries are. Now, I know."

She shook her head. "This isn't fair to you."

"Hey." He traced her ear with his finger. "I'm not looking for casual sex here. I want to be with someone I can have a relationship with."

"But—"

He kissed her again, tracing her bottom lip with his tongue. She shuddered against him.

"I don't need sex to be a part of the package," Jake murmured. "I just want you...however much you're willing to give."

Julie nibbled on her lower lip. "I can have sex with you, you know?"

"Yes, you've told me." He pulled away from her, but grabbed her hand and led her over to a wicker couch. They sat down and his arm went around her shoulders, pulling her close. They leaned back and stared at the stars as music continued to play in the background.

Julie didn't notice any of it. Her mind raced. How could Jake be so accepting? She'd felt his desire for her. What man could accept this arrangement in the long run? She peeked at him from the corner of her eye. He'd tilted his head back to stare upward. He looked lost in thought. Her heart began to ache. She didn't want to lose him.

A lot of asexuals compromised and had sex. She could, too.

"I've had sex before," Julie said, trying to explain where she was coming from.

"Okay," Jake replied.

"So...we could try it sometime if you want."

Jake turned so that they were facing each other. Looking deeply into her eyes, he said, "I told you. I'm in this because I want to have a relationship with you. I'm not looking for some-one just for the sake of having sex with them. I don't mean to be crass, but I've been there, done that. Literally. And it makes me feel as empty as you say sex makes you, though our reasons are different." He picked up her hand and kissed her palm. "Please understand when I say I won't ever ask you to do something you don't want to do. Ever. I want to be with *you*."

Julie wanted to believe him. She knew *he* believed what he was saying. She tried to push aside the doubts that wouldn't stop taunting at the back of her mind.

"Hey." Jake thread their fingers together. "There's some-thing else I wanted to talk to you about."

Julie's stomach twisted nervously. "All right."

"I have to leave tomorrow."

Julie's eyebrows shot up. "I see."

"That's why Lori—my manager—was here earlier. She scheduled Holiday Boys to be on *America, Good Morning*. It was supposed to be sometime next week, but they bumped us up a few days early."

Her mind shifted from worry to excitement in the span of a second. She tried her very best to not act like an overzeal-ous fan. "Oh, are you announcing your reunion?"

One side of Jake's mouth lifted as though he guessed how hard she was trying not to show too much enthusiasm.

"We are." He laughed when she let out a quiet squeal be-fore throwing her arms around him.

"It'll be official then," she murmured against his jaw.

"You didn't believe me before?" he teased, feigning a hurt expression as she pulled back. She grabbed his hand again, intertwining their fingers.

"Of course I did, but there won't be any backing out of it once the rest of the world knows."

He let out an exaggerated shudder. "Heaven forbid." His ex-pression turned serious. "I'll be gone for three to four weeks, depending on how much publicity Lori manages to book, but I'll make sure to keep in touch as much as I can. Lori's sending a team to handle the logistics for the concert."

Julie's good mood dampened slightly, knowing that he'd be gone for so long. "When do you have to leave?"

"First thing in the morning."

She stared at their joined fingers. "I guess I should go so you can get your beauty sleep." She nudged him with her shoulder. "We can't have this handsome mug looking exhausted. It's what brings all the screaming girls to your concerts."

Jake stifled a laugh. He stood up, bringing her with him. "And here I thought my songs and singing were what drew a crowd."

"Nope, sorry, it's just your looks."

She started to walk by him, but he captured her arm and swung her to him so she fell against his chest.

"Is that a fact?" He bent down and blew a loud raspberry against her neck. He chuckled when she shrieked.

"It is," she said, her stomach hurting from laughing so much. "Why do you think I'm here? As soon as you lose your looks, I'm gone."

She could feel his smile against her. He began to suck on her skin. Her playfulness left and she moaned.

"Good to know," he murmured.

"I, uh, I really should get going," she said breathlessly as he continued to nuzzle her. She was going to end up with a hickey tomorrow and she really didn't care.

"Or...you could stay."

She pulled back to look at him. "What?"

"Stay." His expression was tender. "I'll be gone for weeks, and it's still pretty early. We can watch a movie, if you want."

"Yeah." Truth be told, Julie didn't want to leave him for anything in that moment. "That sounds good."

They held hands again as they headed down a set of stairs near the kitchen. Her grip tightened on his as they went. A person could get lost in a house this size.

They reached the basement and entered a room that had a home theater. Chairs covered in thick green velvet took up the middle of the room. A large projector screen was on one side of the wall. On the wall next to it was a large collection of Blu-rays and DVDs.

She raised her eyebrows at him. "I'm surprised you don't stream everything."

"I do that, too." Jake nodded at the movies. "Go ahead and pick something."

She walked over to the collection and pulled out *While You Were Sleeping*. "You can't go wrong with Sandra Bullock."

"Good choice. It's a classic." He took the movie from her and insert it in a Blu-ray player at the back of the room.

They settled in their seats. Jake wrapped an arm around her and she rested her head on his shoulder. Toward the end of the movie though, Julie began nodding off.

"Hey," he murmured against her temple. "The movie's over."

Julie's eyes flew open. She felt like the sandman had punched her.

"I'm sorry," she said with a yawn. "I don't know why I'm so sleepy. Maybe it was the wine earlier. It always makes me a little tired."

"Do you want to spend the night?" Jake offered. Julie stiffened and he immediately held up his hands. "I meant, in one of the guest rooms. I don't want you falling asleep behind the wheel."

She was about to protest when another yawn escaped her. "I don't have anything to sleep in."

"I have stuff you can borrow."

Julie debated for a millisecond. She should go home, but

maybe she and Jake could have coffee together in the morning before he left for weeks on end. She liked that idea very much.

"All right. I'll stay."

His answering smile pushed any lingering reservations she had out of her head. They headed to the top floor. Jake paused outside one door once they reached the hallway.

"This is Dylan's room. The bed's already made, but he stays at his mom's."

Julie didn't miss the hint of sadness she could hear in his voice. Another idea started to form in her head.

"Where's your room?" she asked.

Jake's eyebrows shot up. He pointed over his shoulder to a door down the hall.

Julie bit her lip. "What if I slept with you? Just to sleep," she hurriedly added. "It'd be nice to sleep in your arms tonight."

When he didn't say anything, her face flushed crimson. "Never mind. I—"

Before she could reach for the door handle of the guest room, Jake grabbed her hand.

He tugged her down the hall before pulling her into his room. She barely had time to register the new surroundings before Jake distracted her by taking off his shirt, the corded muscles of his back on full display as he strolled out of sight into a walk-in closet. He came out a short time later carrying a striped top that matched the pajama bottoms he'd changed into. They hung distractingly low on his hips.

"Here, you can wear this." Jake handed her the matching shirt. "I don't think I've ever worn these. Normally, I sleep naked."

Julie's face heated again. "Thanks."

"You can get changed in here." Jake walked into the bathroom and flipped on the light. He pulled a toothbrush still in its plastic packaging out of a drawer along with some toothpaste.

"Thank you," she said again. She waited until he closed the door before she changed into his shirt. It fell to her thighs, keeping her modestly covered. She brushed her teeth and then removed her ponytail. Her hair fell into loose waves around her shoulders and she ran her fingers through it. She still couldn't believe Jake wrote "Enchanted" because of her.

Taking a jittery breath, she left the room. Jake was setting the alarm on his phone. He glanced at her and froze, his gaze skimming over her.

"Do you care which side you sleep on?" he rasped.

She shook her head. "I normally sleep on the right but—"

"I'll take the left. I'm going to brush my teeth real quick. Feel free to get settled in."

After he went into the bathroom, Julie hurried under the sheets, pulling them up to her neck. Her stomach twisted. What if she tossed and turned all night until he shoved her out of the bed? The last time she'd been in a man's bed, it was after she'd had sex with Charlie, and he dumped her shortly after.

She lay against the pillows and stared up at the ceiling as her mind drifted to something more positive. She was about to sleep in the same bed as Jake. Her younger self would be so jealous. Julie let out a snort before she could stop it.

"What's so funny?" Jake asked as he entered the room again.

Julie propped up on an elbow, taking in the sight of his muscled stomach. "Oh, just having a conversation with my inner teen. If you told me twenty years ago I'd be sleeping in the same bed as Jake Reynolds…"

"Oh God, I hope I don't snore," he said as he slid in beside her. "I don't want to ruin the fantasy."

Julie fell back against the pillow with laughter. Jake leaned over and kissed her. She wrapped her arms around him, pulling him closer so that she felt the weight of him. He settled between her thighs and startled nibbling on her neck again.

"You better not give me a hickey," she said, lightly pinching his side. He sucked in a breath at the gesture.

He leaned back to look at her. "You don't want a reminder for when I'm gone?"

"I work in a family-friendly establishment."

He grinned before gently kissing her collarbone. "Fair enough."

He rolled onto his back, taking her with him.

Her fingers rested against his stomach. She began drawing patterns along his skin. She grew fascinated with how he reacted to her, his stomach making tiny jerking movements wherever she touched.

"I don't mean to be crass again," Jake said through choked breath. "But if you keep touching me like that, I'm going to embarrass myself in a way I haven't since I hit puberty."

Julie's fingers immediately stilled. "Sorry."

He pressed her hand to his stomach. "Don't ever think I mind you touching me. But I'm not a saint. There's only so much stimulation I can handle."

Julie nodded but didn't resume drawing shapes on his skin. She kept her hand on one of the ridges of his stomach. Her forehead furrowed.

"What?" he asked.

"I thought you said you ate mostly bagels and whatever quick meal you can find," she murmured.

"Yeah. I'm not the healthiest eater."

"How the hell do you get abs like this, then? I look at a bagel and I swear I gain a pound."

Jake laughed. "I work out a lot. I have a home gym in the basement."

"Because of course you do."

Julie settled against his side and felt his lips brush her hair. It was the last thing she remembered before falling asleep, securely in his arms.

Chapter Sixteen

Jake's hand shot out of the covers and tapped his phone so the annoying sound of the alarm would stop. As he lay there, trying to get his brain to focus, he wondered why he felt so happy.

The events of the previous night rolled through his mind and his eyes flew to Julie.

She faced away from him with her head buried in the pillow, her molten hair hiding her features. He listened to the smooth, even sound of her breathing and was glad the alarm hadn't woken her.

He didn't want her leaving his bed just yet.

Jake carefully extracted himself, then stood and stretched. He glanced at the time on his phone. It was 6:45 a.m. Lori told him the previous night that she was sending a car at 8:00 a.m. While he was tempted to go back to bed, he needed to pack a small travel bag and get going.

Jake grabbed a fresh change of clothes and his toothbrush, and went into a spare bathroom suite to take a shower so he didn't disturb Julie. After getting dressed, he went down to the kitchen to make coffee.

As he waited for the pot to percolate, a familiar sound came down the driveway—Dylan's moped.

He waited to see where Dylan headed—to the front door or the workshop. When Jake didn't hear the front door open, he strode toward the workshop.

Dylan was in the middle of opening a drawer, searching for something when Jake walked in.

"What are you doing here so early?" he asked.

"I'm looking for my earbuds," Dylan said. "I think I left them…yeah, here they are."

Dylan pulled out his earbuds and shoved them in his pocket before turning to look at his dad. "Is that Ms. A.'s car out front?"

Jake folded his arms over his chest. "Yes."

"What, are you guys dating now?"

"I really hope so," Jake said. "In fact, we've had some really interesting conversations lately—"

"Listen, Dad," Dylan said, already making his way toward the exit. "I need to head out. I promised Mom I'd—"

"Stop." Jake's voice brooked no room for argument. Dylan hunched his shoulders. Jake knew that his son was well aware he'd been caught. "This place is off limits to you for the next two months."

Dylan swiveled around. "What? That's not fair."

"Not fair? Do you have any idea how much trouble you could be in?"

"So, I sold a few things in Ms. A.'s store. It's not a big deal."

"Not a big deal? Are you serious?"

Dylan raised his chin defensively. "It was my work to sell."

"Under false pretenses. You forged my name, or whatever name you used, on a legal contract that you had with her store. And then you gave Julie false information to deposit your sales in an account that she thought belonged to someone older—which I guess explains how you had the money to buy that wood. We'll tally that as another lie to add to your growing list. You know you have to be at least eighteen years old to sell anything in her store, right? If she wanted to, she could press charges against you."

Dylan paled. "Is she going to?"

"No, because she's an incredibly forgiving person with a huge heart. One you took advantage of."

"I… I didn't mean anything. I was just trying to save up money for my store."

Jake was trying very hard not to give into the kicked puppy look his son was sporting.

"Next time you see Julie, you're going to apologize to her," he said. "And I mean it—this workshop is off-limits to you."

"Fine," Dylan said. He looked like a small, petulant boy instead of the fifteen-year-old he was.

"And you and I are also going to have a conversation with your mother about this."

"What?" Dylan straightened. "You know how she is. She won't let me do woodwork if you do."

"She and I agreed a long time ago that we would always be upfront with each other when it came to you. I don't plan on going back on my word now." Jake nodded toward the door. "You better go do whatever you promised your mom. We'll talk more when I get back."

Dylan's eyes lifted from the floor to stare at his dad's shoulder. "Where are you going?"

"Publicity tour. For the concert. I sent you and your mom a text about it yesterday evening. Didn't you get it?"

"Mom took my phone away yesterday because I didn't do my homework the other night."

Jake looked up at the ceiling, silently praying for patience. "Are you trying to upset her by not putting any effort into school?"

Guilt flurried across Dylan's face. Jake shook his head. "Yeah, you and I are way overdue to have a *long* conversation. Understood?"

Dylan's jaw tightened before nodding. He started to leave, but Jake stopped him.

"I'm changing the security code on the workshop so I know

you'll stay out. I'd ask for your word, but unfortunately, that doesn't mean much right now. You broke a lot of trust here, Dylan."

Dylan didn't look at Jake again as he left, the door shutting softly behind him. Jake moved his head from side to side, trying to relieve the tension he always got from arguing. He headed back to the kitchen to finish making the coffee.

Julie's upstairs, waiting for you.

He wanted to focus on that and get back to the good mood he'd woken up in.

Jake grabbed two mugs and filled them with coffee. He put them on a tray, along with some sugar since he wasn't sure what Julie liked. He didn't have anything nondairy, but he'd change that soon enough. When he returned to his bedroom, she was already awake, sitting up in his bed.

"Hey," she said. "I thought maybe I overslept and missed you."

"I would have woken you before I left." He leaned over and kissed the top of her head before placing the tray to the side of her lap. "How do you like your coffee?"

"Black is fine." She picked up one of the cups. He took the other and sat beside her on the edge of the bed.

"What's with this?" She brushed her finger against the area between his eyebrows. "You have stress lines. Are you regretting last night?"

"What? Never," Jake assured her, pulling her hand away from his face so that he could kiss her palm. "Dylan was just here. I talked to him about what he did. I don't think I've ever been so tough on him in his life."

"I'm sorry," Julie said.

"It is what it is, and he deserved the punishment I gave him. But I sometimes feel like I take two steps forward and ten steps back with that kid."

"He'll forgive you," Julie assured him. A soft smile formed on her lips as she stared at him.

"What?" He ran his hand over his cheek, feeling the stubble. "Oh, I forgot to shave this morning."

"I like it. You look good with a beard," she said before quickly taking a sip of her coffee.

Jake's heart lightened at her admission. He glanced at the small clock on his nightstand and sighed. He didn't want to leave her yet. Despite what had gone down between him and Dylan, Jake finally felt on the right path with Julie. He hoped he wouldn't have to be gone too long.

"I should probably start getting a move on," he said. "I still need to pack."

Julie let out a soft breath. "I should get going, too. I need to go home and change so I can open the store."

She put her coffee cup on the tray and Jake moved it over to the dresser so she could get out of bed. She pushed back the covers, revealing her long legs. Jake tried not to remember how good they felt straddling his thigh as she made her way into the bathroom.

Slamming the rest of his coffee down, he got up from the bed and started gathering some essentials that he was going to need. He didn't have to bring too much with him. Jake had a penthouse in New York and a mansion in Malibu that had clothes for him, but he had some favorite outfits he liked to wear wherever he traveled. He'd just finished folding a pair of sweatpants into his bag when Julie walked out of the bathroom in her clothes.

"So, will I hear from you while you're on the road?" she asked, tucking a piece of loose hair behind her ear.

"Yeah, I'll need to keep you updated on the concert."

"Got it." She smirked. "All business. No play."

"Oh, I can play if you want." He snickered when her face went red. He swaggered up to her and pushed her hair back so he could kiss her jawline and then her neck. Knowing that it was an erogenous zone for her, he found himself becoming obsessed with that particular area of her body. Julie pressed herself against him.

"Miss me while I'm gone," he whispered against her skin.

"I will," she said breathlessly.

Jake stepped back slightly until his lips were inches from hers. She went up on her toes so that their mouths meshed together. He tasted the minty toothpaste she'd used as his tongue swept against hers. Her arms wrapped around his waist. She held him to her before reluctantly letting go.

"I'll let myself out so you can finish packing," she told him. "I'll text you if I get lost in the house."

He grinned. "Just so you know, if you end up near the library, you won't get any reception."

Julie laughed. "Good to know."

"I'll call you when I land."

She took a couple steps back, her eyes not leaving his. With a sad smile, Julie waved goodbye and left.

Jake turned back to his suitcase and stared at it. Things were just starting to happen between him and Julie while his relationship with his son had worsened. He'd felt so optimistic that their relationship was finally on the right track after they'd gone shopping for wood. Now, they were right back at square one.

Jake really didn't want to leave right now.

A horn honked outside and he grabbed his small suitcase and hurried to the waiting chauffeur. The small airport was only a twenty-minute drive from his house. Tyler and James were already in the private plane, sitting opposite each other in cream-colored leather seats when Jake arrived. Lori was down the aisle, talking to someone on her phone. It sounded like she was trying to negotiate an appearance for them on another show. Going by the satisfied expression on her face, she was succeeding. Jake inwardly groaned. How many shows was he going to have to do before he could come home?

"Hey," he said as he settled next to James. Both James and Tyler were on their phones. He nodded at James. "Mason?"

"Mmm-hmm," James said before going back to his phone.

Jake kept his eyes firmly on the aisle. He'd once walked in on his cousin sexting with his husband. He didn't need to accidentally see a picture of Mason's dick again. His eyebrows pulled together as he briefly thought of James's husband. He liked Mason well enough, but sometimes it seemed that James loved his husband more than Mason loved James. But he made James happy and that's all that mattered.

Jake's mind wandered to Julie. He wondered what her thoughts were on the concept of sexting.

Tyler finished texting and put his phone in his pocket. "Hey, man. What's up?"

Jake shrugged as he stretched his legs out into the aisle.

"Any progress with Julie?" Tyler asked.

"We had dinner last night." Jake smiled. "It was really good."

James glanced up from his phone. "Why don't you look happier, then?"

Jake rubbed his hand across his jaw, feeling the stubble. Maybe he'd grow a beard if Julie liked it.

Smiling, he said, "No, things are good between us. I like her. A lot."

"Well, yeah," James said. "That's been pretty obvious for a while."

"So what's bugging you?" Tyler asked, kicking Jake's leg with his shoe.

"It's Dylan." He explained what his son had done.

Tyler whistled once he was finished. "That was ballsy."

"Foolish is more like it," Jake muttered.

"He's got a dream, man. You can't fault him for that."

Tyler folded his hands together and rested them on his diaphragm, looking completely relaxed. "I remember when you were younger, you did some pretty unwise stuff to make your dreams come true."

"Nothing illegal," Jake countered.

"What's Julie have to say about it all?" James asked.

"She was good about it. Great, actually. She really seems to care about Dylan."

James and Tyler grinned at each other.

"What?" Jake asked.

"Oh to be at the beginning stages of love again," James said.

"What! We've only had one date."

"Sometimes that's all it takes," James told him. "That's how it was with me and Mason. I knew I liked him for a while. But it wasn't until we kissed on our first date that I knew I was in love with him."

"Who's in love?" Paul came up the aisle and sat down on the other side of Jake. Zan followed, his laptop in his hand. He sat down opposite Paul, opened his computer, and began typing without a word.

Paul rolled his eyes. "Zan apparently came up with a brilliant idea for a new book. He's been like this the entire ride from Charlevoix. That's why we're late. He's getting as bad as you used to be, Jake."

"Shut up," Zan muttered as he continued to write.

"Gentlemen." The pilot's voice came over the speaker. "Please fasten your seat belts as we prepare for takeoff."

"No love for ladies on board," Lori muttered as she came up the aisle and sat next to Zan before buckling her seat belt. "Well, boys. You'll be happy to know that I got you on *The Night Show with Jaxon Hall*."

"Nice," Paul said. "You can't ask for a bigger stage to announce a comeback than that."

"I know," Lori said, looking pleased with herself.

"How many shows did you book?" Jake asked.

"Holiday Boys reuniting is huge news, Jake." He barely stopped himself from rolling his eyes, because obviously it was big news. She continued, "I've booked as many appearances as I could. We've got a charity concert to promote, thanks to you, and an opportunity to create buzz for the new album. Once you announce your reunion, everybody is going to be clamoring for the chance to interview you." Lori pulled up her phone. "Now, shall we go over your itinerary once we land?"

Zan shut his computer. "Might as well. Just tell me we have *some* free time during the week. I need to finish outlining my story."

They began to talk as the plane sped down the runway. As it lifted into the air, Jake found his mind going back to what James and Tyler had said about the beginning stages of love.

He wasn't in love with Julie. At least…he didn't think he was.

Did he already miss her?

Yes.

Was he prepared to tell every talk show host and interviewer that he was off the market because he found the woman of his dreams?

Definitely.

Did something inside him ache because he wouldn't see her for a few weeks, wouldn't be able to hold her in his arms?

Absolutely.

But love?

Jake rested his head against his seat and closed his eyes. Yeah…maybe.

Chapter Seventeen

Julie hummed as she opened her store later that morning. For the first time in a long time, she felt hopeful. She wasn't kidding when she told Jake there was already a buzz around town regarding the charity concert. Julie had stopped by the Bridal Barn on her way to her shop to cancel her bridesmaid dress, and it was all Jessica could talk about. Julie didn't think it was appropriate to act excited, especially since she was there for such a somber reason, so she pretended she didn't know anything about it.

Julie couldn't wait for everyone in town to find out that the concert was actually a Holiday Boys reunion concert.

The bell above the shop's door rang around noon. Meg walked in wearing a frumpy T-shirt and leggings. Her eyes were red and puffy.

Julie hurried over to her. "Meg, what happened?"

"Clarice stopped by my apartment," she replied, wiping at an errant tear that streaked down her cheek.

Julie put her arm around Meg's shoulder. "What'd she want?"

"She wanted me to give back my engagement ring. No, she demanded it. She said it was a family heirloom, though I know that's a lie. Lucas bought it on a business trip last year."

"Meg, I'm so sorry," Julie said. "What'd you do?"

Meg laughed, the sound slightly hysterical. "You know how my apartment overlooks the bay?"

Julie's mouth dropped open. "You didn't."

"I did. I ran outside and threw it as far into the water as I could."

"What did Clarice do?"

"She started to rant about how she always knew I was unfit for her son, that she was glad he called it off before I could ruin his life."

"I swear, Meg, if I ever see that woman again…"

"I don't think she'll be bothering me anymore. Especially when I told her exactly what I thought of her. We're talking eighteen years of holding back on what a poisonous bitch she is."

Pride burst inside Julie. "Did you really?"

"Yep," Meg said. She grinned miserably before she let out a quiet sob. "I guess things between Lucas and me are well and truly over. He'll never forgive me when Clarice tells him what I said today."

"Meg, you deserve better than him. You need a man who will walk through hell and back for you."

Meg hiccupped as she tried to catch her breath. "Well, next time Prince Charming shows up in town, send him my way, will you?"

Julie pushed back a wet strand of her friend's golden-brown hair that was sticking to her cheek. "I promise. And I'm so sorry you're going through this. I know it's not going to get any easier anytime soon, but it *will* get better."

"You're suddenly an expert in love?" Meg said, nudging Julie in the side with a slight smile.

"Maybe," Julie replied, trying to be evasive.

Meg peered at Julie intently. "Did something happen between you and Jake?"

Julie shook her head. "We can talk about that some other time."

Meg's eyes widened. "Um, no. If something happened between you and Jake, I need all the juicy details."

"Come on. You're upset."

"This will cheer me up. I promise."

"Well…"

Julie told Meg about her date with Jake and how she'd spent the night in his arms.

Meg sighed when Julie finished, her tone sappy. "I guess Prince Charming already came to Holiday Bay."

"I'm pretty sure Prince Charming has an equally charming best friend, who grew up next door to you."

"Who? Tyler?" Meg sounded bitter. "He's dating some supermodel out in California. He wouldn't want the girl next door who annoyed the crap out of him when we were kids. Besides, as far as I'm concerned, I'm done with relationships." Her expression grew fierce when she saw the brief disbelief on Julie's face. "I'm serious. I'm done with all of it. No more dating or falling in love. I spent half my life in a relationship with Lucas. I'm a free bird now, and I'm going to spread my wings. Nothing but one-night stands in my future and—"

Julie grabbed Meg and hugged her again.

"It's okay," Julie murmured as Meg's hysteria turned into frantic tears. "You're going to be okay. You're so much stronger than you know."

Meg scoffed but didn't argue with Julie. She pulled away and rubbed at her face. "I must look a mess."

"It's just me here. No one to judge you."

"But what if a customer walks in?"

Julie shook her head. "What are the odds that a customer will walk in right now? It's always slow this time of day." She motioned to the back of the store. "Why don't you use the bathroom to wash your face, and then I'll drive you home."

Meg sniffed but nodded. She walked down an aisle and disappeared from Julie's view. A few seconds later, she heard the bathroom door quietly close. Julie went to grab her car keys and purse when Dylan walked into her shop.

His eyes looked red, as if he'd also been crying. Julie's shoulder sagged. It seemed to be the morning for it.

"Dylan, hi."

"Ms. A., I—"

"Dylan, I think at this point, you might as well call me Julie."

Dylan wiped at his nose with his sleeve. "I wanted to say I'm sorry. I shouldn't have lied to you and told you my dad was the one creating those woodwork projects."

Julie contemplated how to handle this. She finally asked, "Why did you, out of curiosity?"

"I want to open a shop of my own someday. A place where I can sell my stuff. My mom is completely against the idea. She wants me to go to law school. Any money I save, she puts in a college fund. I don't want to go to college, though. I want a place like yours."

Julie smiled sadly. Places like hers were dying. If it wasn't for the concert, Julie would've had to declare bankruptcy soon or go crawling to Farmington. But she hoped Dylan would succeed someday. He was talented, and despite not being happy with him, she hated how miserable he looked.

"Dylan, I'm sure if you asked your dad, he'd loan you the money to open a store."

Dylan started shaking his head before she even finished. "No. I… I don't want anything to do with my dad's money."

The way he said it so vehemently took her by surprise. "Why? Your dad would do anything for you. I know if you—"

"I don't want his money. Not ever."

"Okay," she said in a soothing voice when she saw he was getting upset.

"He…that's all he thinks about."

"What?" Julie stared at Dylan in confusion.

"He was never around when I was growing up because he

always had to do another record, another show. All he cares about is making money."

"That's what you think?" Julie whispered.

"That's what I know. All he cares about is being successful."

"That's not true," Julie said gently. "He's an incredibly caring man. For example, I know that he doesn't have the best memories of Holiday Bay—"

Dylan's eyes widened. "He told you about that?"

"Yes, he did. And yet, he's still willing to help—to use his success—to look out for people here. I mean, he talked Holiday Boys into doing a reunion concert here, of all places, when arenas in bigger cities would be a much more suitable venue. And I know with absolute certainty that he loves you, and he'd give you the world if you let him."

"You know for certain," Dylan said sarcastically, as if he didn't care what the answer was, though she knew he did. Very much.

"Yes, I'm certain. I can tell how much he loves you by how he talks about you and how proud he is of you." Julie straightened her shoulders. "Now, then. What are we going to do about our business arrangement?"

"I didn't think we had one anymore," Dylan grumbled.

"I'll tell you what. If you can get *both* of your parents to cosign on your vendor agreement, you can continue to sell items here."

Dylan's head shot up. "Are you serious?"

"Of course," she said before she added in a joking tone, "You're one of my most popular vendors. It's purely for business reasons on my end." She leaned against the store's counter, her face turning serious. "I know what it's like. To start a business and be willing to do whatever it takes to succeed. But you have to do things the right way. If you lie to me again, then I'll terminate our contract permanently."

Dylan nodded. He turned to leave but looked back at her. "For what it's worth, I don't hate the idea...you dating my dad, I mean."

She bit her lip to keep from grinning. "Thanks. I appreciate it."

After he left, Julie let out a tired sigh. What a day it was turning into.

"Did you just say Holiday Boys is doing a reunion concert here?"

Julie swung around to see Meg practically bouncing on her feet.

Oops.

After a long day at the shop, which included keeping Meg from freaking out while also making her promise to keep the news about Holiday Boys a secret, Julie finally collapsed on her couch, kicking her shoes off so she could put her tired feet up.

She was about to turn on the TV when her phone rang. Her tiredness disappeared when she saw Jake's name on her screen.

"Hi," she said.

"Hi, yourself," Jake said.

"Did you just get in?"

"No, sorry. I meant to text you earlier, but we pretty much went straight from the airport to a meeting with our new record label. I've been in meetings all day."

"No worries," Julie said. "I'm glad you made it safely."

"Do you think if you get a chance, you'll be able to watch *America, Good Morning* tomorrow?"

"I can, yes."

"We're going to be making the announcement. Be prepared. They'll probably mention the video."

Julie put her palm over her face. "That thing is going to haunt me until I die."

Jake let out a deep chuckle. "I can't say I regret that you made it."

"Me either," Julie said. She cleared her throat. "Dylan stopped by the shop today."

"Oh? How'd that go?"

"He apologized for what he did."

"Good, I'm glad."

Julie hesitated. "I told him he could sell his projects in my shop if you and his mom both cosign on a new contract for him."

Jake let out a breath. "That's really generous of you."

She shrugged, even though he couldn't see it. "I get where he's coming from, even if I don't approve of how he went about it. He wants to follow his dream, and he's got the talent to back it up. He reminds me of you in a lot of ways."

"He has talent I'll never have," Jake said.

"He's got your drive. Despite his recent bad choices, he's going to be okay. If he puts his mind to it, I think he'll be successful in whatever he wants to do."

Jake was so silent that Julie had to check her phone to see if he'd hung up.

"You there?" she finally asked.

"Yeah. I wish I was with you right now."

Julie smiled, her grip on her phone tightening. "I wish you were here, too."

"Soon, okay?"

"Yeah."

"And if you have any issues tomorrow with people bothering you or reporters, send me a text and I'll have my publicist handle it."

"Thanks, Jake. We'll see how it goes tomorrow, okay?"

"All right. Well, I should probably let you go. I need to get some sleep."

"Good night."

"Good night."

He hung up and Julie put her phone on the couch, her stomach twisting with apprehension.

She hoped the band's reunion announcement went well, though she didn't look forward to being in the spotlight again.

Julie pulled her knees up to her chest and rested her chin on them.

She stayed like that for a long time.

Chapter Eighteen

Julie paced in front of Meg's TV. *America, Good Morning*'s hosts had announced they had some very special guests before they'd gone to commercial break, and the anticipation was making her antsy.

"You're making me nervous just watching you," Meg said. "Sit down already."

Julie flopped down on Meg's couch. Her leg started bouncing up and down.

"Hey, it'll be fine," Meg said. "Jake isn't going to throw you to the wolves. His publicist already contacted you this morning about what to say if the press showed up, right?"

"Yeah," Julie said. "And it'll be good for the store. That's what I keep trying to remember."

"You've got this," Meg assured her right as the hosts came back on TV.

The female host, Gretchen, had platinum blond hair that looked like it was permanently windblown. She wore a violet silk blouse and pencil skirt that went down to her knees. Her cohost, Darryl, was a man in his late fifties with dyed black hair and a blinding white smile,

"And now," Gretchen said. "The moment we've all been waiting for. Ladies and gentleman, I am beyond excited to introduce you to our next guests. You might be more aware of their individual success stories, but twenty years ago, this band was *the* hottest group to ever hit the airwaves. Let's give a warm welcome to the… Holiday Boys."

The crowd outside the studio window went crazy as all five band members appeared on the soundstage.

"Gentlemen, it's wonderful to have you here," Gretchen said.

"It's good to be here," Paul replied.

"This is a huge treat for me," Gretchen told the camera before smiling at the men. "I was a big fan of yours when I was a teen. Your posters covered every inch of my bedroom walls."

"And who was your favorite?" Darryl asked, flashing his white smile at the camera.

"Well…" Gretchen gave the band a side-look. "I have to confess that I had more pictures of Jake on the wall."

Meg rolled her eyes. "Of course she did."

"And what brings you all together today?" Darryl asked.

"Well," James said. "After a lot of discussion, we've decided to do a reunion album."

The crowd outside, who could hear everything over the outdoor speakers, went crazy.

"In fact," Jake said. "We'll be doing a charity concert next month in Holiday Bay, Michigan, with proceeds going to small businesses in the area."

"Holiday Bay," Gretchen said. "That's where you're originally from, and the origin of your band name, correct?"

"Paul and I grew up in the neighboring town," Zan explained. "But the five of us met at a singing competition in Holiday Bay, so we all have a lot of appreciation for our namesake."

"Does this have anything to do with a video made by Julie Alleen a few weeks ago?" Gretchen asked. Julie's video popped up on a large screen behind them. Julie moaned, covering her face.

"Julie went to school with us," Tyler said. "When we found

out small businesses in our hometown were struggling due to outside influences, we wanted to do what we could to help Holiday Bay get back on track. It's an incredible place with a lot of heart, and if anyone gets a chance, they should visit. There's a lot to do. Aside from the amazing shops and businesses, there's swimming in the bay in the summer and ice fishing in the winter."

"If you're doing a color tour along Michigan's coast," James added, "the bay is incredible during this time of year with the changing leaves. It's worth stopping by and saying hi."

Gretchen narrowed her eyes slightly on Jake. "Speaking of Julie, would you care to comment on Julake, the ship name your fans gave you two?"

Jake gave what Julie knew was his professional smile. "It's very clever."

When he didn't expand, Gretchen opened her mouth to ask him another question, but James interceded.

"One hundred percent of the proceeds from the concert will go to the Holiday Bay Small Business Association. Each small business owner will receive a portion for their store. We'll also be adding a donation link on our website to anyone who wants to help a small town get back on their feet."

Jake looked at the camera and smiled. It felt like he was staring right at Julie. "Holiday Boys will also be donating ten million dollars to get the ball rolling."

Her mouth dropped open as the rest of the segment started to wrap up.

Meg shook her arm. "Did he just say ten million? And that's not even including the rest of whatever money they raise. Julie, you and the rest of the town won't have to worry about money for years."

"I… I can't believe it."

She didn't hear the rest of what anyone said on the show before it went to commercial again. Her phone started buzzing.

Julie glanced at it blankly before unlocking her home screen. The different members of the town's business association were messaging each other in their group chat, asking if others had seen the announcement.

Julie opened a new text and messaged Jake. Are you serious?

In less than a minute, he replied. Absolutely.

Julie's eyes teared up as sweet relief washed over her. She would finally be able to stop worrying about her finances. She was going to be able to invest in her store like she'd always wanted. She would have the resources to build a stronger online presence in addition to a local one. Maybe she would even earn enough extra income that she could put more money toward her mom's care. Just as importantly, other stores could stay in business if they chose to. And Julie knew most of them did. These stores symbolized the dreams of so many families in Holiday Bay.

Jake and his bandmates just saved their town.

Julie walked into her mom's apartment the next Monday, feeling lighter than she had in a long time.

Her mom looked at her and smiled. "Julie!"

Julie's heart warmed at her mom's instant recognition. She'd had two plans in mind for hanging out with her mom that day. Depending how she reacted when she saw Julie, they would either stay at her mom's apartment, or she'd check her mom out of Red Oaks so they could spend the day at Julie's house. It looked like they were going with plan B.

"Hi, Mom." Julie kissed her mom's cheek. "What would you say about getting out of here for a bit? I thought I could make us lunch at my place."

"That would be lovely."

Julie helped her mom into her coat—she was always cold these days, no matter the temperature—and they walked out to Julie's car. As they drove down the road, Julie half expected her mom to start talking her ear off like she normally did whenever she was having a good day. Instead, she sat silently in the passenger seat.

"Everything okay?" Julie asked. "You're awfully quiet over there."

"My got up and go, has got up and went," her mom replied. Julie's lips quirked upward. How many times had she heard that expression growing up?

"If you're not up to it, I can take you back," Julie offered. Her mom didn't say anything, so Julie said, "Mom?"

When her mom continued to sit in silence, Julie glanced at her. What she saw made her heart fly up her throat. Her mom's eyes were pointed toward the ceiling, her mouth hanging over. Her skin was ashen and clammy looking.

"MOM!" Julie yelled. She took her foot off the gas pedal, unsure what to do. She frantically repeated, "Mom!"

Her mom rolled her head toward her and Julie's skin crawled with fear. It was like looking into the face of a zombie.

"Whhhass," Her mom replied, her speech slurred.

Julie knew the signs of a stroke. Her grandma had ministrokes for several months before her death.

Julie slammed her foot on the gas and sped the car as fast as she could to Clarington, which had the closest medical facility.

It took twenty painful minutes to get there, Julie pleading with her mom the entire time.

"Mom, stay with me. I'm going to get you to the doctor."

"I don't need a doctor," her mom said as the medical facility came into view. Her voice was slow and weak but she was no longer slurring.

Julie turned into the emergency room entrance, her tires squealing. She threw the car into Park and flung the door open, not bothering to shut it. Running into the entrance, she found a woman in scrubs walking by.

"Please help me. I think my mom just had a stroke."

The nurse calmly signaled for someone behind the desk to send assistance. She went out to the car and opened the passenger door. Julie's mom was slumped in her seat, her breathing uneven. "Can you tell me your name?" the nurse asked as she removed the stethoscope from around her neck.

"F-Fran," her mom answered.

"And how old are you?"

Her mom didn't answer so Julie said in a shaken voice, "She has Alzheimer's." Even on a good day, her mom couldn't answer that question.

An orderly came out with a wheelchair. They got Julie's mom into it and rolled her into one of the exam rooms that had curtains for walls. After helping her mom onto the hospital bed, the nurse immediately hooked her up to a vital signs monitor. She left them, and a pretty woman about Jake's age entered. She wore a lab coat and had a stethoscope around her neck.

"Hello, Jane. I'm Dr. Rodriguez," she said as she walked over to the computer in the corner and pulled up the patient information. "Can you tell me how you're feeling?"

"Okay...tired," her mom replied. Her face still had that sickly pallor to it.

"And who is this?" the doctor asked, pointing to Julie.

Julie held her breath as her mom looked at her with a frown. She finally said, "Daughter."

Julie breathed a sigh of relief. Her mom didn't say Julie's name, but at least she recognized her on some level.

"Can you tell me what happened?" the doctor asked Julie.

Julie went over what took place in the car. The doctor took notes on the computer before going over to her mother and giving her an exam.

Dr. Rodriguez gave a nod when she was done. "I'd like to monitor her blood pressure for a few hours. I'm also going to order a CT scan." When Julie looked worried, the doctor gave her a reassuring smile. "It's just a precaution. It's encouraging that Jane is alert and speaking clearly, but with her Alzheimer's, it does put her at a higher risk for further brain issues. Let's see what the test results say and then we can go from there."

Julie nodded. "Thanks."

She sat with her mom for the next two hours, the heart monitor going off whenever the blood pressure device gave a reading it didn't like. Julie bit her lip as she took in the numbers, which read 154/98. That was too high.

"What is that noise?" her mom said as the machine went off again, her hands moving restlessly over the hospital blanket.

"Your blood pressure is high. The machine is letting the doctor know what your status is," Julie explained.

Her mom was silent for a few minutes as the chime continued to go off. Her tone was agitated as she repeated, "What is that noise?"

Julie took a deep breath. "It's alerting the doctors that your blood pressure is too high."

They had the same conversation on repeat for the next half hour until a nurse came in and quieted the machine.

The same orderly from earlier followed. He gave Julie and her mom a smile. "I'm here to take you for your CT scan, Mrs. Alleen."

"Will it take long?" Julie asked.

"Not too bad. We should be back in about forty-five minutes," he said. He pressed some levers on the hospital bed to release the brakes, and pushed her mom out of the room.

As Julie waited, she pulled out her phone. She saw that she had a couple of missed messages from Jake. Though she desperately wanted to talk to him, she called Veronica first. When Veronica answered after a few rings, Julie explained what had happened.

"Are you going to come see her?" Julie asked.

"I really can't take the time off work right now. Let's see how serious it is first," Veronica replied. Julie barely kept her temper in check. Their mom was in the hospital from a potential stroke, and Veronica still hesitated to come into town and help.

"Fine, I'll keep you posted," Julie snapped before ending the call. She called Jake next.

"Hey," she said.

"Hi," Jake replied, the sound of his voice lifting her spirits. "I was afraid I missed you today. I tried getting a hold of you earlier."

"Sorry about that," Julie said. She went on to explain what had happened with her mom.

"I'm so sorry, Julie," he said once she finished. "Is there anything I can do?"

"No, I'm just really glad to hear from you." Julie leaned back in her chair, exhaustion taking over. "Where are you right now?"

"About to board a plane to California. We're booked to appear on some talk show tomorrow morning. I don't even remember which one at this point."

"Have safe travels, okay?"

"Thanks."

The orderly came back into the room, pushing her mom's bed back into place.

"Listen, I have to go," Julie said.

"Keep me updated."

"I will." She disconnected the call. She asked the orderly anxiously, "Will we have the results soon?"

"It might be another couple of hours. Some people from a car accident just came in, and Dr. Rodriguez is assisting with them."

Julie nodded. She watched the orderly hook her mom back

up to her vital signs monitor. After he left, Julie held her mom's hand while she told her all about the charity concert. Ten minutes into her story, the machine started beeping again.

"What is that noise?" her mom asked.

Julie sighed. It was going to be a long day.

Julie could barely keep her eyes open. It was well past 2:00 a.m. They had taken her mom into a private room and asked Julie to go to the waiting room until they had her mom situated.

As she stared blurrily at the Scrabble puzzle on her phone, someone sat beside her. Looking over, she was stunned to see Jake smiling back at her.

"Wh…what are you doing here?" she asked.

"I took a detour from California." He wrapped his arm around her shoulders and kissed her temple. Julie leaned against him, resting her head against his collarbone. She breathed in his cologne, comforted by his reassuring heat.

"Won't you miss your show?" she asked.

"I own a private jet," he said before adding hesitantly, "I can only be here a few hours and then I need to head out again." He rubbed his head against her forehead and she smiled, despite the stress of the day. His whiskers scratched her skin. He was growing a beard again.

"Any word on your mom?" he asked.

"They're moving her to a private room. I'm still waiting to hear the results of her CT scan," she said just as Dr. Rodriguez entered the room. The woman paused when she saw Jake, her eyes momentarily going wide before her face shifted back to something more professional.

"I wanted to give you an update before my shift ended for the night," the doctor said.

Julie jumped to her feet. Jake followed more slowly. He wrapped an arm around her waist, giving it a reassuring squeeze.

"I believe your mom had a transient ischemic attack, or what we call a TIA. Think of it as a mock stroke."

"So…she's okay?" Julie asked.

"We'll want to change some things in her medication regimen. I'm going to send her primary doctor my notes along with the recommendation that we up the dosage of her current blood pressure medicine. For now, we're giving her something here to get that blood pressure under control. I also want to run a few more tests to confirm the diagnosis."

"She'll be okay though, right?" Julie's hand drifted to where Jake's rested on her waist and gripped his fingers.

Dr. Rodriguez hesitated before saying, "I want to keep her here for observation for a couple more days, but she can go home after that. That's not to say she's a hundred percent in the clear. We typically view TIAs as a warning sign for an impending stroke. The important thing we need to focus on right now is keeping her calm and getting that blood pressure down."

Julie's stomach knotted. *An impending stroke?* She tried not to let her concern show as she said, "Thank you for the update."

The doctor gave Julie a small, reassuring smile. "There's really nothing more you can do tonight. Why don't you go home and get some rest."

Julie nodded and the doctor turned to leave. She paused before saying to Jake, "My daughter is a big fan of yours."

"I appreciate the support," Jake said, and the doctor left.

Julie started to yawn. "I guess I should head home."

"I had a taxi drop me off here, so why don't I drive you home in your car? I don't think you should be driving tonight."

"I can drive," Julie argued, right before she yawned again.

"I'm not going to take the risk of you falling asleep behind the wheel." Jake tugged on her hand and she meekly followed.

As they began the drive back to Julie's house, she drifted

off to sleep. She jolted awake when Jake pulled into her driveway. A taxi was already there, waiting to take Jake away from her again.

"And he's off again," she said, trying to keep the sadness out of her voice.

He cupped her cheek and turned her head toward him. Leaning over, he brushed his lips once...twice against hers before pulling back.

"If you need anything, anything at all, you call me, okay?"

"I will," Julie said. "Thank you for being here for me tonight."

"I'll be here anytime you need me."

He bent his head and kissed the base of her neck and then he was out of the car. He got into the taxi and the driver started the engine. Julie watched it go until it disappeared into the darkness.

Chapter Nineteen

Jake walked out of the LA store, his gift for Julie gripped tightly in his hand. He was probably smiling like an idiot, but he didn't care. He couldn't wait to give her his present. He could just imagine the expression on her face. At least, he hoped she would enjoy it as much as he thought she would. She deserved it, especially after the week she'd had. Thankfully, her mom had been released from the hospital a few days ago and was back at her assisted-living facility.

As Jake made his way to the studio where they were doing another TV show, his phone dinged, notifying him that he had a text. He'd messaged Julie earlier that morning, complaining that he'd walked in on James sexting his husband—*again*—but he never got a response from her. He was slightly worried that he might have offended her.

Grabbing his phone, he saw that the text was from Julie. He opened it and almost tripped over his own feet as he read what she'd wrote.

I want you inside me.

Jake read it twice to make sure he hadn't misread her words. He could very clearly picture himself inside her. He quickly looked away from the phone, trying to force his mind elsewhere before he popped a boner in the middle of the street.

He put the package he carried under his right arm and started typing, I'm out in public, as much as I appreciate this.

Take me to bed or lose me forever.

Jake paused. Wait. He was pretty sure that was from a movie. Are you quoting Top Gun?

I want you to paint me like one of your French girls.

Jake burst out laughing. That was definitely from *Titanic*. Cute. What was the first quote from?

Ghostbusters. What? No good? :)

I love you was what he wanted to write. He sucked in a breath, realizing that it was true. Holy shit, he'd fallen in love with Julie Alleen. Maybe a part of him had been in love with her since he saw her that day in the high school hallway. Forcing himself to focus, he wrote, They're perfect. Just like you.

...Is that something you'd want to do? Sexting?

Jake paused, unsure how to answer. He finally typed, I'm open to whatever you want to try—whatever you're comfortable with.

I'll think about.

His face was soft and unguarded as he stared at her response. So when someone grabbed his arm and kissed his cheek, he didn't react fast enough. Camera flashes went off, blinding him briefly. When his vision cleared, he saw Lori hanging on him.

He jerked his arm away. "Are you stalking me?"

She raised an eyebrow at him. "We're outside of the TV

studio. And I wanted to say hello to my favorite Holiday Boy."
She smiled brightly at the paparazzi standing nearby.

He wanted to yell at her to leave him alone, that he was
taken. But the idea of starting an argument in public left him
cold. Gritting his teeth, he opened the door to the building and
went inside, not bothering to see if she followed him.

"Jake," Lori called out.

"I've got nothing to say to you." He continued to walk.

"Do you know what today is?" she asked, trailing behind
him.

"Don't really care," he responded.

"Daddy died eighteen years ago today."

That got Jake to stop walking. He closed his eyes briefly,
feeling sick that he'd forgotten it was the anniversary of Big
Poppa's passing. Old grief washed over him.

"I'm sorry, Lori," he said.

She caught up to him and leaned against the wall beside
him. "He was always so proud of you. You know that, right?"

"I do."

"From the moment he met you, he told me, 'Keep an eye
on that boy, he'll be a star someday.' And he was right. He always had an eye for real talent."

Jake didn't know what to say to that. He was still pissed
at that little stunt she'd pulled outside, but he didn't doubt the
sincerity in her voice as she spoke about her father.

"I should get ready for the show," he finally said.

"Wait." Lori straightened from the wall. "I've been wanting to talk to you."

Jake's guard instantly went up. "About what?"

"I want you to let me represent you full-time, both with the
Holiday Boys as well as your solo career."

"Rick Morgan handles my solo career," Jake said.

Something twisted on Lori's face before it smoothed back

to normal. "Rick has enough clients. I can give you that one-on-one attention that you deserve."

And if that didn't scare Jake, he didn't know what would. "I'm happy with Rick."

Lori went ridged at his continued rejection. "Do you know what it's like to be a woman in this business? Do you have any clue how hard it is to break in with good ol' boys who run this industry?"

"You've done just fine on your own."

"Because I'm the daughter of Phil 'Big Poppa' Cummings. Just ask any of those sexist jerks and they'll say I wouldn't have even got my foot in the door if I wasn't a Cummings. They've shown me zero respect despite me helping Holiday Boys become the success that you are."

"I'm sorry. I really am." And for a second, Jake actually meant it. Then he remembered how many times Lori touched him without his consent. "I've got to go."

As he walked away from her, she said, "You know this is what my dad wanted."

He didn't turn back to acknowledge what she said, even as the guilt gnawed at him.

Julie walked to her store a week later, feeling happier than she could ever remember being.

When she wasn't attempting the art of sexting by sending Jake over-the-top lines from movies, they would speak on the phone for hours. She would tell him how excited people in town were for the concert, and that they were already seeing an uptick of tourists in town. They spoke about whatever random topic popped in their heads. Julie began to look forward to their calls, and was always sad when they ended.

She was counting the minutes until Jake came home.

As she turned the corner toward her shop, she saw a familiar Mercedes-Benz parked outside Kyleigh's Knits. Her stomach lurched when she realized it was Harris Farmington's car. The billionaire stepped out of the knit shop moments later, his face furious. He didn't notice Julie as he slid into his back seat and slammed the door. Once the car was out of sight, Julie ran across the street.

Kyleigh stood behind her counter, an absent smile on her face as she worked on her laptop.

"Did you…?" Julie started to ask, too afraid to hope.

Kyleigh looked at her and smiled. "I told him to take his offer and shove it."

Julie's shoulders dropped in relief. "Oh, thank goodness."

"You'll be happy to know that several other shop owners told him the same thing. It sounds like Farmington will have to look elsewhere for his new distribution center." Kyleigh walked over to Julie and hugged her. "Thank you."

"I didn't do anything," Julie said, a blush forming on her face.

"If you hadn't made your video, this never would have happened."

"Oh, that…"

"I can't believe Holiday Boys are going to be here in little over a week," Kyleigh said. "Did I ever tell you I dated Paul in high school?" When Julie shook her head in surprise, Kyleigh continued. "We went to the same performing arts camp during the summer. I thought it was love at first sight, but what did I know, I was just a kid. We broke up right after Holiday Boys got signed." She made a *pfft* noise, but there was sadness in her voice. Julie reached out and gave her hand a reassuring squeeze. Kyleigh gave a look of *What can you do?*

"I almost wish I could go to the concert, though," she added. "Despite Paul, I do enjoy the Holiday Boys' music, but I'm hosting a booth. What about you?"

"Same."

"And it's not like you won't see Jake another time." Kyleigh gave her a knowing look.

"What do you mean?" Julie did her best to look innocent.

"Oh, please." Kyleigh gleamed. "I've seen Jake Reynolds go in and out of your shop multiple times over the past month."

"You didn't tell anyone?" Julie asked. She wasn't too surprised that people saw Jake around town. She was surprised he never got swarmed by fans whenever he stepped outside, other than the occasional person or two. His publicist was good, but she couldn't believe the woman was *that* good.

Kyleigh lifted a shoulder. "It was none of my business. Besides, he's from Holiday Bay. We protect our own."

Julie's heart warmed. Jake might have mixed feelings about the town, but they still considered him part of their community. She and Kyleigh discussed the upcoming concert a little more before Julie headed back to her store.

A woman leaned against the front window. She had brown hair pulled into a tight bun on top of her head and large hazel eyes. She looked familiar, though Julie was sure she had never met her before.

The woman straightened when she saw her, and Julie tensed. Was she a reporter? She had received a few phone calls from reporters after the *America, Good Morning* show, but thankfully, Jake's publicist had taken care of that.

"Are you Julie Alleen?" the woman asked.

Julie pulled her keys out of her jacket pocket and quickly found the one for the store. She unlocked the door before answering.

"I am. What can I help you with?"

"I want you to leave my son alone, for starters."

Julie's forehead wrinkled. "Your son?"

"Dylan Reynolds."

Julie took a second to examine Dylan's mom. He had inherited her eyes and mouth, but otherwise, he was his father's son.

"You're Angelika?" Julie said, and Angelika nodded.

"Won't you come in?" Julie asked. She stepped inside and Angelika followed.

The other woman looked around the shop, her eyes landing on Jake's poster, which still had the lights around it. Her mouth turned down in disgust.

"Dylan told me that you're dating Jake," Angelika said, her eyes swinging back to Julie.

Julie lifted her chin. "I am."

"Is that why you let Dylan sell his stuff in your store? As a way to get to Jake?"

Julie flinched at the accusation. "I didn't know they were related when Dylan first started bringing his work in here to sell. I assume he told you I wasn't aware he was the one making the projects."

"Then you'll have no problem telling him he can't continue."

"I told him he could if he received both your permission and Jake's."

"Well, he doesn't have mine," Angelika snapped. "I'm not going to let Dylan turn into his father. Obsessed with following a dream."

"But… Jake is a success. He made his dream happen."

Angelika glared at her. "You don't have a damn clue what that dream cost my family, so don't speak about things you don't know."

Julie kept quiet. Jake's relationship with his ex was none of her business. She held her hands up passively. "Let me show you something."

She hurried to the back storage room where she had moved the Craftsman nightstand Dylan had made. She planned to give it back to him if he couldn't get permission to continue selling his work.

Julie carried the table to the front of the store and placed it in front of Angelika. "It's beautiful, isn't it?"

"Yeah, so?"

"Dylan made it."

Angelika's eyes widened before she looked over the table. Her face lost some of its severity when she said, "He made this?"

"Yes." Julie ran a finger over the smooth surface. "Dylan has such amazing talent. It's not some pipe dream. He could make a living from this."

Angelika glanced at Julie. "You must really want to impress Jake."

Julie raised her chin. "It has nothing to do with him. Your son has talent. That should be embraced, not shamed."

The other woman's tense shoulders relaxed, but only a little. "I don't want him to turn into his father."

"There's nothing wrong with Jake," Julie said defensively. "He's one of the kindest, most generous people I've ever met. Dylan would be lucky to take after him. He already does in so many ways."

Angelika stared at her before she shook her head sadly. "You're in love with Jake."

Julie froze. "I… I'm…"

"Do yourself a favor before you get in any deeper. Google his dating history. Jake's the kind of guy who has a woman in every city, and when he can't find someone, he has his manager, Lori." Angelika pulled out her phone and tapped on an app. A picture of Jake appeared, with Lori kissing his cheek. Julie couldn't look away from the expression on Jake's face. He looked like he was in love. "This was taken last week. They've been having an affair for years. He wasn't faithful a day in our marriage. He won't be faithful to you. Guys like Jake can't change. Not when they enjoy sex as much as he does."

Without another word, Angelika left the store, not realizing how damaging her words were. She'd just ripped the Band-Aid off Julie's biggest fear, something she'd tried her damnedest to suppress since she had told Jake she'd give them a chance.

Julie went into the bathroom and splashed cold water over her face. When she looked up and glimpsed her reflection, she saw how pale she was.

Angelika's words rang in her ears like a broken record that wouldn't stop.

Guys like Jake can't change.

Not when they enjoy sex as much as he does.

Julie remembered how quickly he had reacted to her when she'd pressed herself against him. He said he was a faithful guy, but could he *truly* stay happy with her? Especially if he craved sex as much as his former wife said. And wouldn't she know? They were married for years.

It wasn't as if Jake had ever told Julie he loved her. How could she expect him to be faithful when he knew she was ace? She laughed somewhat hysterically. Had she really thought he'd be satisfied with a few naked pictures of her? How naive was she?

Julie took a shaky breath in through the nose and out through the mouth in an attempt to calm herself. It didn't work.

She closed her eyes, but could still see the picture of Lori and Jake, how happy he looked with his manager's lips plastered against his cheek. And it was taken a week ago. Right after he'd come to see Julie when her mom was in the hospital. Around the same time she'd sent him her first naked picture. Bitter tears stung her eyes as her cheeks heated with humiliation. She really was stupid to think he cared for her like she cared for him.

Julie grabbed a paper towel with trembling hands and patted her face before heading back to the front of the store. She moved Dylan's table back in the storage room. After taking a calming breath, she went back to the front and sat behind her counter.

Her laptop was next to her, the screen black. Her fingers twisted together before she moved one hand to the keyboard.

Her index finger hovered over the power button. She really didn't need to look up Jake's dating history. He had told her he'd slept around.

But had he slept around while he was married, like Angelika claimed?

A couple of tourists stopped in, pulling her from the temptation to start googling Jake.

She forced a smile to her lips. "Welcome."

"Hi," the man said. He looked annoyed as he carried several large, heavy-looking bags in his arms.

"This is such a cute store," the woman said as she picked up a porcelain flower. She turned and saw Jake's poster on the wall before swinging back to Julie.

"You're the woman who made that video."

Julie cringed. "That would be me."

"I would die if I was that close to Jake Reynolds."

"Honey, I'm standing right here," the man said.

The woman patted the man on his cheek. She walked over to the stand that held the different Holiday Boys merchandise. She picked up a knit hat and brought it over to the counter for purchase.

"How exciting that he came here, huh?"

"Yes, I was very lucky," Julie said, a pained smile on her face.

After they left, Julie found herself staring at her laptop again.

Against her better judgement, she opened up the internet and googled Jake's dating history. Before she knew it, several hours had passed, and she was sick to her stomach.

No matter how kind the articles were regarding Jake's professional life, article after article laid out his love life in explicit detail. The amount of women he'd allegedly slept with was staggering. And between all the women in his life, there was Lori, the woman he'd been having an affair with for years, just as Angelika said.

Julie wrapped her arms tightly around her midriff. Bile rose in her throat.

Angelika had guessed right. Julie was in love with Jake. A man who never settled with one woman, even when he was in a relationship with them.

If it was all true, then what the hell was he doing with Julie?

Memories of Charlie and her high school boyfriend slammed through her head. How quickly they had dumped her once sex was no longer on the table, no matter how emotionally involved she'd become with them. She never felt one tenth of the emotion for them that she did for Jake.

She moved on from Charlie. She didn't think her heart would ever recover if things soured between her and Jake.

She almost jumped out of her skin when her phone rang. Reaching for it, her stomach ached even more when she saw that the caller was Jake.

For the first time, Julie declined the call.

Chapter Twenty

"Can you repeat that?" Jake asked his son as they spoke on the phone.

"Mom said I could sell my stuff in Julie's shop. She co-signed the contract for Pieces of Home. I just need your signature now."

"What? Why? I mean, I'm happy for you, Dylan, but your mom seemed pretty adamant that you focus on college."

"She went to speak with Julie, and Julie showed her the nightstand I made. Mom told me it was really good. She said that if I agreed to still give college a chance, then she would sign the contract."

Jake's mood—which had been awful lately thanks to a recent lack in communication from Julie—lifted slightly. "That's great, Dylan. Though, I'll have to verify this with your mother. Last time I spoke with her, she made it clear that she didn't want you focusing on woodwork."

"I'm not lying, Dad." Dylan was defensive.

Jake rubbed his temple. "I'm not saying you are, but I need to make sure your mom and I are on the same page."

"Fine. So, when you get back, can I use the woodshop?"

"Fat chance. You're still grounded for lying."

Dylan made a noise of protest. "But Julie—"

"Since when did you start calling her Julie?"

"She told me to."

Jake smiled, liking the idea of Julie and his son bonding,

even though it reminded him that he hadn't spoken to her in five days.

A TV assistant stepped into the green room. "Ten minutes."

He nodded. "Listen, Dylan, I'm about to go on TV. We'll talk more tomorrow."

"Okay, good night, Dad."

"Night—oh, wait. When did you speak to Julie last?"

"The day you left town. I went by her store yesterday but she was busy with customers so I didn't go in. Why?"

"No reason. Good night."

They ended their call and Jake switched back to his text messages. The last time he had heard from Julie was a short text saying she was busy getting ready for the concert. That was two days ago.

It made Jake feel off…untethered. He'd gotten used to speaking to her for hours a night.

"No word yet, huh?" James asked as he sat in the chair next to him. Zan, Paul, and Tyler were on the other side of the room, laughing as they watched the late-night host's opening monologue on TV. It was the band's third late-night show that week. Lori had their schedule packed so tight, Jake barely knew what city he was in. The concert was in three days and she still had them booked for the next two nights.

He shook his head and shoved his phone in his pocket. "She said she was busy getting things ready for the concert."

Jake's thumb began to tap anxiously against the arm of his chair. James watched him, a small smile appearing on his face.

"What?" Jake asked in irritation.

James shook his head. "Nothing."

A wave of frustrated anger rushed over Jake. What the hell was going on? How could he and Julie go from constant communication to…nothing?

Lori walked into the room in a skintight black leather skirt and a silk black shirt. She had her phone in her hand, typing rapidly. Once she was finished, she tossed it on a nearby counter.

"All right, guys, it's time to go into the studio. Jake, a word first."

Jake's stomach twisted, not eager for a rehash of their conversation from the other day. Tyler, Paul, and Zan got up from their chairs and left the room.

"I need to use the bathroom before we go on," James said, getting up from his chair. He glanced between Lori and Jake and murmured quietly to Jake. "You good?"

Jake nodded shortly. James went into the private bathroom, closing the door behind him.

Jake turned his attention to Lori. "What's up?"

Before he knew what was happening, Lori threw herself into his lap, kissing him hard on the lips. He pushed her off and stood up.

Jake swiped at his mouth, his hands shaking. "Don't ever do that again. Do you understand?"

Lori folded her arms over her chest. "So you haven't reconsidered?"

Jake stared at her like he'd never seen her before. Maybe he hadn't. "What part of *no* are you not getting?"

"Don't you realize what the two of us could be like together?" When Jake looked at her blankly, she said, "We would be the most powerful couple in the music industry, answerable to no one. Record companies would crawl to us, and we could set things on our terms. Think about it, Jake. It'd be perfect—we'd be perfect—just like that night we had sex."

Jake's jaw clenched. "Our sleeping together was a mistake. But since Holiday Boys have reunited, I've tried to treat you with nothing but professional respect."

"Is that what you think?" Lori's lip curled. She brushed at her skirt, her long red fingernails picking away at an invisible piece of lint. "Is this because of that prude in Michigan?"

"Don't talk about her that way."

"Why not? She can't give you what you need. I can."

The color drained from Jake's face. Lori *had* overheard them that day in the studio when Jake had "hypothetically" discussed Julie's asexuality with James and Tyler. Who knew what she would do with that information.

She took a step closer to him and put her hands against his chest. "You know this is what my father wanted. Us, together. He told me it was his greatest wish before he died."

Jake took several hurried steps back so that Lori's arms dropped to her sides. He put his chair between them, giving them added distance.

"Everything all right in here?" James asked as he stepped back into the room. James had his phone in his hand. He tapped something on it then shoved it in his pocket.

"Tonight's my last stop," Jake snapped. "I'm headed back to Holiday Bay tomorrow."

"But…" Lori started to say.

"I'm not arguing with you. Cancel my remaining appearances. I'm done."

Lori looked like she wanted to deck him. With a furious glare, she grabbed her phone off the counter before stomping out of the room.

Jake stood beside James, trying to take a deep breath to calm some of his anger. Tension rolled down his body, putting him on edge.

"Jake…" James started to say.

"Don't," Jake said.

"I heard what happened in here. She kissed you against your will. That's not okay."

"It's fine, all right. Let's just focus on the interview."

James put his hand on Jake's shoulder. "I know Lori's good at her job, but her personal conduct toward you is straight-up sexual assault. We should start putting feelers out for a new manager now. Big Poppa would understand, he—"

"Would he?" Jake felt his stomach twist again. "Do you know how many times he used to hint that he'd be okay with me asking Lori out? She wasn't wrong in what she said. It would have made him ecstatic having us get together."

"Jake, you're not obligated to be with her. You made that family rich beyond their dreams. You repaid Big Poppa tenfold. You don't owe him anything else anymore."

Jake sighed, feeling weary down to his soul.

"Yeah, I know. I was going to talk to you guys anyway once the concert was done," Jake said as the show's assistant rushed into the room, frantically waving them out the door. "I can't deal with Lori anymore. Every time she gets near me, I feel sick."

James looked relieved as they walked down the hall toward the studio. "Sounds like a plan."

Closing his eyes briefly, Jake thought of Julie. One of his favorite memories of her was the morning after they'd slept in the same bed. Her hair had been tousled from sleep as she drank the coffee he'd given her. She'd looked like an angel.

He couldn't wait to get Julie back in his bed.

Despite whatever was going on between them, he felt a sense of calm as he thought of her. He'd see her soon.

With that thought in mind, he plastered on his famous professional smile and walked into the studio.

When Jake walked up to Pieces of Home the next day, Julie was by her car, loading boxes filled with merchandise.

"Hey," he said, shifting the package he carried from one hand to the other." She jumped in surprise. "Sorry, I didn't mean to scare you."

"It's okay." She wouldn't meet his eyes as she bent down to pick up another box. He put the package under his armpit so he could grab the box from her and slide it into the car.

"I've been trying to get a hold of you," he said as casually as he could. "Is your mom okay?"

"She's fine. I've just been busy." She waved her hand at the boxes. "Things have been crazy lately, the closer we've gotten to the concert. Business has really taken off. Your fans have been arriving all week, and I've been trying to get things ready for my booth."

"Yeah, I got your text." Jake noticed a few tourists across the street. They spotted him and started talking to each other excitedly. One grabbed his phone and began taking pictures of them. Jake had a feeling *Julake* would trend again soon.

"Look, can we talk inside?" Jake asked.

Julie opened her mouth but noticed the people photographing them. She gave a sharp nod and shut her trunk. As Jake followed her inside, he flipped the open sign on the store's door to Closed so they could have privacy.

As Jake turned to face her, he asked, "What's going on?"

The store lights highlighted the dark circles under Julie's eyes. "I told you, I've been bu—"

"Busy, right." Jake ran a hand through his hair in agitation. She was being distant. Even when he first came to her store after she posted that video and she'd been starstruck, she hadn't been like this. It was as if the warm, vibrant woman he'd fallen in love with had been replaced by a pod person.

"Dylan said you spoke with Angelika," he tried. "She's going to let him sell his stuff in the store."

Julie looked at a spot past his shoulder. "I'm glad."

Her short answer had his frustration boiling over. "What is going on with you? I thought we were growing toward something here. Why am I getting the silent treatment? Did I do something? Because I don't understand how we could go from talking every night to one cold text."

Julie's eyes sparked with anger. "Sorry I couldn't drop everything to be at your beck and call."

"When did I ever ask you to?" Jake folded his arms over his chest. "No, that's not what's going on here. Everything was fine until earlier this week." He stiffened. "Which was right around the time Angelika came in and spoke with you, right?"

"Jake, I…" Julie played with the hem of her trench coat. "You and I come from such different worlds—"

"We really don't. We both live in Holiday Bay."

"That's not what I mean."

Jake went stock-still, inspecting Julie's face, taking in every conflicted emotion. "What did she say to you?"

Julie swallowed hard. "Just what I already knew. That you enjoy being with women."

"And let me guess. I'm an unfaithful pig who can't keep it in my pants."

Julie visibly swallowed. "Like I said, you and I come from different worlds. You like sex, and in the end, caring about me won't be enough."

Jake took in her resolve and his jaw clenched. "So, that's it. You'll take her word—a woman you barely know—over mine."

"Do we really know each other that well?"

It would have been kinder if she'd sucker punched him in the stomach. "I thought we did. These past few weeks I let you in more than I've ever let anyone." Jake walked over his poster that still hung on her shop wall. The pain of the past five days—hell, the past twenty years—swarmed him.

"Do you know what my marriage to Angelika was like?" His throat was tight and he had to force the words out. "Angelika and I fought all the time. She constantly accused me of infidelity, despite the fact that I never once slept with anyone else while we were married. Our marriage was hell, when all either of us wanted was to not subject Dylan to the same type of bullshit we grew up with. And yes, after we got divorced, I did sleep around, but not nearly as much as the tabloids said." Jake swung back to face her. "Julie, I told you before that I want this. I want you, in any manner you can give me. But I can't go through that again. I can't go through being constantly accused of things that make me sick to my stomach. I told you before, after seeing how my dad's infidelity and abusive behavior destroyed my mom, I swore I would never treat a woman like that, and I never have."

Jake stopped, unable to put into words how badly his own marriage had hurt. He looked at Julie, pain tearing him apart.

"I never thought about settling down again," he continued, "until I met you. The thing I've come to realize lately is that I love you." Julie sucked in a breath. Jake gave a brittle smile before he said, "I want to be with you more than anything. Being able to talk to you on the phone every night helped me get through all those endless interviews and the long, grueling hours of travel. When I'm with you, I feel like I'm home. I've never felt that way before. Not once. Not even with Angelika. I want you in my life. But you have to trust me. If you can't, I won't go through the accusations again. I can't." Jake walked to her and kissed her cheek. "Think about it. If you want this, find me at the concert."

He started to leave, but he remembered her gift, which he still had under his arm. He'd been so excited to give it to her. Now, he just felt empty inside. "I got you this in California. I…"

He couldn't say any more, so he put it on the counter and left, feeling like he was leaving a part of himself behind in the store. He forced himself to keep walking. He heard several people call out his name. Even though he hated the type of celebrity who wasn't hospitable to their fans, he sped up his pace and jumped into his car.

Jake drove at a speed that probably would have gotten him arrested if a cop had stopped him. He turned into his driveway, screeching the tires when he came to a sudden stop outside the workshop. He went inside and strode over to the table that had his project on it—the one he'd been working on for Julie. He stared at it before picking up a nearby hammer and throwing it hard across the room. It hit the wall, busting a hole in the plaster.

Jake ran a hand over his beard—the one he'd grown for Julie. He stared at the box he'd been making for her booth and debated busting the damned thing apart. Instead, he picked up his phone and called Dylan.

"Dad?"

"You want to help me finish this box?"

"I thought I wasn't allowed in the workshop."

"This one time to help Julie—because you owe her that—and I'll be here to supervise so you don't take advantage and work on something else."

Dylan was quiet before he said, "Yeah, I'll be there soon."

Jake was in the process of cutting wood for the box's lid when Dylan entered. Jake waved at the table where the bottom part of the box was.

Dylan grabbed the electric hand sander and began working along the box's edges. Jake didn't say anything as he walked to the table and slapped the wood down.

Dylan eyed his dad, turning off the sander when he took in Jake's tense expression.

"Everything okay?" he asked.

"Fine," Jake said as he began to frame the lid.

"What happened to the wall?" he asked, nodding toward the obvious hole.

"Hammer slipped out of my hand," he muttered.

"And it defied gravity and went vertical into the wall, instead of down to the ground?"

"Something like that." Jake's tone was clipped.

Dylan didn't press his dad anymore, and for that, Jake was grateful. They worked together in companionable silence until one in the morning.

When Dylan started nodding off while polishing some Petoskey stones, Jake said, "Why don't we call it a night? It's too late for you to be driving your moped. I can give you a ride back to your mom's."

"Actually, I…" Dylan hesitated before looking at his dad uncertainly. "I messaged Mom earlier. If it's all right with you, can I stay here tonight?"

Something tight inside Jake shifted and then loosened. "Yeah…yeah, you can stay here."

And for the first time since Jake moved to Holiday Bay, Dylan spent the night.

As Jake lay in his bed, a part of his heart—the section that had taken a beating every time he tried to love someone—healed slightly, knowing his son was under his roof. Jake's love life might be a mess, but maybe his relationship with Dylan had gotten back on track.

They spent the following day putting the final touches on the box. When Jake got up the day of the concert, he grabbed Julie's box and put it in his car before heading to the venue. The concert was later that evening, but the band still needed to do a sound check. He felt good about the event itself. The band had been doing rehearsals the entire time they were on their publicity tour. They had fallen into their usual routine as though the past fifteen years hadn't existed.

The first person Jake saw when he arrived at the fairground was Lori.

"Where's the booth for Pieces of Home?" he asked, carrying the crate-size box.

Lori put a hand on her hip, ignoring his question. "Did you think about what I said the other night? About us?"

Jake's patience had reached its limit. "There *is* no us. Your behavior the other night was inappropriate and unprofessional. What happened between us years ago was a serious lapse of judgement on my part, and if I'd known I'd ever have to see you again after that night, I would never have slept with you." Jake clutched the chest tighter. "And since you can't keep it professional, maybe it's time you find another band to manage."

Lori snapped straight. "You're firing me?"

Jake didn't bother answering. He needed to figure out where Julie's booth was.

As he started to walk away, Lori said, "If you fire me, I'll sue you for sexual harassment."

Jake whipped around to look at her. "That's a damn lie and you know it."

"But who do you think the public will believe? Me, who's only ever sung your praises? Or you, a disgusting womanizer?" She walked up to him, pure hatred on her face. He took a step back in surprise. Not that he was afraid of her, but he realized it wasn't the first time he'd seen that look from her directed his way.

"You think you can sleep with any woman you want and then discard them like trash. I've devoted twenty years of my life to you, and how do you treat me? Like another notch on your bedpost. I've given you every opportunity to see how much we make sense, and you treat me like my feelings don't matter. You're a terrible person, Jake. And maybe it's time you got a taste of your own medicine."

She didn't wait for his reply as she sauntered away. Jake swallowed back the bile that rose in his throat before he forced his legs to move. His mind raced. He needed to talk to the guys. As soon as they did their encore performance after the show, he'd tell them what was going on. In the meantime, he'd get a hold of his attorney. Marcy and Lori never got along. He was positive Marcy would love nothing more than to wipe the floor with her.

As he made his way into the barn, Jake passed several people already setting up their stalls. A few vendors waved at him. Putting on his public persona, he smiled impersonally and continued walking.

"Can I help you, Mr. Reynolds?" a security guard asked.

"I'm looking for the booth for Pieces of Home."

"It's this way," the man said.

He guided Jake to a table in the center of the building. Julie must have been there at some point in the past two days, because her tables were already set up with the items from her store.

"Can I trust this to be safe here?" Jake asked, nodding to the box in his hands.

"I'll watch over it personally," the man assured him.

Jake put the box on the back table of the booth, wondering what Julie's expression would be when she saw it. Would she be happy to see it? Sad because it would remind her of how they left things? Would she even feel anything about it at all?

Moving his head to relieve some tension, he made his way through the barn and over to the concert area. James and Tyler were standing on the stage. Paul was at the sound station, speaking with one of the engineers. The video he'd made featuring the different stores in town flickered across a large screen that made up the main stage's backdrop. Zan sat on a speaker nearby, drinking coffee and talking on his phone.

"You look like crap," Tyler said when Jake walked onto the stage.

"Thanks, man," Jake muttered.

"Is everything okay?" James asked.

Jake ran a weary hand over his face. "I found out why Julie stopped speaking to me. Apparently, Angelika got to her and told her how unfaithful I supposedly am."

"What?" Tyler said. "That's the dumbest thing I've ever heard."

"I never understood why Angelika thought that about you," James added. "You were living like a monk any time I came to visit you. And it wasn't like you didn't have opportunities to cheat."

"You know what Angelika's childhood was like," Jake said. "Her dad was really rough on her, which led to a lot of life-long insecurities."

"So you've told us before," Tyler said. "But she's moved on. You should be able to as well."

James folded his arms over his chest as he looked at Jake. "What are you going to do?"

He let out a tired sigh. "I don't know. I want to be with Julie. I can see myself growing old with her. But I can't go through another relationship where I constantly have to defend myself."

"And what about sex, man?" Tyler asked. "You're sure you can live without it?"

"I want Julie in my life," Jake said. "I want her more than I want anything else, including sex."

Someone cleared their throat behind him and Jake turned to see Lori glaring at them, her posture rigid.

"If you three are done gossiping, it's time for your sound check."

As she walked by them and headed toward the exit, Jake watched her go, fury rising inside. He looked at his friends and muttered, "We can talk later...about a few things"

They nodded, James giving him a knowing look. Jake walked over to the microphone and tapped it. The sound of a live mike echoed through the venue.

He didn't regret recommending they do a charity concert. He knew it would help the town. It would help Julie.

But he wanted to get it over with.

Because if Julie didn't show up tonight, he would have his answer as to if they had a future together or not.

Chapter Twenty-One

Julie waved goodbye to her departing customers before glancing at the clock. The concert was set to start in two hours. She'd been busy throughout her day. Holiday Boys fans stopped into the shop in droves to see where she'd challenged Jake Reynolds. They talked to her like she was a celebrity herself, which she found amusing in a time where she didn't think she would ever smile again. She'd picked up her phone more than once to call Jake and tell him how they were treating her. He would have gotten a kick out of it. The fans also bought a majority of whatever she had left in the store that wasn't already at the fairground.

The day had not only been financially rewarding, but being busy kept her mind off Jake. She'd had nightmares the last two nights, her brain replaying how he'd looked before he left the store, as though the world had disappointed him for the last time. She'd woken up with her cheeks wet, her pillow soaked from the tears she'd spilled in her sleep.

As she stood behind the store counter, her mind groggy, she debated if she would even go to the concert. Grabbing her phone, she called Meg.

"You're going," her friend said as soon as she answered, having had this conversation with Julie the past two days.

"Meg, it's going to be awful. Being that close to him."

"Did you forget that you're the whole reason he's doing this concert in the first place?"

"Of course I haven't," Julie replied. "I just don't know what to do about everything."

"Then let me break it down for you," Meg replied. "He told you he loved you, right?"

"Yes."

"And you love him, too."

"I…"

"Oh please, don't pretend you aren't crazy about him. You've been in love with him since ninth grade. You loved him before he became the famous guy he is today. And you finally have a chance at happiness with said guy. Why are you so willing to throw it all away?"

"You didn't read what those articles said. They say he's addicted to sex."

"Did you ask him about it?" Meg countered.

Julie stayed silent.

"Yeah, exactly," Meg answered her own question. "Why are you willing to listen to some stranger's write-up about what they *think* his life is like, when you can go directly to the source?"

Julie gnawed on her lip. "Because I'm scared."

"Of what?" Meg said gently. "Of Jake turning out to be like Charlie?"

"Charlie said he loved me, too, but he dumped me as soon as I said no to sex."

"Jake's known about the no-sex rule for weeks now. He still wants to be with you."

"But—"

"Oh for Pete's sake." Meg was impatient again. "Julie, I want you to repeat after me… I am worthy of love."

"Meg, I—"

"I want to hear you say it."

"I am worthy of love," Julie repeated.

"Awesome. Now stop listening to every moron out there who's writing crap about Jake to increase their website views. Jake loves you. Look at everything he's done for you. Don't you realize how lucky you are to have someone who loves you like that? Who'll put you first?"

Julie frowned, knowing she was tiptoeing into a sensitive area. "Meg, I'm sorry. I didn't mean—"

"Go get your man, Julie." Meg disconnected the call.

Sighing, Julie put her phone in her purse and walked to the door. She needed to head over to the fairground before they allowed general admission in. No matter what happened with Jake, she had a booth to run.

She stepped outside, enjoying the warmth that June brought. The evening was expected to be warm, but not hot—perfect for the Holiday Boys' outdoor concert.

"Oh good, I was hoping to catch you."

Julie startled, her gaze flying to the woman standing in front of her. She frowned. What was Jake's manager doing there? Angelika's words filtered through her mind. This woman had been having an affair with Jake for years. Or at least, that's what Angelika thought. Julie remembered the sincerity in Jake's voice when he said he was faithful. The hurt expression when he'd read her doubt.

"I heard that there's been a little bit of a misunderstanding between you and Jake," Lori said. When Julie didn't react—other than to lift her chin defensively—Lori continued. "I know it must be daunting to have Jake gone for periods of time, but there's no reason to break up with him. I assure you I'm no threat to your relationship. In fact, I think it's the perfect arrangement."

Julie stared at her in confusion. "What are you talking about?"

"Well." Lori's expression looked innocent enough. "I understand that you're not willing to have sex with Jake because you're asexual."

Julie's breath caught in her throat. "He told you that?"

"Of course, he tells me everything." Lori stared at her nails as though she was bored. "You see, I'm not looking for a commitment, so it really is the perfect solution. He's always had this urge to settle down with someone, and while the sex between us is utterly fantastic, I'm not looking for anything more. So why not kill two birds with one stone? He gets a nice little homebody to listen to him gripe at the end of the tour, and he gets someone to fulfill his physical desires while he's on the road. That's how it was while he was married to Angelika."

Julie couldn't speak, her heart crushed by hurt and betrayal. How could Jake tell this vile human being something so personal about her?

"He is incredible in bed," Lori said, her expression turning to satisfaction as she thought about some particular memory. "The things that man can do with his tongue. He's so gifted at eating a woman out. Not that you would know anything about that, huh?" She smiled as Julie flinched. "But as I said, I'm not looking for commitment. So, are we in agreement?"

"I think you should leave," a man said as he came up to them.

In her shock, Julie hadn't noticed anyone else approaching. Lori swung sideways, her face going slack, but she quickly recovered.

"James, why aren't you at sound check?"

"It ended a half hour ago, and I wanted to speak with Julie." James glanced at Julie and gave her a tight smile before turning back to his manager. "Lori, you have been a problem for Jake for as long as I can remember. He's told you in every way possible—other than a restraining order—that he doesn't want anything to do with you. Your obsession with sabotaging Jake's relationships ends tonight."

Lori looked defiant. "I don't know what you're talking about."

"I never understood why Angelika had it in her brain that Jake was unfaithful to her, when we both know Jake never looked at another woman while he was married to her. I mean, I certainly noticed when you first took over the band that you booked us for events on days that were important to Jake and his family. His wedding anniversary, Dylan's birthday. You've been working behind the scenes for years, trying to seclude Jake from those who love him so he'd have no one but you."

"You're delusional," Lori said.

James continued as though she hadn't spoken, "And after overhearing what you said to Julie, I've had my suspicions confirmed. You lied to Angelika, didn't you? Told her a bunch of times about how Jake was cheating on her so you could break them up."

Something twisted across Lori's face. "If she was foolish enough to believe it, then she didn't deserve Jake in the first place. I saved him from her."

James shook his head. "Ah, there's the real Lori. What I don't understand is why? You don't love Jake. You never have."

"You don't know anything. Jake wouldn't have had sex with me the way he did unless he was in love with me."

Julie flinched at that, but James merely laughed. "It was a drunken one night stand for the two of you and nothing more. What? Did you think you were so good in bed that you could trap him into a relationship? That he'd be too addicted to your body to ever want to let you go?"

Lori's eyes flared with anger. "I don't have to stand here and listen to this. I have to get to the concert."

"No, you don't."

Something in his face made her stiffen. "What are you talking about?"

"When I was younger, I was too wrapped up in my own

problems to say anything about your conduct. I'm not afraid now." James raised his chin. "I'm terminating your employment with Holiday Boys. You're no longer our manager."

"You don't have the authority."

"I guarantee you that when I tell the guys how you spoke to Julie tonight, they'll be in agreement. Who do you think the record company will side with? Us or you?"

Lori's hands clenched at her sides. "I'll sue you for wrongful termination."

"You go ahead and try," James said calmly. "And I'll share with the courts and anyone who asks all of the texts, emails, and voicemails you've left the entire band, telling us how bad of an idea this concert is. I'll be able to show how much you complained about doing a charity event for our hometown. It won't be a good look for you, Lori."

Lori looked ready to fight. Her hands curled up at her sides.

"Don't even think about it," he said. "Jake might put up with your crap because he feels obligated to your dad, but I won't have any issue pressing charges against you for assault."

Lori stared daggers at James. "I'll sue Jake for sexual harassment."

James shook his head, a look of loathing crossing his face. "You really don't give a damn about Jake, do you?"

"Of course I do. I love—"

"No...you don't. You want him because there's a lot of power in dating Jake Reynolds, especially in the music business. But he doesn't want you, and you can't accept that."

Lori looked like she was about to deny it and then she threw her head back and laughed. Julie shivered at how unhinged she sounded.

"Look at you," Lori said. "Acting like Jake's knight in shining armor. Jake is nothing but a puppet dancing on the strings I pull. I helped create him, just like I did all of you. And you think you can suddenly call the shots and get rid of me? I don't think so. I'll sue him and take him for every penny he's worth. And if I get to destroy his relationship with St. Prude over here—" Julie's palm itched to smack Lori across the face at that insult"—then all the more fun for me."

James shook his head. "See, I figured you'd pull garbage like this at some point. That's why I took the precaution of protecting Jake, being the knight in shining armor that I am." He pulled out his phone and pressed something.

Lori's voice came through clearly on the recording, *Don't you realize what the two of us could be like together? We would be the most powerful couple in the music industry, answerable to no one. Record companies would crawl to us, and we could set things on our terms. Think about it, Jake. It'd be perfect—we'd be perfect—just like that night we had sex.*

Jake's voice was angry as he replied, *Our sleeping together was a mistake. But since Holiday Boys have reunited, I've tried to treat you with nothing but professional respect.*

Is that what you think?

James stopped the recording. He tilted his head as he looked at Lori. "Now, that does sound like sexual harassment, but the harasser certainly isn't Jake."

Lori stiffened. Knowing she was finished, she stomped by James.

"Lori," he called out, and she stopped. "If I see you anywhere near Jake again or, for that matter, the music industry in general, I *will* press charges for harassment and stalking, do you understand? You're done."

Lori's hands went into fists again but she didn't look back once as she continued to walk, her gait slow and measured. James turned back to face Julie once Lori was out of sight.

"Well, now that that's done." James smiled at her. "How've you been, Julie?"

Julie's mouth hung open. She closed it quickly. "I, uh, I'm doing okay."

"Great," James said. His tone was pleasant, as if nothing monumental had just happened. "How's your sister?"

"My...my sister?" Julie felt like someone had knocked her sideways. When Holiday Boys first became famous, people labeled James as the sweet one in the group. But the way he'd handled Lori's termination without batting an eye made it clear he wasn't someone people should mess with. Julie was impressed, even though she felt emotionally wrung out.

"Yeah. Veronica?" he said.

Julie tried to get her brain back online. "I'm surprised you remember her."

James chuckled. "You never forget your first—and last—girlfriend."

Julie heard a crowd coming down the street, and she turned to see people headed their way. Some were wearing Holiday Boys merchandise.

"Is there somewhere private we can talk?" James asked.

"Sure." Julie opened her shop door and they walked inside.

Now that she had a moment to collect her thoughts, Julie looked James over. It had been years since she'd seen him in person. He had graduated high school the same year Jake had, and left town with the Holiday Boys shortly thereafter. He was the same height as Jake, but he was stockier due to the physical labor he did while doing home renovations. They had the same hair color, but their eye coloring was different, with Jake having blue eyes and James having brown.

Julie walked over to a shelf and straightened a plastic flower. "What did you want to talk to me about? I'm sure it wasn't to find out how Veronica is doing."

James smiled, as though he was proud of the way she was behaving so collectedly after the upsetting encounter with Lori. "True. I wanted to talk to you about Jake."

Julie figured as much. She didn't say anything as she waited for James to say what he needed to.

"I can understand why you would think Jake wouldn't be faithful to you. Especially when you encounter horrible people like Lori."

Julie looked down at the ground. "Did Jake tell you I'm ace?"

"In a matter of speaking."

Julie's cheeks burned. "So, he pretty much told everyone."

"No, Jake wouldn't do that. He gave an example of a hypothetical situation during a private conversation. I was able to deduce who he was talking about."

Julie laughed without humor. "Lori says otherwise."

"Lori has an enormous talent for eavesdropping on conversations she has no business listening to." James's face turned angry. "Jake only spoke to Tyler and me about it. He needed someone to talk to, and the three of us have always been closer than brothers. It was while we were speaking that we pointed out the obvious."

"Which was what?"

"That Jake's crazy about you. I don't think I have ever seen him so torn up about anyone as he's been about you." When Julie only stared at him miserably, he said, "Did Jake ever tell you why Holiday Boys broke up?"

Julie shrugged. "He said it was because he had a problem with the record company."

"He would say that." James's lips quirked into a sad smile. "He quit because of me."

"What do you mean?"

"He quit because he didn't like how the record executives were treating me. I knew back then that I was gay, but it was a different time, and people weren't as open-minded as they are now. Big Poppa and the record executives told me that if I came out, it would destroy the band. They even made me sign a contract stating I wouldn't say or do anything to expose I was gay, or I risked getting sued for 'detrimental damage to our image.'"

"That's awful," Julie whispered.

"Jake thought so, too. Dealing with that kind of pressure—to always have to lie and be on alert of slipping up—caused me to have severe anxiety. It got to the point where I was having panic attacks on stage and couldn't perform. I began to worry every time I went out, thinking if I looked at a man the wrong way, people would guess the truth, and I would destroy everything we'd worked so hard for."

"I'm so sorry you went through that," Julie said.

"I'm okay now. I have a wonderful husband and the fans have been amazingly accepting. But back then, it was a different ball game, and it finally became too much. Jake came over to pick me up one day so we could go to the recording studio. I couldn't even get out of bed. That's when he had enough. He walked into the executives' offices and told them to shove their contract up their asses. He publicly announced later that day he was done with the band."

James clasped the back of his neck. "People were irate. The record company sued him. Fans felt betrayed. People said he only cared about himself and not the others in the band. But after I explained to Tyler what had happened to me, he announced his plans to leave the group as well, and Holiday Boys officially broke up."

James looked at her intently. "Jake went through hell, but he did it because he loves me. That's the kind of person he is. He was willing to give up everything for me and risk his career, because he's loyal. He's the most loyal guy you'll ever meet. Do you understand where I'm going with this?"

"Yes," Julie said, her voice thick with emotion.

James's face turned to satisfaction. "Good, because I'm telling you now, Julie, that guy deserves the world, and he'll give it to you in return if you let him. He won't betray you.

He doesn't know how." James patted her on the shoulder. "I need to get going. Will I see you at the concert?"

Julie nodded and he smiled.

After James left, Julie walked slowly back to her counter, her mind whirling with everything he said.

Could she put her painful experiences of the past behind her and trust Jake with her heart? She wanted to—and hadn't he proven himself time and time again since they had reunited?

He sacrificed his privacy for her, something he told her that he prized. He'd confided his darkest secrets to her. As Meg had pointed out, he put together this concert and had done everything he could to save her business, not to mention the other businesses in town, despite how he felt about Holiday Bay. He confessed to writing "Enchanted" because of her, a song which helped her get through some tough times in her life.

He'd done so much for her. And not just her. Her mind drifted to Dylan. She knew Jake would do anything for his son, and was willing to fight for Dylan's happiness. James's story only solidified that Jake was loyal to those he loved.

And he *loved* Julie.

She loved him, too, and wanted to be with him.

But could she trust him with her heart?

The answer was simple and obvious.

Yes, she could.

The realization swept over her, making her feel elated. She knew she had screwed up with Jake, but he hadn't closed the door on them. He told her to think about if she wanted a relationship with him, and she did. Now she had to prove it to him.

She went to grab her phone. Her hand brushed against the package Jake had given her the other day. She'd been unable to open it after he'd left, so she'd tossed it on the counter. It'd been sitting there for the past two days, a painful symbol of the potential end of their relationship.

Curiosity getting the better of her, she ripped open the brown paper packaging. Julie sucked in a breath.

In her hands was a first edition *Anne of Green Gables*.

Her eyes teared up. Jake remembered how much she loved the story. It must have cost him a fortune…and she'd left it on the counter for anyone to steal. She wanted to kick herself, but her heart was too busy filling with overwhelming love for Jake. She'd focus on kicking her own ass later.

She picked up her phone and called Meg.

"Hey," she said once she heard her best friend's voice. "I need you to do something for me. Can you watch my booth at the concert?"

"Why?" Meg asked.

"I'm taking your advice." Julie grinned. "I'm going to go get my man."

Julie heard the crowd roar as she walked toward the barn where the vendors were. Music echoed over the loud speakers, the familiar chords of one of Holiday Boys' first hits starting to play. Julie hurried into the building and made her way to her booth. Despite the fact that the concert was beginning, there was a large crowd of people around her stall.

"What on earth," she muttered, holding the rolled-up poster board she had under her arm closer to her.

Julie made it to the front of the crowd and saw a security guard standing close to a box. Julie's breath caught in her throat. It was the one Jake had shown her a drawing of. It only had its base the last time she saw it.

The box had a treble clef burned into the lid, and a fossil rock embedded at the bottom of it. Julie's eyes misted when she recognized the stone as being the one she had found the night Jake kissed her for the first time. Meg was showing the box to someone before lifting the lid. On the inside of it,

Jake had scrawled, *For the redheaded girl who leaves me enchanted*, along with his name.

Meg saw her and waved her over. "Jules!"

"What is going on?" she asked, pointing at the crowd.

"The word is out that Jake Reynolds made a public declaration for you. People are going crazy that he basically confirmed 'Enchanted' is about you. A decades-long mystery has finally been solved! I posted this on an auction site on your behalf about an hour ago, and bids are already at eighty thousand dollars."

"Are you serious?"

"Man, when that guy goes for a romantic gesture, he goes big." Meg noticed the poster board under her arm. "What's that?"

"My own romantic gesture. I just wanted to stop by and see how you were doing before I went out there."

Meg gave her a knowing look. "Stop stalling."

Julie nodded, taking a deep breath.

As she walked away, Meg shouted, "Good luck!"

Julie stepped onto the field of the fairground. The place was packed. She could see the five guys on stage. Lights flashed around the crowd, and the sound coming through the speakers was clear. Despite not having performed together in fifteen years, they sounded amazing. Jake and Tyler were at the front, while James, Paul, and Zan stood behind them. They did dance moves to the song that matched their video from years ago. The crowd sang with them, every lyric shouted back to the band with a deafening roar.

Julie did her best to get to the front of the stage, though it wasn't easy. She got elbowed a few times. Once she got closer, she could see Jake scanning the crowd, lines of worry on his forehead, despite how electric the energy was in the air.

She finally reached the front. She knew the minute Jake

saw her. Relief blazed across his features. He visibly relaxed and a brilliant smile formed on his lips.

Unrolling the poster board, she held it high in the air. He stopped singing as he mouthed what she had written. Jake threw his head back and laughed. Jumping down from the stage, he pushed past security and hopped over the metal barrier placed between the crowd and the band. Jake grabbed Julie and whirled her in a circle.

She dropped the sign to the ground. Their lips met, fusing together. Her hands went around his neck, pulling him closer.

The crowd around them erupted in cheers.

A couple of bystanders glanced down at the sign before giving each other bemused looks. They didn't understand the context of what she had written. They didn't need to. Julie and Jake understood each other perfectly.

The sign summed up their relationship in two words.

Challenge Accepted.

* * * * *

Harlequin® Reader Service

Enjoyed your book?

Try the perfect subscription for Romance readers and get more great books like this delivered right to your door.

See why over 10+ million readers have tried Harlequin Reader Service.

Start with a Free Welcome Collection with free books and a gift—valued over $20.

Choose any series in print or ebook. See website for details and order today:

TryReaderService.com/subscriptions